KV-370-820

# Kitten

*Published by Phaze Books*
*Also by Mychael Black and Shayne Carmichael*

*The Power of Two*

*Kitten* (eBook)

*Onyx*

*The Cowboy and the Thief*

*The Duke's Husband*

*Tombstone Ranch* (Shayne only)

*Dominion*

*The Adventures of Captain Chase Sykes and Navigator Duncan
Sampson*

*Dark Needs* (print collection)

*Kitten 2* (eBook)

Cincinnati, Ohio

This is an explicit and erotic novel
intended for the enjoyment
of adult readers. Please keep
out of the hands of children.

www.Phaze.com

# Kitten

a novel of homoerotic fantasy by

# Mychael Black
# Shayne Carmichael

**Kitten** © 2007, 2008 by Mychael Black and Shayne Carmichael

All rights reserved under the International and Pan-American Copyright Conventions. No part of this book may be reproduced or transmitted in any form or by any means, electronic or mechanical, including photocopying, recording, or by any information storage and retrieval system, without permission in writing from the publisher.

This is a work of fiction. Names, places, characters and incidents are either the product of the author's imagination or are used fictitiously, and any resemblance to any actual persons, living or dead, organizations, events or locales is entirely coincidental.

Cincinnati, Ohio

A Phaze Production
Phaze Books
6470A Glenway Avenue, #109
Cincinnati, OH 45211-5222
Phaze is an imprint of Mundania Press, LLC.

To order additional copies of this book, contact:
books@phaze.com
www.Phaze.com

Cover art © 2007, Silver Blaze
Edited by Kathryn Lively

eBook ISBN-13: 978-1-59426-885-4
eBook ISBN-10: 1-59426-885-1

First Edition – January, 2008
Printed in the United States of America

10  9  8  7  6  5  4  3  2  1

Warning: the unauthorized reproduction or distribution of this copyrighted work is illegal. Criminal copyright infringement, including infringement without monetary gain, is investigated by the FBI and is punishable by up to 5 years in prison and a fine of $250,000.

# Part One

# Chapter One

"I know you're there. Who are you?"

The rustling leaves sounded loud to Shaun as he tried to hide further in the bushes. Holding his breath, he flattened himself as close to the ground as possible. When the man who had spoken moved slightly, Shaun scrambled backward. Unable to stop the sound, a low, warning pulse erupted from his throat and he stilled completely.

The man, who had been lying on his back, rolled slowly onto his stomach and peered into the brush. "You *are* a were. I won't hurt you. My name is Ashley." He got up and held out his hand. When Shaun didn't respond, the man named Ashley straightened his back. "Come," he said, using the authoritative inflection of a Master; although in his case, apparently one without a pet to control.

An enraged snarl filled the air but was quickly bitten back as the command almost shocked Shaun into obedience. Crawling forward, he slowly left his hiding place.

"I thought so." For a moment, Ashley stilled, looking Shaun over.

Muscular and sleek, Shaun knew he was a rare find even when only half-shifted, especially with his black-and-white striped fur.

"What is your name? If you know the command, then I know you can speak."

"Shaun." Clad only in a black loincloth, very little of him was covered. With fluid motion, he moved to his hands and knees in front of Ashley.

"You don't belong out here."

Ashley reached out and hummed softly. It was a technique used by Masters to calm their pets. He traced the outline of the tattoo etched into Shaun's skin, just at the nape of his neck. It was a procedure done when a were was captured. Once a Master took possession, the star would take on the form of the Master's initial, signifying ownership. Shaun's tattoo was still that of a perfect star, showing that he was unclaimed. The soft trill brought a visible relaxation to Shaun's tense body, though he tried to fight against the effect. Biting at his lip, his head lowered, allowing Ashley to touch him.

"I won't hurt you," Ashley murmured. "How long have you been free?"

The words might have been meant as some form of comfort, but Shaun didn't take them that way. Lifting his head and raising his chin higher in a defiant manner, he said, "For more than two months. I've lived out here on my own."

"You need proper bedding and a bath," Ashley said matter-of-factly. He picked up a cigarette butt from the grass beside him and stood slowly, pushing the butt into one of his jeans pockets. "Come."

Because he was given no choice in the matter, Shaun hissed angrily; but, nonetheless, he followed slowly behind the man. It would do no good to beg to be left out here. He already knew what a prize he'd be viewed as.

Home was no more than a few minutes away. Ashley was grateful that he'd found a place so far outside of the city, but close enough for work. Five minutes later, he held his front door open, standing to the side to let Shaun go in first. Shaun seemed apprehensive as he stepped past him. Once inside, Ashley watched as Shaun took several deep breaths. Apprehension, it seemed, gave way to curiosity, and Shaun slowly prowled around the perimeter of the room, poking into everything.

Closing the front door and locking it, Ashley smiled. He'd had chances in the past to take in a pet, but he'd never found the right one to replace the emptiness within him. Then this beauty had practically fallen into his life. Ashley wasn't surprised that a part of him was already working out the possibility of keeping Shaun with him, of claiming him.

"Would you like something to drink?" He went into the small kitchen, watching Shaun over the bar.

Pausing as he tried to pry open one of the small jars he'd picked up, Shaun looked over at him with a touch of suspicion. "Water."

"Water it is." Ashley took out two glasses and filled them both with ice cold water from the pitcher in the refrigerator. Then he went into the living room and held out one of the glasses to Shaun. "Drink. I will get your bath ready." With that, Ashley walked out, heading down the short hallway to the bathroom.

As Ashley walked away, Shaun shook his head in confusion, staring at the glass in his hand. Aware he needed a bath, he set the jar down and padded silently behind Ashley as he drank.

Setting his glass on the sink counter, Ashley got down on his knees and started the bathwater. Watching from his position, Shaun hadn't expected Ashley to join him. Chiding himself, he should have realized it, though. A Master expected nothing more than a well-behaved pet at his heel, to show off to his contemporaries, and to be a warm body in his bed. If Shaun had any form of luck, cruelty wouldn't be the order of the day. That's about all he could hope for. After finishing the water, he set the glass on the sink.

When the water was deep enough, Ashley turned it off and stood. As he turned around, he looked surprised to see Shaun in the doorway. "I was going to come tell you that your bath is ready. If you don't mind, I'd like to sit and talk while you bathe. If you wish for me to, I'd be happy to wash your hair." Sitting down on the toilet lid, he made no move to take off his clothes.

Just as a well-trained pet would, Shaun took off the

8

small loin cloth and laid it on the edge of the sink. Stepping into the tub, he sank down into the water. The heat felt damn good as he leaned back against the porcelain edge.

"Why?" Shaking his head, Shaun frowned, repeating his question more fully. "Why would you want to wash my hair?"

Ashley just shrugged. "Why not? It would take a fool to not see that you're beautiful. If you don't wish me to, then I won't."

Even though it was part of his nature to adore being touched and petted, Shaun wasn't sure he wanted this stranger to touch him. Yet controlling his own natural instincts while being petted was an impossible task. Leaning slightly toward Ashley, he drew in a slow breath. The earthy scent reached him, a mixture of sunshine and grass underneath the faint smell of tobacco.

"I don't like strong scents," Ashley said with a smile, "and I hate cologne. The best smells in the world are chocolate, nature, and a man's arousal."

"You don't stink." Small favor to be grateful for. As he looked over Ashley, curiosity began to get the better of Shaun. He actually liked the smell, but the man was too far away to do anything more than catch his scent from the air.

"I should hope not," Ashley chuckled. "I took a shower this morning." He slid off the toilet lid and to the floor, kneeling close to the bathtub. "Is that better?"

As Shaun leaned over slightly and turned his head, Ashley was no more than a few inches away from his face. A small chuffing sound came from him before his nostrils flared with the deep breath he took. Inching slowly forward, he got a bit closer. "Yes, you like chocolate." The scent itself came from the direction of Ashley's hands and made Shaun lower his head as he leaned as far over the edge of the tub as he could. "Sweet."

"I love chocolate," Ashley said rather breathlessly.

A heady, muskier aroma slowly tinged the air. It was

one Shaun knew very well: Ashley wanted him. Its influence on Shaun was undeniable, yet he fought it. Drawing back, he reached for the bar of soap and washcloth and began washing.

"Will you let me wash your hair?" Ashley asked softly after a few minutes of silence. "I don't have to get in with you to do it."

Shaun gave him a wary look. As he thought over what Ashley asked, he could see nothing bad behind the request. "If you want." Stretching in the tub, he sank beneath the water to wet his hair before he sat back up. Then he wiped the water from his face and settled to let Ashley wash his hair.

Ashley moved closer and picked up the bottle of shampoo. After pouring a generous amount in his hand, he began working his fingers through Shaun's hair, gently untangling it. "So beautiful," he whispered.

Closing his eyes, the massaging of Ashley's fingers served to relax Shaun very nicely. The tiniest flicker of sound eased from his throat, barely perceptible but there. Small tilts of his head guided Ashley's hands as his own fingers kneaded slightly on the porcelain tub's rim.

Ashley picked up a nearby cup and filled it with water. He slipped his hand beneath Shaun's chin to tilt his head back gently. "Shh," he murmured, smiling. "I'm only rinsing."

A touch of nervousness had returned with the feel of Ashley's hand, but Shaun relaxed, letting Ashley rinse out the shampoo. It was a strange thing for this man to want to do this. Blinking up at Ashley, he saw the smile but didn't return the gesture.

When he finished rinsing the shampoo out, Ashley set the cup down and moved away. "Thank you," he said as he sat on the floor, leaning against the wall. "I haven't done that in…" He closed his eyes as his words trailed off. "For some time," he finished quietly.

"It means something to you?" Shaun was not at all certain what to make of Ashley. Slowly standing, water ran down his body in little rivers, dripping back to the tub. Lifting his hands, he pulled back his hair to wring out the water.

"More than I should probably dwell on," Ashley said. "I used to do it for my lover. He was a were as well, although I loathed the thought of calling him my 'pet.' I'd forgotten how relaxing such simple acts could be. Thank you for allowing me that small pleasure."

The concept of a were as a lover to any mortal was completely alien and unknown to Shaun. They were pets and nothing more at the hands of men and women. Staring at Ashley blankly, Shaun couldn't even grasp the idea. He just took the towel hanging nearby and quickly dried himself as he got out of the tub.

"Are you hungry?" Ashley looked up from where he sat, weariness showing in his pale blue eyes. "I haven't eaten since I left work."

Nodding slightly, Shaun laid the towel down and picked up his loincloth. Refastening it around his hips, it barely covered his groin and left most of his ass showing. Then he ran his fingers through his hair, trying to give it some semblance of order.

Ashley struggled to get up, finally finding a good handhold on the sink counter. As he stood, he eyed Shaun and shook his head. "You can't keep going around like that. Follow me. We look to be about the same size; maybe you can wear something of mine." He walked down the hall to his bedroom and started rummaging through the dresser. A moment later, he pulled out a pair of gray sweatpants and a white T-shirt. "It's not much, but it'll be much more comfortable than that."

As Ashley held out the pants and shirt to him, Shaun just stared at him again. Normal clothing was rarely given to pets. Hesitantly, he reached out and took them. Untying the loincloth, he laid the scrap of material on the dresser before he slipped on the clothes.

"Looks good on you," Ashley said with a smile. As he turned, he doubled over and grabbed the edge of the dresser, hissing through gritted teeth.

The sound of Ashley's pain drew Shaun's attention quickly back to the man. Reaching out, he gripped Ashley's arm, supporting him. "Are you all right?"

Ashley laughed, although there was little humor to it. "Yes, yes. Thank you. Just an old back injury that likes to flare up if I move wrong." Looking up, he gave Shaun a weak smile. "How about that dinner?" With a groan, he righted himself, grasping Shaun's hand briefly in gratitude.

"I can help," Shaun said somewhat hesitantly. Letting go of Ashley, he stood there, uncertain. "In half-form, I have energy to ease pain; I just can't fully heal anyone."

Ashley hesitated for a minute, then nodded. "I suppose it would help if I plan on cooking. What do I need to do?"

"Just take off your shirt and lay down on your stomach on the bed."

Nodding, Ashley turned and pulled his shirt off. Then he stretched out on the bed, pillowing his head on his arms. Deep scars criss-crossed his back, but Shaun said nothing about them. After removing his clothes, Shaun approached the bed slowly. Leaning over, he rested his hands lightly on Ashley's back before slowly rubbing them over his skin. Heat radiated from him, giving his touch an immediate anesthetic effect as he massaged.

"Oh, God," Ashley moaned. "That feels good, Shaun. Really good." Moving his arms up to grip the edge of the mattress, he slowly stretched, the muscles tightening and releasing beneath Shaun's hands. Ashley turned his head to the side and closed his eyes.

"It is easy to relieve pain, but I can't do anything about why you are in pain," Shaun said as the warmth from his touch seeped deeper into Ashley's skin, relaxing the muscles beneath.

"No one can. What's done is done. I tried. I tried to stop them, Shaun. I loved him with everything I was, and they took him from me." Ashley shook his head suddenly.

"Thank you; it helped more than you can imagine." He rolled over and smiled, reaching up to stroke Shaun's cheek softly.

With the unexpected touch, Shaun purred. He adored being petted. He tilted his head and rubbed instinctively into Ashley's palm.

"So soft." Ashley cupped Shaun's face in his hand, then slid his hand back over Shaun's head. Shaun's hair was black and white, like his fur, and even though his body was that of a man's, his fur still covered his body. "Kitten."

The deeper rumbling of the purr formed before Shaun could stop it. His innate nature sought and craved the feel of a hand running over him. Sitting at the edge of the bed, he let Ashley touch him. As he closed his eyes, small movements of his head and face nudged those hands, guiding them.

Moving his fingers slowly over the soft fur, Ashley sighed. "Am I insane for wanting this? For wishing I could do this forever?" He moved his hand slowly, brushing the pad of his thumb over Shaun's lips.

Anything Ashley said might as well have been in a foreign language. Shaun wanted nothing more than for that hand to continue petting him. When Ashley's hand neared his lips, his tongue darted out, tasting at the salty flavor of Ashley's skin. The faint rasp of his tongue bathed the length of Ashley's finger as the steady thrum of his purring rose around them. He had to lick; he had to be petted. When Ashley didn't pull his hand away, Shaun proceeded to wash his entire hand. He wanted to curl up near Ashley, just to feel that touch.

"Kitten," Ashley whispered, lifting his other hand. Starting at Shaun's cheek, Ashley stroked his fingers slowly over him, moving down Shaun's neck to his shoulder. "Come," he said softly, gently urging Shaun down to the bed. "Dinner can wait for a bit. This is more important, needed."

The one word spoke deeply to the animal inside

Shaun, and was the true nature of the control humans had over his kind. He needed no encouragement and instantly curled against Ashley. Tipping back his head, he exposed his throat, craving that touch. It couldn't stop just yet; he wasn't ready for it to.

Turning on his side to face Shaun, Ashley petted him, his fingers stroking the soft fur of Shaun's throat, then down the middle of his chest. Then he leaned forward just enough to kiss the tip of Shaun's nose.

The flick of Shaun's tail darted sporadically in the air before it curled against Ashley's hip. With the close proximity of Ashley's face, Shaun turned his head to rub his cheek against Ashley's before he quickly began licking it. The arch of his body followed the path of Ashley's hand, never allowing it to stray far from him.

"Sweet Kitten," Ashley murmured, turning his head slightly to brush his lips over Shaun's.

Ashley never stopped petting. His hand slowly moved over Shaun's neck, shoulder, and down his side. Shaun gave him a quick lick before he continued downward to Ashley's jaw. Once satisfied with his taste of Ashley, he stopped giving Ashley a tongue bath and rested his head on Ashley's chest.

"Don't leave me," Ashley said quietly. He rubbed his cheek over Shaun's hair as he curled his fingers on Shaun's hip, petting the fur there.

Shaun remained where he was, content to let Ashley pet him, the soft thread of his purring never stopping as long as he was being petted. As he dozed, an occasional flick of his tail would bat near Ashley's hand. Anything more was beyond him just then.

# Chapter Two

The smells of steak, shrimp, and mixed vegetables filled the small apartment, and Ashley hummed along to the radio, not paying much attention to the song that was playing. His back wasn't giving him any trouble and he figured he had a certain Kitten to thank for that.

He stopped after flipping the steaks and shrimp over in the pan. Kitten. Good God, he'd already given Shaun a nickname. Chuckling to himself, he started humming again. A few minutes later, Shaun wandered into the kitchen, yawning and stretching.

Ashley smiled. "Good evening," he said as he got out two plates and the silverware. He set two places at the small dining room table before turning back to cooking their dinner. "I hope you got some good sleep. I know I desperately needed that nap."

Shaun nodded. It'd been awhile since he could sleep safely and not be on high alert. He watched as Ashley set the table. At first, he wondered if somebody else was coming over for dinner. Moving toward one of the cabinets, he slid to the floor and sat cross-legged, not too far away from Ashley.

"Is a guest coming?"

"No. Why?"

Ashley looked down at him, cocking his head to the side. He took the pan from the burner and put the steaks and shrimp on a large serving platter, then surrounded them with the steamed vegetables. Glancing over at the table then back at Ashley, Shaun gave him a confused look. Pets were expected to eat on the floor, and Shaun waited patiently for Ashley to give him a bowl of food.

Though the scents of steak and shrimp were mouthwateringly delicious, he didn't expect he'd be given even a morsel of it.

Ashley took the food to the table, then crouched down on the balls of his feet before Shaun. "I do not take pets. Although I do have…unusual tendencies, I will not take a living creature as a pet without consent. Your place is at the table. I would be delighted if you would join me."

"But you have taken me as your pet." As far as Shaun was concerned, there was no other reason Ashley would have let him into his home. He was a were, nothing but a pet to humankind.

Ashley sighed and stood, pulling Shaun to his feet. "No, I have not. I brought you here because I could not bear to see you survive out there. I am a Master, Shaun, but not in the sense of owning a pet. Illian—my former lover—was my sub, my submissive lover. It was something we both consented to. I do not believe in *owning* a pet."

"You brought me to your home because you didn't want to leave me in the woods?"

"Call it a weakness if you will," Ashley said as he steered Shaun to the table. "Now eat. There is plenty here and if you are still hungry when this is gone, I will gladly fix something more for you." Ashley sat down in his own chair and looked at Shaun expectantly.

Bewildered, Shaun paused for a moment beside the chair before finally settling into it. Looking over at Ashley, he wasn't sure if he dare reach for the food or not. "I couldn't hunt in the park because people would have noticed."

Nodding to the plate full of food, Ashley said, "I imagine so. Now eat your fill. There is no reason to fear me, nor should you fear any repercussions for anything. Most people wouldn't allow even a family dog to sleep with them in their bed, yet I often requested Illian sleep however he wished, which was usually half or full-shifted."

Tilting his head, Shaun regarded Ashley with a good bit of curiosity. It was beyond unusual that any Master would give his pet such freedom. Returning his attention to the food set out before them, he carefully transferred one of the steaks and a couple pieces of shrimp to his plate. Unlike most pets, most of whom had been trained from a young age, he knew how to use such things as forks and knives.

"This Illian, he was like me. A cat?"

"No, no. Illian was a wolf in true form. Not a werewolf, who doesn't have a choice; but a shape shifter who chooses to shift back and forth. I rescued him from a pet hunter and fell in love immediately." Ashley's expression turned thoughtful for a moment before he continued. "Someone found out that I treated him as a lover and not a pet. I was reported and they came in while I was at work. I knew the moment it happened, like a stab to my heart. The scars on my back, and thus my back problems, came about as I tried to save him."

Shaun stopped in mid-bite to stare at Ashley in outright shock. When he found his voice, he asked in a whisper, "You risked your life to try to save a shifter?"

"I risked my life for what I believed in, for the one I loved more than life itself. And I would do it over again should the need ever arise."

"You risk much in your beliefs." Shaking his head, Ashley's words were beyond Shaun's comprehension. "I wasn't raised as a pet, but I still know a lot of the ways of human masters."

Shaun's appetite soon got the better of him and he fell silent as he ate. He devoured the steak and a few pieces of shrimp before he took more of the shrimp. He wasn't much for vegetables and would only occasionally eat them. Most times he'd turn his nose up at them altogether. His primary weakness, however, was sweets.

"Will you stay with me?"

Looking up from his plate, Shaun blinked at Ashley. Unless he wore the mark of a master, anybody could and would enslave him the moment they saw him. Shaun would lay any amount of gold on the possibility that another wouldn't be as kind as Ashley was proving to be. "I think it's the other way around. Outside that door, I am free game to whatever Master takes me."

Ashley smiled and stood. "Excellent." He went into the kitchen and opened the refrigerator. After several seconds of grumbling, he crowed happily. A moment later, he walked up behind Shaun. "Close your eyes and open your mouth, Kitten."

Settling back in the chair, Shaun's stomach felt nicely full for once. Eyeing Ashley with curiosity for a second, he finally closed his eyes and opened his mouth. Ashley brushed the hair from his neck, revealing his tattoo. Just as Ashley slipped the piece of chocolate candy into his mouth, he pressed his lips to the tattoo. The design pulsed and when Ashley pulled away, the star had taken on the shape of the letters A and G.

The luscious flavor of sweet chocolate melted over Shaun's tongue, and he barely felt the stinging pain at the nape of his neck. Yet he was aware Ashley had taken him as his pet, and he was forever branded with Ashley's mark unless Ashley sold him. Something in him rebelled, trying to reject the notion, but he'd already been trained to accept it.

"I wasn't always a pet."

"You are not a pet now," Ashley whispered, turning Shaun's face toward his. "But you are safe." He kissed Shaun softly then, his tongue sliding across Shaun's lips before he pulled away slightly. "I didn't do it because I want a pet. I did it to keep you safe."

Shaun wasn't sure how close he truly wanted Ashley to be, and he didn't yet fully trust in any of this. "I think I understand why you did. It just doesn't make much sense. Most would prefer to own me for themselves or want the gold I could bring them."

"I will not lie to you," Ashley said as stroked his hand over Shaun's hair. "I desire you greatly, but I will not take a lover if he does not want me as well. You are safe here, although if you venture out—or if we venture out together—then it might be prudent to put on the air of you being my pet."

Shaun wanted that touch and his head tipped toward Ashley's hand. The simplest touch made his body long to feel the smooth strokes. "Others will expect you to treat me as they would. There is no way to hide what I am."

"In public, there will be no choice." Ashley slid the fingers of both hands through Shaun's hair.

First Shaun's head nudged to one hand then the other, trying to get the full effect from both. A purr started in his throat, though it died off as he spoke. "If you want to do this, I can only be grateful you are willing to keep me safe."

"I only ask one thing in return," Ashley said. Leaning close, he brushed his lips across Shaun's. "One kiss. Please."

Shaun opened his mouth to speak, but when he felt the touch of Ashley's lips, he remained silent. His tail twitched with a small frenetic burst of nervousness, yet he didn't pull away.

"Kitten." The word was more breathed than said as Ashley brought their mouths together, his tongue sliding over Shaun's lips before slipping into his mouth to taste.

It felt strange to be coaxed into a kiss, but Shaun couldn't help but respond to it. A small sound rose in his throat as Ashley's tongue stroked over his. Tipping his head slightly upward, he pressed their lips more tightly together, the gesture a small sign of acceptance.

"Thank you," Ashley said, pulling away slowly. "Bed? I'll pet you until you're asleep."

That's all Ashley had to say. Blinking up at him, Shaun nodded. He could curl anywhere for hours as long as a petting was part of the offer. This place was already starting to look like heaven.

Taking Shaun's hands in his, Ashley led the way back to the bedroom. The dishes could wait until tomorrow.

Saturday was for cleaning. Right now, he had a Kitten to pet.

Sitting on the edge of the bed, Shaun watched him with bright curiosity. Ashley could tell Shaun was a bit more comfortable now, rather than apprehensive as he had been before. Not being forced into any of this, or being chained and treated as a normal pet, he knew it would help Shaun to accept himself and his new home.

Shaun stretched out on the bed and quickly curled up on one side, giving Ashley room to climb in. Ashley got into bed and tugged the covers over them as he pulled Shaun to him. Settling on his side to face Shaun, he moved closer, unable to resist the urge to nuzzle the soft fur at the hollow of Shaun's throat. He exhaled softly, loving the way the fur warmed beneath his lips. His right hand stroked over Shaun's side and down to his hip. When Shaun's tail flicked his hand, Ashley reached out and played with it.

Nudging in against him, Shaun seemed very comfortable. His head fell back, eyes closing as Ashley petted him. When Shaun's fingers kneaded gently on Ashley's chest, Ashley gasped and pushed closer, fingers stroking Shaun's tail.

"Kitten."

The flex and clawing of Shaun's nails continued to knead against Ashley as a soft, rippling purr vibrated from the werecat's throat. Ashley kissed Shaun's chest, then started to pull away slightly as he felt himself growing hard again. Shaun looked at him and blinked, a questioning look in his eyes.

"I want you," Ashley groaned. "Want you so bad it hurts." He reached out, just to keeping touching, petting. "Won't ever stop petting you, Kitten."

MYCHAEL BLACK / SHAYNE CARMICHAEL

# Chapter Three

As had become Shaun's habit over the last few weeks, he sat cross-legged on the couch, waiting for Ashley to come home. His eyes kept drifting between the door and the leash and collar on the nearby small table. He knew the minute Ashley walked in that they were going shopping. In public, Ashley would have to treat him as a normal pet, but he was too excited at the chance to shop to care.

The door opened and Ashley smiled immediately. "Hello, Kitten. I'd hoped to get home sooner." He closed the door, set his keys on the bar, and dropped his bag to the floor. Then he walked over to Shaun and held out a hand to him. "I've been looking forward to our shopping trip. Have you, Kitten?"

Bounding from the couch, Shaun nearly tackled him before the bag hit the floor. "You promised me." A soft purr vibrated from his throat as he rubbed his face on the front of Ashley's shirt.

Laughing, Ashley hugged him tight. "Yes, I did. Are you ready?"

Nudging against Ashley with the hug, Shaun nodded eagerly before tipping his head back slightly to him, ready for the collar.

"Kitten..." The pet name was whispered as Ashley stared at him. "Please...a kiss?"

Nodding slightly, Shaun hummed softly in anticipation as he leaned in toward Ashley.

Ashley smiled just before his mouth covered Shaun's. His tongue slid across his Kitten's lips, then between them. He moaned happily, content enough to drink in his

21

Kitten's taste—rich, sweet, and earthy. Fingers in Shaun's hair, Ashley held on and knew he was caught—hook, line, and sinker. Shaun's fingers curled in the front of his shirt as he nudged closer to Ashley. After allowing them both a few more minutes of indulgence, Ashley pulled away slowly, peppering Shaun's cheek with kisses until he reached his Kitten's ear.

"Shall we?"

Seeming vaguely disappointed when the kiss ended, Shaun's expression quickly changed to one of excitement as he waited for Ashley to put the leash and collar on him. No ordinary leash and collar, the black leather was chased with an intricate silver filigree design. When Ashley had put it on the table the night before, Shaun had studied it at length.

"I don't like this whole collar business," Ashley said as he stepped away to get the collar and leash, "so I decided that, if we're going to use them, they have to mean something." Picking up the collar, he fingered the design absently as he walked back over to Shaun. "I wanted something special, something only for us."

He slid the collar under Shaun's hair and fastened it around his neck, taking great care to make sure it wasn't too tight. "I had this made for you yesterday. I was afraid it wouldn't be done in time for our shopping trip, but there were no orders in front of mine."

The small chain that dangled from the edge of the leather glistened against Shaun's black and white fur. He reached up to touch the collar. "I thought you did. I've never seen anything like it in the pet department of the stores. It's somehow special, but I'm not sure how."

Ashley smiled as he slid his hand through the loop at the end of the chain. "Because it's ours," he said simply. After fastening the leash, he grabbed his keys and opened the door. Once Shaun was out, he closed and locked it. "There are some nice stores just a block from here. Do you like leather?"

"Normally I don't like much when it comes to

clothing. It tends to make me uncomfortable."

Nodding, Ashley said, "Okay, we can work with that. I'll take you into the shops and you can find what you like. How does that sound?" He looked over at Shaun and smiled as they stepped out onto the busy sidewalk.

As they walked, people turned their heads and stared. Some looked like they'd seen a god, while others simply looked envious. Ashley held his head up and smiled proudly, never once letting Shaun fall behind. He made certain they walked together — side by side, Shaun in half-form.

Appearing oblivious to everybody else, Shaun wondered if he could talk Ashley into buying a few things for him. He wouldn't push it, though he really did want another loincloth that covered more than the one he wore. It was about the only thing he could wear in his half-form. Giving Ashley a surreptitious side glance, Shaun found his Master was watching him.

"Are we going to get something to eat, too?"

"We'll do whatever you want, Kitten," Ashley said, smiling. "Are you hungry now?"

Shaun nodded.

"Then eating it is." Ashley stopped in front of a restaurant and perused the menu pages taped to the window. "Do you like Chinese?"

When Shaun nodded again, Ashley opened the door and entered the restaurant. A young woman greeted them, but addressed Ashley. "Is it just you and your pet tonight, sir?"

"Yes, and I would like a private table, please."

"Right this way."

Ashley smiled over at Shaun as they followed the woman to a table behind a partition. It was low to the floor, with a short chair and a pile of silk pillows. Nodding to the pillows, Ashley said, "Sit, Kitten," as he sat on the chair. Looking up at the woman, he continued. "Please just bring us both some water for now."

Shaun settled on the floor near Ashley's leg. The press

of his body wedged tightly to Ashley as he glanced up at him. Then his attention was diverted by the glimpse he caught just beyond the edge of the partition. Others were dining and many had their pets in tow as well. All of the weres were kept leashed and close to their owners. None of them were allowed to be in their full animal form in the restaurant.

The most common pet was wolf, and there were several in the restaurant, ranging from silver to black. From his position, Shaun could also see at least two cats. One was a panther, and the other a lion. Within the werecat breeds, tigers and lions seemed to be the most common, though any white version of either was a highly rare and prized creature. That alone explained the curious, and rather envious, stares Shaun and Ashley received.

"You are much more beautiful," Ashley said, dropping a soft kiss on the top of Shaun's head. The tender display caught them a few stares and Shaun tried to ignore them. It was uncommon for owners to show tenderness to their pets, but Ashley didn't seem to care.

"What can I get you this evening?" the waitress asked as she set their waters on the table.

"I will have the shrimp lo mein, with steamed rice. My pet will have the shrimp and fish treats." Ashley handed her the menus.

A small, pulsing purr echoed Shaun's approval before he laid his head against Ashley's leg, rubbing his cheek against him. Content for the moment, a bright inquisitive gaze roamed over what he could see. He wasn't the only one looking. The panther was watching him with just as much curiosity.

"Oh, that smells wonderful," Ashley said as the waitress put their food in front of them a few minutes later.

"Anything else I can get you?"

"No, this is quite fine for now. Thank you." After she left, Ashley picked up one of the shrimp from Shaun's bowl and held it in front of Shaun. "Open wide, Kitten," he

MYCHAEL BLACK / SHAYNE CARMICHAEL

coaxed teasingly.

Shaun opened his mouth to take the offering of shrimp and licked at Ashley's fingers. After eating the first piece, he mewled softly, begging for more.

Picking up a piece of fish, Ashley rubbed Shaun's lips with it, teasing him as he lifted it up. When Shaun's head was tilted back, mouth open expectantly, Ashley kissed him. Shaun licked Ashley's lips playfully before he lowered his head to snag the piece of fish from Ashley's fingers. When a man moved around the divider and crouched down in front of him, Shaun blinked but didn't say anything.

After studying Shaun for a moment, the man looked over at Ashley. "Exquisite markings on this one. I'd like to offer a lel standard gold for him, if you're interested."

Eyes narrowing, Ashley all but growled, "He's not for sale."

The man shook his head. "A pity. I have a white female. You wouldn't consider breeding him, would you? I'll offer a half cut of the sales on the litters. Why don't you think about it?" Digging into his pocket, he pulled out a gold card case and opened it. He took out one of his business cards and placed it on the table in front of Ashley. With a smile, he straightened from his position. Giving one last look at Shaun, the man returned to his own table.

Ashley said nothing; he just glared at the man as he walked away. Then he looked down at Shaun. It was still a considerable sum to breed, but there was just no way he could do it—not to himself, and not to Shaun. He then smiled and picked up another shrimp, feeding it to Shaun before he started on his own dinner. All the while, he kept glaring at anyone who looked their way, his right arm tightening around Shaun's shoulders. He remained quiet for the rest of their meal. He knew this was something they'd have to talk about: his resistance to such things. When he was done, he pushed his dishes away and left the money on the table with the check.

25

"Are you done, Kitten?"

"I'm done." In a graceful movement of muscle, Shaun stood and moved with Ashley toward the door.

Back outside, away from the others, Ashley let out the breath he hadn't been aware he'd been holding. He stopped walking suddenly and turned, pulling Shaun close for another kiss. This one, however, held a touch of desperation in it as Ashley all but clung to Shaun, not caring what others might think. Shaun's lips molded tightly to his as a soft, rolling purr filled the kiss.

Drawing back, Shaun looked at him questioningly. "Is something wrong, Master?"

Ashley rested his forehead to Shaun's and closed his eyes, breathing in his Kitten's scent. "Just unnerved, Kitten," he said quietly. "I can't stand the thought of sharing you, even if it's only to breed."

"I thought you would want the gold." Shaun sounded relieved.

Ashley remained silent for several seconds, drawing back to look into Shaun's eyes. Then he just smiled. "No amount of money can replace you." Leaving it at that, he took Shaun's hand and led him toward one of the shops a few doors down from the restaurant.

It was market day and the shopping square was filled with people. Before they entered the store, Shaun caught sight of the Institution's center stage sale of werecreatures. If he hadn't escaped them, he'd be one of the ones performing for prospective buyers. Saying nothing, he simply edged closer to Ashley as they walked.

Sliding his arm around Shaun's shoulder, Ashley said, "You are with me now."

"They would have eventually caught me," Shaun whispered as he plastered himself to Ashley's side. Ashley's fingertips brushed the dark tattoo on his neck and a soft, rolling purr vibrated Shaun's throat with the touch.

As soon as they walked into the shop, Ashley pulled him to a corner out of the way. "You're safe now, Kitten. I promise you that." He smiled and kissed Shaun softly. "Now, let's go see what you can find." Turning Shaun around, he steered his Kitten toward the back of the store where the pet supplies were kept.

With a nod, Shaun smiled at him. "I know. I belong to you."

As they wandered the aisles, Shaun nosed around and stopped occasionally to look at something that had caught his interest. When they reached the clothing section, his steps considerably slowed, but he didn't say anything.

Smiling, Ashley leaned closer to whisper in his ear. "Yes, Kitten?"

Shaun quickly gave him a side glance before he shook his head slightly. Swallowing the sigh, Ashley just shook his head. This was going to take a lot of work on both of their parts. He resorted to watching Shaun closely, noting which things his Kitten lingered over.

"Oh. This is a nice one, Kitten." He picked up a soft, velvety black loincloth. Holding it up against Shaun, he smiled. "It looks beautiful. You like it, yes?"

Shaun nodded quickly. "I like it."

"Then we'll get three," Ashley said as he picked up two more. "Is there anything else you wanted to look at?"

Shaun blinked and shook his head. "I was hoping you would buy me one."

Ashley grinned. "I was hoping you would speak up and tell me what you wanted. Guess only time will lead to that." Giving him a kiss, Ashley started for the cashier.

Shaun trotted happily behind Ashley and waited patiently beside him as he paid for the clothing. He wasn't quite used to being allowed to say what he wanted. He knew it placed a burden on Ashley to have to read him, but he really didn't understand it any other way.

Once the items were bagged, Shaun walked obediently beside Ashley as they left the store. Not too far away, a woman was inspecting one of the werewolves. The Institute dealer stood beside her as the woman ran her hand over the wolf's soft fur.

"He's very responsive, ma'am. The Institute has certified him as fully trained in a number of arts to be most pleasing to a new Mistress."

As her hand lowered to the wolf's genitals, the were's hips quickly nudged against her. Lowering his eyes, the wolf glanced away as Shaun looked at him. Shaun knew him very well; the were had been trained to perform, and had little to no control over his own responses. Shaun had run from the Institute before they could advance him to that particular training.

"And what are you asking for this one, Shafel?" the woman asked as her fingers lingered over the wolf's cock.

Giving the werewolf one last glance, Shaun smiled at him. He hoped the were's new owner would be as kind as Ashley was to him. Shaun had seen the wolf at the Institute a few times and even knew his first name.

Ashley growled and gripped Shaun's hand tighter. Shaun followed hurriedly behind him, trying to keep up. Not understanding why Ashley was suddenly impatient to get home, Shaun eyed him silently.

The second they stepped into their apartment, Ashley dropped the bag from the store and ran to the bathroom. Seconds later, Shaun heard him throwing up, then the toilet flushed. Bewildered, he headed toward the bathroom and hovered in the doorway. Watching Ashley with concern, he finally stepped forward and laid his hand on Ashley's shoulder.

"I'm fine, Kitten," Ashley muttered. He slid a hand up over Shaun's as he wiped his mouth with the hand towel from the counter. "Just a demon from the past I'd never thought I'd see again."

Taking his Master's hand, Shaun pulled Ashley back to his feet. "Somebody bad enough to make you sick?"

"That woman…the one inspecting the wolf." Ashley looked up at him. "She sold Illian to me. She beat him to within an inch of his life on a regular basis."

"I was hoping Kal would be treated nicely. Like you

treat me."

Resting his head on Shaun's shoulder, Ashley drew in a shaky breath. "In this city, they don't care," he growled.

"A friend of mine might. I knew him before I went to the Institute. He works with the CPG. He might know somebody who could, maybe, do something?"

Shaun knew there was some kind of movement among the mortals who wanted laws to protect the weres, but the idea had yet to fully catch on. One of his neighbors in his old neighborhood had been an activist, and Shaun had occasionally helped him. He just wasn't sure if Chester could do anything about this.

"CPG?" Ashley blinked in confusion. Then it seemed to dawn on him. "The Creature Protection Grid. Yes! Who is he? We'll get in touch with him about her, whether she buys Kal or not."

"Chester was seriously into it, and I helped him every once in a while before I was taken. He told me some of the enforcers were sympathetic to helping weres. You just had to know which ones. We could go see him tomorrow. I don't think it would bother him that I'm a weretiger."

Ashley nodded. "Then we will do that."

While there was no guarantee Chester could help, it made Shaun feel better to at least try. Sliding his arms around Ashley, he clung to his Master as he nuzzled Ashley's neck.

# Chapter Four

Ashley knocked on the nondescript wooden door, then looked over at Shaun. "I sure hope he can help."

Looking around somewhat nervously, Shaun's gaze kept returning to the yard next door before he finally pulled himself together. He'd talked Ashley into getting off work early to do this because he didn't want to chance running into his parents, and for his own reasons he refused to take any form other than fully human right now.

A minute later, a young man opened the door. His dark brown hair stood in peaks at odd angles and he was dressed in an overly large gray T-shirt and jeans. Blinking at Shaun, he looked completely surprised. "Shaun?"

Shaun gave him a hesitant smile. "Hello, Chester. I thought we could talk to you?"

"Damn, Shaun." Grabbing a hold of Shaun's hand, Chester dragged him into the house as he threw a smile at Ashley. "Come on in."

Ashley closed the door and returned Chester's smile, though his own seemed a little more wary. "Hi," he said, extending a hand to Chester. "Ashley."

"Nice to meet you, Ashley." Chester gave Ashley's hand a quick, firm shake before he turned back to Shaun. "I was so fucking pissed off when your parents threw you into the Institute. The Palmers and Mrs. Jenners tried to petition the Institute to get you, but by the time the paperwork cleared, they said you had escaped."

"I didn't know," Shaun said, surprised. "Thanks for trying, Chester. Tell them thank you for me."

"Guess we did come to the right guy." Ashley looked at Shaun. When Chester gave him a curious look, Ashley continued. "Do you know Illa Jacobs? She's a well-known purchaser and breeder of wolves."

Chester shook his head. "Not a name I've come across, but I can check the files to see if there's anything on her. Why?"

"Illa Jacobs sold me my first…pet," Ashley explained. "When he came to me, he was badly beaten, clearly mistreated in some of the worst ways possible. We saw her yesterday, looking to buy another wolf. I fear for any others that might be in her possession."

Chester didn't seem all that surprised. "What's your area?" Moving toward his desk, he opened a file cabinet and began leafing through the folders.

"We're in New Roth, Chester." Shaun answered for Ashley.

Darting a quick look at Ashley, Chester seemed to catch on quickly to the unique relationship since Ashley made no attempt to reprimand Shaun. "Okay, let's see what I got."

As Chester opened one of his folders, he hummed softly for a moment before he said, "You are in luck. Enforcer Narson runs the twenty-seventh district. He has an excellent record for pushing punishment as far as he can. And as far as Illa Jacobs goes…" Trailing off, he closed the folder and went to his computer. After a moment of typing, a status file appeared on his screen.

Reading the text, Chester murmured, "Oh, this is a nice lady. There've been several complaints placed against her. Maybe it's time to match her with Narson and see what comes up."

Moving to stand behind Shaun, Ashley slid his arms around Shaun's waist and rested his chin on his shoulder. Shaun rested his hands against Ashley's and purred softly as he turned his head slightly to look at him.

"It doesn't surprise me in the least to know she has complaints lodged against her." Ashley shrugged. "I'll see her in prison for a very long time if I can."

After clicking a button to print out the report, Chester looked over at Ashley. "I can give you what the CPG has on her. But I'll warn you, there's nothing Narson can do about the prior complaints. They've already been dismissed by other Enforcers. But if you talk to him, he might tell the Area Commander to forward any more reports with her name on them. He's not going to be able to do anything until somebody files another complaint."

Sighing, he took the paper from the printer and handed it to Ashley. "I can see you're Shaun's owner, and I'm glad to see you're concerned about the situation."

"I don't keep pets," Ashley said as he took the paper. "I claimed Shaun to keep him safe, not to declare ownership. I care greatly for him. Thank you very much."

Chester smiled wryly. "Not many would see it that way, but it's good to hear you know the distinction."

"He does make me happy and keep me safe, Chester."

Nodding to Shaun, Chester smiled at both of them. "I wish you luck taking care of Jacobs."

"Thank you," Ashley said. Kissing Shaun's shoulder, he whispered, "Are you ready to go, Kitten?"

"Can I come see you again, Chester?" Shaun asked uncertainly.

"Sure, any time you want, Shaun. You could always help me stuff envelopes again." Chuckling, he took hold of Shaun's hand, giving it a squeeze before releasing it.

"It was a pleasure meeting you, Chester." Ashley shook Chester's hand again and opened the door. He held it open for Shaun, then closed it behind them. "Well, that went better than I'd expected."

As they left Chester's house, Shaun took hold of Ashley's hand. "I thought he might help. He was always very loud about the CPG."

"Home, Kitten?"

"Sounds like a good idea to me." Shaun only looked in the direction of his old home once before he completely dismissed his old life.

"You okay?" Ashley asked him, nudging Shaun's shoulder gently with his as they walked.

"I'm fine." He gave Ashley a reassuring smile before getting into the car.

The trip home was quick, but quiet. Ashley's thoughts kept wandering back to Illa Jacobs, then to Illian, and finally to Shaun. He'd loved Illian with everything he was, and now he was headed in the same direction with Shaun. He only wished it was mutual. He wanted the closeness he'd had with Illian; he wanted it with Shaun.

"Home sweet home," he said as he parked the car in front of their apartment building. Giving Shaun a half-smile, he got out.

Shaun led the way to their door. Once inside, Ashley set the keys and papers on the counter and went into the kitchen. It wasn't often he drank, but he needed a drink now. He pulled out a bottle from the cabinet and opened it, pouring a small bit into a glass sitting on the countertop.

"Ashley?"

"Kitten...I'm so sorry..." Ashley knew he wasn't making much sense, but after Shaun's reaction last time, he wasn't sure how to broach the subject now. "I just..." He sighed and took another drink of the bourbon.

Tilting his head, Shaun's expression became curious as he moved closer to Ashley. The playful nudge of his body pushed against Ashley's as Shaun lifted his head for a kiss. A teasing flick of his tongue licked at Ashley's lips and he purred softly.

"Kitten..." Ashley murmured, tongue sliding out to lick Shaun's. "I want you so much..." The second the words were out, he wished he could have taken them back.

Shaun's lips drifted over his cheek before Shaun lowered his head to bury his face against Ashley's neck. Ashley knew it really wasn't a subject Shaun knew how to deal with quite yet. He shivered and let out a ragged sigh.

"Come on, Kitten...let's go lay down, maybe have some petting time."

# Chapter Five

After that night, Shaun shifted to full tiger form and remained that way for weeks. During the day, he roamed the neighborhood, playing with the children at the nearby park. Not surprisingly, during this time the reported cases of attempted child kidnappings severely decreased. It seemed a white tiger was an excellent deterrent to the black market engineers who sporadically captured children for illegal genetic experiments. Though the laws were harsh against people who genetically altered mortals into weres to sell on the black market, it was still a thriving business. As a result, neighborhood parents had taken to allowing Shaun to baby sit their youngsters in the park while they enjoyed the much-needed peace.

Shaun considered the neighborhood his territory. His range included the entire street and the houses behind his own, as well as the park. Each day, he spent hours learning the rhythm of the small community. Everybody seemed to have their own routine: those who went to work, those who stayed home, the children going to school and coming home. The quiet and noise of the street fluctuated, depending on the time of day, and Shaun became familiar with it all.

In the afternoon, he would return home to find Ashley waiting for him. The scent of dinner being prepared would lure Shaun to the kitchen. Always sitting patiently beside the cupboard, he'd wait for Ashley to feed him.

Late at night, he'd curl beside Ashley in the huge bed. After the appropriately deemed time for petting, Shaun would contently fall asleep. Sometimes he'd wake up in the middle of night and watch Ashley sleep. As the nights passed, he began to relax and soon came to rely on Ashley's presence.

Come morning, he would wake to find Ashley nestled up against his back. It became his habit to wake his Master with a lick to his face. Shaun's life took on a regular schedule, and it went a long way into settling him into accepting Ashley and the life he offered.

As summer began to slowly take on its full strength, the days in the park lengthened as the children spent every free moment of their time playing outside. Lounging on the grass, Shaun was surrounded by kids. Some of them climbed on him, wanting a ride, but most were content to simply pet him. The lazy rumble of his purr constantly sounded as he rested his head on his paws, blinking sleepily.

"How would I know to find you here?"

Raising his head, Shaun chuffed softly as his head stretched forward toward Ashley. Yawning widely, his canines flashed before he licked Ashley's hand. In this form, he had no problem being affectionate; everything else was just a bit harder. Although, as his Master, Ashley had every right to force him to do whatever he wanted.

"Missed you," Ashley whispered as he turned his hand over to stroke the soft fur of Shaun's throat. "Have you eaten today? I had to leave early this morning."

Shaun shook his head. Slowly standing, he gently head-butted one of the three children near him. It was time for them to go home, and he would make sure they got there safely before he went home with Ashley.

Giggling and laughing, the boy and two girls raced ahead across the park, and Shaun playfully gave chase. The long line of his sleek body stretched out to its full length and gracefully balanced with each hit of his paws to the ground. His speed was nowhere near what he was capable of, but then he was only playing.

Ashley stayed where he was, content to watch them until he couldn't see them anymore. Resting his head on his knees, he started to doze off. A low whistle startled him awake and he looked up to see two men standing not far from him, both of them looking quite…interested.

"What's a hot thing like you doin' out here all alone?"

The other one sneered at Ashley, mouth widening in a slow, leering grin. "How about we find out just how hot he really is?"

Ashley's heart jumped into his throat and his muscles tensed, ready to bolt at any second. Then he saw all six hundred pounds of muscle and fury that was Shaun suddenly lunge toward them. The first man had just reached out to grab Ashley when his companion's eyes widened impossibly.

With their attention diverted, Ashley scrambled backward, bumping into a shrub. Both men took off running in the opposite direction of the enormous white tiger running full throttle toward them. When one of them hesitated, Shaun went after him. Ashley was left shaking, almost becoming one with the bush behind him as he watched the men and Shaun dart across four lanes of traffic.

Chaos ensued as several cars swerved in order to avoid hitting the fleeing men and the tiger. The blare of horns and drivers' cursing became a jangled noise, yet none actually stopped to see what was happening. The full length of Shaun's body covered the ground easily and he launched at the man's back. Bringing the man swiftly down, Shaun's teeth clamped at the back of his neck. The rest of his body pinned the struggling man against the pavement at the side of the road.

*"Shaun. Stop. Let him go!"*

Ashley's command reached the animalistic fog hazing Shaun's mind. Fighting the urge to tear into the panicked mortal beneath him, Shaun let him go. Roaring out his rage, he let the offender scramble up as he backed off. Without a backward glance, the man ran as Shaun padded down the side of the road toward the crosswalk. Ashley jumped to his feet and ran, dropping to his knees when he reached Shaun and throwing his arms around Shaun's neck.

"Thank you. Thank you so much, Kitten."

The rapid-fire flick of Shaun's tail betrayed the agitation still quivering through him. He didn't know why his Master had been afraid, but it had been because of those two men. His instinct to protect his Master was a force that couldn't be overridden by anything else. With Ashley's affectionate nuzzling, Shaun gently butted against him. The initial reaction slowly began to fade with Ashley's influence on him, and Shaun calmed considerably. A soft purr rumbled from his chest as he turned his head, lavishing his own form of kisses to Ashley's face.

"Come on, love," Ashley said, standing. "We need to make a stop at the police station to report what happened."

Tilting his head, Shaun stared up at Ashley, blinking before he obediently stood. Circling behind Ashley, he came up against the side of his Master's leg, nudging against him. Smiling down at him, Ashley stroked a hand over his head, petting the silky black and white fur.

"You're so beautiful," Ashley whispered as they walked. "A prayer answered."

Shaun stayed close to Ashley as they made their way from the park to the police station. Several appreciative stares from others followed them, but Shaun paid no attention to any of them. When they approached the station, Shaun waited for Ashley to open the door. No one seemed disturbed by the presence of a tiger in their precinct. Weres were too common of a sight.

Ashley spent several minutes talking to various people, giving his statements and reports on what had happened in the park. He described the two men to the police, and when he finished he turned back to Shaun.

"It's done. Let the police take care of it. Shall we head home?"

Settled on his stomach, Shaun lifted his head.

Blinking lazily, he ambled to his feet and led the way back down the corridor and to the exit. The walk home was quiet and easy, Ashley's hand never leaving Shaun's head. When they got home, Ashley locked the door behind them. Then he slid straight down the door, taking in a long, ragged breath. Turning to face him, Shaun nudged against his Master. He wanted more petting. Rubbing his muzzle against Ashley's chest, his soft purr was the only sound between them.

"Sometimes I wish I was a werecat," Ashley said as he slid his hands over Shaun's head and back. "Maybe then I could be more to you than what I am." Closing his eyes, he let his head fall back and allowed himself to remember, just for a moment, what it felt like to touch someone. It had been entirely too long, that much was certain.

Unable to speak in full cat form, Shaun sat back on his haunches. A tingle of electricity raced in the air around him as he slowly shifted. The mass of his body decreased and the larger bulk of his muscle contracted, becoming smaller and streamlined. His muzzle retracted, forming the smoother lines of a human face as his paws became hands and feet. Shaun sat cross-legged in front of Ashley, watching him quietly.

"You don't want to be like me."

Ashley opened his eyes. After a moment of silence, he finally spoke. "I have my reasons to want just that. I want to be something more to you than what I am, and because I'm human, that will never change."

Motioning helplessly with his hand, Shaun gestured to himself. He was in half-form, fur still covering his entire body. Even in full mortal form, he wouldn't be mistaken for anything but what he was.

"I wasn't always like this. Right before my eighteenth birthday, I shifted. Until then I was normal, or at least I thought I was normal. Two days after I shifted for the first time, my parents sold me to be trained as a pet. That was six months ago. I spent my eighteenth birthday in the training institution. I was supposed to graduate from school, not be trained to a collar and leash. I don't know who I am anymore; I just want everything to be back the way it was." A half sob silenced Shaun, and it took a moment for him to continue. "I ran away from them"

Ashley reached out with one of his hands, cupping Shaun's face tenderly. "I don't want a pet. I want a companion. Your safety is the only thing that prompted me to claim you, Shaun. As far as I'm concerned, your soul, your life, your heart—they are all yours. I want to help. I want you to know that you are special."

Needing the comfort of Ashley's touch, Shaun nuzzled his Master's hand. "I don't know who I am. They tell me who I am, but I don't know the truth anymore. I don't want to be this way, but I can't help it."

Ashley scooted closer, settling on his knees in front of Shaun, and tilted Shaun's head up to see his eyes. "What do you need from me, Shaun? I'm not asking what you think you need. I'm asking what *do* you need? You are not at the institute; you are with me. You are beautiful, more beautiful than you think, and I want so much for you to see that."

Blinking back tears, Shaun stared at him. He'd never really thought about what he might need. Even in the short time he'd spent in the institute, Shaun's sense of self had been skewered. "I want to stay here with you. I'm happy here."

"Your place is here. With me," Ashley whispered. He pressed a soft kiss to Shaun's lips, then pulled him close.

Confusion warred with a mixture of pain in Shaun and he curled up against Ashley. "Will you always keep me?"

"How could I not?" Ashley murmured against Shaun's hair. "I've fallen in love with you."

Lifting his head, Shaun gave him an inquisitive look. "You have? Why?"

Ashley smiled and brushed the backs of his fingers over one of Shaun's cheeks. "Because of who you are, Shaun. You are the most beautiful being I've ever seen, and I'm beyond honored to have you here with me." Ashley slid his thumb slowly over Shaun's bottom lip. For a moment, nothing existed but those amber eyes staring back into his own.

Shaun smiled and a contented purr rose in his throat. "I can love you, too, you know." Shaun pressed a soft kiss to the ball of his thumb.

"Then I am doubly blessed." Ashley leaned down to kiss him softly, whispering his pet name of 'Kitten' on Shaun's lips.

Purr deepening, the tip of Shaun's tongue began tasting Ashley's mouth, slipping deeper inside. Shaun's initiative in making the kiss more momentarily shocked Ashley. The purrs and the touch of Shaun's tongue, however, served to wash that away. Ashley opened to him, letting Shaun do what he wished. Although he gave Shaun's tongue a few teasing licks, he wanted this be what his Kitten would make it. He whispered 'Kitten' into Shaun's mouth, the name escaping in a soft moan.

Shaun playfully nipped at Ashley's lower lip before continuing his exploration of Ashley's mouth. Ending the kiss, Shaun's head dipped down toward Ashley's throat, lavishing a series of kisses, licks and nips over his skin.

"Love you, Kitten," Ashley whispered. "I love you so much." Unable to stop the soft moans escaping him, he simply tipped his head back, letting Shaun explore. And if Ashley had to sneak away for a bit of private time later, then so be it.

Pulling back slowly, Shaun smiled at him. "What's for dinner anyway? I'm starving."

Ashley chuckled and kissed Shaun's nose. "What would you like, Kitten?"

"Steak?" Shaun grinned. "And chocolate?"

"Mm," Ashley hummed, "I can do steak. And I bought some new chocolates yesterday, dark chocolate truffles with milk chocolate centers." He kissed Shaun's forehead and shifted, standing them both up.

Scrambling from Ashley's lap, Shaun made a quick

detour to his bedroom. He needed to at least put on his loincloth. Once it was fastened in place, he hurriedly headed out to the kitchen to join his Master. The promise of a new treat was more than enough of a lure.

Catching him in the hallway, Ashley smiled devilishly. "Close your eyes and open your mouth, Kitten."

A sudden flare of his nostrils tried to catch a hint of whatever Ashley had in his hand. Smiling briefly, Shaun closed his eyes and opened his mouth. Ashley's mouth covered his then, tongue sliding a piece of sweet chocolate into Shaun's mouth.

"Enjoy," Ashley whispered.

The taste of the chocolate drew an instant mewling sound of enjoyment from Shaun. His Master gave him a home, safety, and love, and spoiled him outrageously. Resting his hands against Ashley's chest, his nails kneaded into the fabric of Ashley's shirt. Wanting to share the chocolate, he kissed Ashley back. Ashley's fingers slid through his hair, holding him close as they kissed. When Ashley pulled slowly away, he rubbed his nose along Shaun's.

"Help me cook dinner?"

"I know how to cook." Letting go of his shirt, Shaun turned his head, giving Ashley's cheek a quick lick.

"Good. You get started, and I'll meet you there in a few minutes." Ashley gave him a quick wink before heading for the bathroom.

Shaun sidestepped Ashley to continue down the hall into the kitchen. Busying himself, he got the steaks out of the refrigerator and set them on the counter. Knowing Ashley liked vegetables, he hunted through the crisper and brought out the vegetables to make him a salad. He might even be enticed into eating a bite or two, but it was a big maybe.

# Chapter Six

With Shaun busy, Ashley took the chance and took off his clothes, dropping them into the hamper by the sink counter. He draped a towel over the toilet seat lid and sat down, leaning his head back against the shelving above the toilet. His strokes started slow, leisurely pulls from the base to the tip of his cock, his other hand rolling and tugging his balls. As the pleasure built, images of Shaun flashed through Ashley's mind, his imagination feeding him sounds of Shaun breathing and panting, coming as Ashley filled him. That was all it took.

Barely biting back a moan, Ashley came, heat pouring over his hand. "Kitten…"

\* \* \* \*

After unwrapping the steaks and turning on the stove, Shaun set the steaks to frying as he cut up the salad. As he reached for the bowl to put everything together, he suddenly stilled, aware of the rippling thoughts reaching him. He could feel the odd vibration from his Master and knew what was happening. Understanding Ashley had his own needs, he had to smile at the thought of what Ashley was doing. The sensation warmed through him. It was a part of being loved.

Ashley sidled up behind him a few minutes later, dropping a soft kiss to his shoulder while reaching around to steal a sliver of carrot from the salad Shaun was preparing. "Mm, very good, Kitten. Maybe one of these days I'll be able to coax you into eating a vegetable or two," he teased.

Making a face at Ashley's comment, Shaun said, "I'm not that fond of vegetables." He caught the scent of spent sex on Ashley, but didn't say anything. He tried not to draw in the odor, but it was next to impossible. A soft sound escaped his throat as he busied himself slicing the rest of the carrot and cucumber.

"Are you okay, Kitten?" Ashley turned him slowly around, hands sliding up his arms. As Ashley looked at Shaun, realization seemed to set in his eyes. "Kitten," Ashley whispered, a smile flitting across his lips.

Shaun wanted to lick Ashley and learn him, learn what his Master smelled like, tasted like. Yet, he knew it might be misunderstood. "I'm okay," he said quietly, meeting Ashley's gaze.

Running his fingers through Shaun's hair, Ashley smiled. "I will never pressure you into anything. You know that, right? But you are welcome to do whatever you wish, whenever you wish. I will not take things farther. You are in control."

Tilting his head, Shaun relished the feel of Ashley's hand in his hair. Closing his eyes, he focused for a second on the familiar tinge of Ashley's closeness and the musky undertone surrounding him.

"I know enough about you to know you wouldn't. It isn't that. I just don't want to make anything worse on you." He understood Ashley had his needs, and he really didn't want to make the situation any harder on him.

"Oh, Kitten." Ashley pulled him close, nuzzling Shaun's cheek before whispering in his ear. "You could never make anything worse for me. You are the only one who fuels my fantasies. When I pleasure myself, it is you I think about. Your needs are just as important, if not more so, than my own as far as I'm concerned."

Shaun wanted and needed to be close to his Master. Everything he craved was in Ashley's hands. The solid foundation of safety, security, and love were everything to him. It kept his fear and uncertainty in the future at bay.

"Master." A soft, lilting purr came from him, the word woven in the melody as he licked Ashley's cheek softly.

"Love you, Kitten," Ashley murmured. His head

turned just enough to catch Shaun's tongue and lick it. "If exploration and taste are what you want, then I am at your mercy." He stroked his fingers over the back of Shaun's neck.

As much as he wanted to, they still had dinner to take care of, and from the smell of the steaks, they were nearly done. Still, Shaun took a bit of advantage as a soft growl spoke to Ashley before his arms snaked around Ashley's neck. His darting tongue followed the slow withdrawal of Ashley's and slid into his Master's mouth.

Ashley hummed softly. When the steaks started to sizzle, however, he broke the kiss with a chuckle. "Damn. Guess that's our cue that it's dinnertime."

Shaun had managed to become pleasantly occupied and he rumbled his disappointment when Ashley drew back. "You go ahead and dish out the steaks." Turning back around, Shaun picked up the salad and the silverware, and carried them to the table.

Ashley set their plates on the table and pulled his chair closer to Shaun's. "Let me feed you. Please?"

Once he'd gotten their drinks, Shaun settled in the chair. Eyeing Ashley, he wasn't surprised at all by the request. It had become a fairly normal thing for them. Nodding in answer, he rested an elbow on the table as he leaned in closer to Ashley.

After cutting a bite-sized piece from Shaun's steak, Ashley picked it up with his fingers and lifted it to Shaun's lips. "Open for me, Kitten."

Shaun's eyes remained steadily on his Master as he opened his mouth obediently. With a smile, Ashley placed the steak on his tongue, letting his fingers brush Shaun's lips as he pulled his hand away.

"Sweet Kitten."

Somehow it just tasted better from Ashley's hand, and when he took the next piece of meat, Shaun drew Ashley's hand back to his lips to lick the juice from Ashley's fingers.

Biting at his lip, Ashley groaned. The next bite he cut

was for himself and he smiled as he ate it. "Very good, Kitten," he said, a look of complete rapture on his face.

Shaun preened slightly. "I've always liked to cook."

"I'll remember that. Let you cook more often."

When dinner was done, they cleaned the table and dishes in a companionable silence. Now in a playful mood, Shaun nudged against Ashley while his Master tried to do the dishes. He occasionally swatted Ashley with his tail as he waited for Ashley to finish washing up. He even tried to get Ashley's attention with a series of playful vocalizations as he prowled the perimeter of the kitchen several times. Each time, he returned to stand beside Ashley at the sink.

Having finished with the dishes, Ashley glanced over at Shaun, giving him a wide smile. "Does my Kitten want to play?"

Shaun glanced between Ashley and the front door. "Can we go for a walk?"

Tossing the towel onto the counter, Ashley chuckled. "Certainly." He grabbed his keys and stuck them in his pocket. Taking Shaun's hand, he walked out of the apartment. As soon as the door was locked, he let go of Shaun. "Catch me if you can, Kitten." With that, he took off toward the park.

Shaun gave his Master a sporting chance and didn't take off after him right away. An alert gaze tracked Ashley just before Shaun broke into a lazy run. Others were out and about, taking their own pets for an early evening walk. Shaun just wanted to play and didn't let Ashley get too far away from him.

As he closed in on Ashley, he veered off to the side, disappearing behind a group of trees. He slowed and silently prowled, coming up behind Ashley. Without a sound, he carefully crouched not too far from his Master and started slinking through the grass. Raising his head slightly, he took in a deep breath. The next instant, he was on Ashley, the twisting force of his body sending them both rolling as he entangled himself against his Master.

Ashley's breath left him in a rush and he spent several minutes laughing too hard to catch it again. When he finally managed to control it, he flopped back onto the grass, his arms sliding around the sleek body of the half-shifted werecat above him. Looking up into Shaun's eyes, he couldn't help but smile. Shaun happily bathed his face as long fingers kneaded into Ashley's shoulders, purring and rumbling. Laughter took over and Ashley rolled them over suddenly, planting a quick kiss to Shaun's nose before scrambling to his feet. He backed away slowly, grinning and taunting Shaun.

"Oh, Kitten…"

Moving slowly, he headed along the south side of the park. The area was surrounded by trees, creating a small cul-de-sac. He might as well have had a ball of yarn or a juicy steak, pulling it along.

Springing up, Shaun slowly advanced on Ashley. The sleek, graceful step was reminiscent of a stalking cat. His tail gave an impatient twitch as more distance grew between them.

"Here, Kitten…" Ashley darted to the right, slipping behind a clump of bushes and weaving his way through them. He whistled to Shaun, still using the sing-song tone he did when he'd called Shaun's name. "Come find me, Kitten." Too busy watching, Ashley spun around at the last minute, colliding with Shaun. The motion sent Ashley sprawling backward onto the ground, laughing. "You're good."

Grinning with his own self-satisfied air, Shaun dropped to his hands and knees and quickly crawled over Ashley. His hands and legs kept Ashley pinned so he couldn't escape this time as Shaun lavished him with kisses and licks. Starting at Ashley's face, Shaun's head dipped to continue beneath Ashley's chin and to the line of his throat. Chuckling, Ashley stretched beneath Shaun's weight, tilting his head back to expose more skin. With words beyond him, all he could do was make soft sounds of appreciation, letting his Kitten know just how proud and happy he was. Nuzzling in against his throat, the throaty sounds from Shaun deepened. Then Shaun lifted his head.

"I caught you twice. Should I let you catch me?" The grin on Shaun's lips was impish and just as teasing as his words.

Ashley managed to pull his arms free at least and pulled Shaun down for a kiss. "Run, Kitten," he whispered.

Instead of running, however, the thrum of Shaun's purr softened as his lips molded to Ashley's. Humming softly into Shaun's mouth, Ashley slid his arms around his Kitten's neck, holding him close, petting. He opened for Shaun, letting him explore as he petted, stroking his fingers through Shaun's hair. Spreading his legs, he let Shaun settle between them comfortably. Okay, so maybe he wasn't quite ready to move either.

Odd, how their bodies seemed to fit perfectly together. Ashley's petting drew a constant purr from Shaun, the rhythm rising and falling in slow waves. Shaun explored every inch of his mouth and it was several long moments before he stopped. Pulling back slightly, Shaun stared down at him. How Ashley could lose himself in those eyes. He smiled softly, moving his hand down just enough to slide his fingers slowly along Shaun's jaw.

"You are everything to me," he whispered.

"You are my Master."

Cupping Shaun's face, Ashley pulled him back down, wanting another kiss. He could kiss Shaun until the end of time, just relishing the way his Kitten's lips felt on his, the raspy surface of Shaun's tongue as it slid over his own. He could drown himself in the purrs that slipped into his mouth, those sweet sounds that let him know his Kitten was happy.

"Love you, Kitten. Now run. There's chocolate waiting for good Kittens who get their exercise," Ashley teased, winking at Shaun.

"Do I get an extra piece if you catch me quickly?"

Before Ashley could answer, Shaun scrambled off of

him and darted toward the river. Closing his eyes, Ashley allowed his mind to settle a bit more. He could feel Shaun—anywhere the werecat went. He opened his eyes and followed the thread connecting them, the invisible—but very real—tendril of energy radiating from the tattoo on Shaun's neck. Its twin echoed somewhere deep within Ashley, within his heart and deeper still, in his soul. It was something Ashley had willingly let happen to him.

He emerged from the trees and started for the river, knowing that's where he would find his Kitten. He moved slowly, slinking in between the trees and the bushes, taking his time. He could feel Shaun, knew his Kitten was near. The closer he got to Shaun, the stronger the pull became.

Shaun gained a bit of distance from Ashley before his Master decided to follow after him. Ducking behind a downed tree, he waited patiently. He didn't dare lift his head to get a clear view since it would give away his position. Curling in a small depression between the bottom of the tree and the ground, Shaun rested his chin on his hands.

A moment later, Ashley's body covered his, and his Master nuzzled the soft skin just behind his left ear. Shaun had thought it would take some time for Ashley to find him since he was pretty well hidden. The initial surprise faded as he stretched slightly beneath the weight of his Master's body. The soft, lilting purr returned and Shaun tilted his head enough to give Ashley easy access to him.

"You found me."

"I did," Ashley murmured.

The more Ashley played with him, and the longer time they spent together, the more accustomed Shaun grew to moments like this, when even the faintest hint of arousal felt completely natural.

"Can we go home?"

"Yes."

Ashley gave him a last nip and got up, holding out a hand for him. Slipping an arm around Shaun's waist,

Ashley pulled him close as they walked, his head resting easy on Shaun's shoulder. Night had already fallen and only a few people were out on the streets. Through the open windows of the houses they passed, the everyday sounds reached Shaun. Everything was normal and peaceful, and the soft breeze carried the fragrance of nearby blooming flowers.

"I vote for movies and curling up on the couch." Ashley looked up at Shaun and smiled. "Don't suppose my Kitten would object to snuggling?"

Giving him an 'are you kidding me?' side glance, Shaun said, "I'll race you home." With a sudden burst of speed, he sprinted off down the street and around the corner toward their home.

# Chapter Seven

Before Ashley had a chance to open his mouth, Shaun neared their building. Shaking his head and laughing, Ashley just took his time, almost too tired after their park excursion to even think about racing now. When he reached the front door, he swatted Shaun's butt and stuck his tongue out at his Kitten before unlocking the door. The flick of Shaun's tail caught him in the face in retaliation before they walked into the house. Heading straight for the kitchen, Shaun got some snacks for them, then came back into the living room.

Picking a hair out of his mouth, Ashley closed the door and locked it. He stripped as he made his way to the living room, leaving a trail of clothes behind him. Pausing in front of the entertainment center, he wondered what movie to put on.

"What do you want to see, Kitten?"

"A good scary movie."

"Scary, as in 'you climbing into my lap' scary?" Ashley asked him, giving him a smile and a wink. "Or scary, as in 'making you look over your shoulder for the next two nights' scary?"

"Looking over my shoulder sounds good."

"*Candyman*."

Pulling a DVD case out of its place, Ashley put the disc into the player and grabbed the remote. Picking up the quilt on the back of the chair, he settled down on the couch, covering them both before snuggling tightly against Shaun. After several minutes of squirming, he got back up, turned around, and untied Shaun's loincloth.

"You're wearing too many clothes, Kitten."

After the small piece of material was gone, Shaun settled back against him. Keeping the bowl of snacks nearby, he offered Ashley some. Ashley shook his head, just happy to get close, to touch. He slid an arm around Shaun's waist, holding him as he started the movie.

When the bowl was nearly empty, Shaun leaned over to put it down on the end table. Shifting position, he stretched over Ashley's lap. After resting his head against Ashley's thigh, he returned to watching the movie. When it got good, he jumped slightly. With the movements, Ashley lost track of the movie, his attention more diverted to Shaun's position. He hadn't been hard a few minutes ago. But now he was fighting to get his mind off of his Kitten and his cock. With every small move from Shaun, Ashley ran his hand over his Kitten, feeling the movements of the muscles just beneath the flesh.

Shifting and sliding, Ashley managed to slip out from under Shaun and stretched out behind him, leaving Shaun to nestle back against him. He kept a tight hold on Shaun, petting and stroking, his hand wandering idly over Shaun's side, his hip, his thigh.

Turning his head slightly, Shaun smiled up at him as the cozy warmth surrounded them both. The movie forgotten, Ashley leaned forward and kissed Shaun softly. He licked Shaun's lips, fingers curling around his Kitten's hips to keep him still. The slightest movement on Shaun's part and the moan lodged in Ashley's throat would slip free.

Shaun's lips parted and with a slight shift of his body, Ashley deepened the kiss, moaning softly into Shaun's mouth. He wanted to touch—God, he wanted to touch—but he kept his hand where it was, almost fused to Shaun's hip in an effort to keep from moving lower.

Shaun made a soft noise and twisted, exposing himself to Ashley. Unwilling to rush this, Ashley kept the focus on their kiss, his tongue playing with Shaun's. He slid his hand over Shaun's belly, then down to trace the crease where Shaun's hip met his pelvis, just barely skirting everything else. He wanted Shaun to want this too. Shaun's muscles tensed and the slight rise of his hips pushed into the touch.

He could never deny his Kitten for long. Ashley pulled from the kiss and kept his eyes locked with Shaun's as he slid a single fingertip down the line of Shaun's cock. He wanted to see Shaun come, wanted to see pleasure etched across his Kitten's face as Shaun cried out to him. Lowering his head, Ashley licked at the nape of Shaun's neck, tracing the outline of the tattoo with the tip of his tongue.

The heat of an electrical strike rushed through them both the instant Ashley's tongue touched Shaun's tattoo. Shaun's legs parted further as his hips rose again. He cried out softly as he reached for Ashley's shoulder. Licks turned to nibbles and Ashley curled his fingers around the shaft of Shaun's cock, rolling his thumb over the head, slicking it with the drops leaking from the tip. With the connection wide open between them, he poured every ounce of love into the movement of his lips and teeth on Shaun's neck as he stroked him.

*I know you can hear me. Let yourself go. Come for me, Kitten.*

Head shaking wildly, Shaun rolled onto his back, legs wrapping around Ashley's, pulling him on top. For a brief moment, Ashley was almost too stunned to react. The tip of his cock brushed across Shaun's entrance and every rocking motion of Shaun's hips nearly drove him out of his mind. The pros and cons of what he was so close to doing weighed heavily on him, and the insistent movements, the pleading sounds, served to make his indecision worse. Just before giving in, he shifted, sliding his cock up alongside Shaun's. Wrapping his fist around both of their cocks, he rose up slightly on his other arm and stared down at Shaun.

"Come on, Kitten," he urged as he started to stroke them both. "Come for me. Let me feel you…"

Golden eyes stared into Ashley's, begging him as

Shaun writhed beneath him. Fingers curled tightly around Ashley's arms, Shaun whimpered, the sound desperate. Knowing he had no choice now, Ashley caught Shaun's mouth in a kiss before letting go. With a shift of his hips, his cock pressed against Shaun's hole and he reached blindly into the coffee table drawer for the small bottle of lube he kept there. He slicked himself quickly, then pushed.

The powerful muscles in Shaun's legs kept Ashley locked to his Kitten even through the pain he knew Shaun was feeling. Ashley knew nothing could stop the connection between them now. Panting heavily, the rock of Shaun's hips demanded Ashley take him. Although he fought like hell to gain some sort of control, Ashley found that he really had none now. Even if he just stayed still, Shaun would continue to ride him until they both came. But he couldn't stay still; he wanted to feel, wanted to give Shaun everything he could. Sliding a hand between them, he started stroking Shaun again.

"Kitten," he groaned. "So tight. Hot." Dear God, Shaun was tight as fuck. The notion hit Ashley then, like a ton of bricks. Shaun was a virgin. "Oh. Fuck…"

Pulling out, he had only a second to catch his breath before he plunged back in, mouth coming down on Shaun's as he started driving into him with deep but easy strokes. With every push of his hips, his hand mirrored the movement on Shaun's cock.

The heated friction inside Shaun's body kept him straining into each thrust. Tension increased like lightning strikes, rippling along his nerves, and he couldn't hold back from it. A deep tremor raced through him, driving him nearly off the couch as his body internally exploded. A harsh sound tore from his throat, crying out Ashley's name as he came. Barely seconds later, his release filled Ashley's hand. In his mind, barriers fully collapsed, leaving him totally open and vulnerable to Ashley. A flare of energy warmed through him in waves as he gave into them—as he gave into Ashley.

"Shaun!"

Several hard thrusts drove Ashley deeper inside him. Ashley jerked against him, filling Shaun with his release. Breathing heavy and ragged, Ashley released him to slide both arms tight around him. Shaun could not refuse to answer his Master. Lifting his head, he nuzzled in against Ashley's throat as he held onto him, feeling Ashley's need for closeness. The slow, soothing pulse of a purr rumbled as he nuzzled his Master's skin. Ashley pulled out slowly and rolled onto his side, pulling Shaun with him.

"I love you," Ashley whispered.

Shaun felt so tired. He murmured as his body nestled against his Master. More than likely they'd be sleeping on the couch because he really couldn't move. He hurt all over, but it didn't matter.

# Chapter Eight

Once dinner was finished, Ashley stood and cleared the table. When he returned, he held a box in his right hand and took one of Shaun's hands in his other. "Come, Kitten. I have a special treat for you."

Curiosity got the better of him, and a bright, inquisitive look followed Ashley. Taking hold of his hand, Shaun asked, "A special treat?"

"A very special treat," Ashley said as he led him into the living room. "I bought it just for you." Once Shaun was seated on the couch, Ashley undressed and curled up beside him, turned just enough to face him. He opened the box, but held the lid so that Shaun could not see the contents. "Close your eyes and open your mouth, Kitten."

Shaun's tail twitched in anticipation, batting at Ashley's hand. He wanted to see what Ashley had for him. Closing his eyes, he opened his mouth for Ashley.

"This," Ashley said, "is for you." He placed the small piece of hard chocolate on Shaun's tongue.

As Shaun closed his mouth, the rich chocolate taste began to melt on his tongue. A hint of spices subtly flavored the taste, drawing an appreciative purr from him. Oh, he liked this, and he wanted to share it. He opened his eyes and leaned toward Ashley, the tip of his tongue darting out as his gaze rose to Ashley's.

Popping another piece in his own mouth, Ashley pulled Shaun close, feeding him the chocolate as they kissed. The candy melted on their tongues, flavoring the kiss with chocolate, cinnamon, and ginger.

"I wonder," Ashley murmured, "what would happen if I just bathed in this stuff."

Thinking he would never stop licking Ashley if he did, Shaun couldn't answer him. His tongue darted over Ashley's, taking more of the taste, now flavored with Ashley. A deep purr rumbled as he moved, trying to get close enough to his Master to satisfy his own craving.

Ashley laughed into the kiss and leaned back, letting the box slide to the floor. Then he pulled away from the kiss and stroked chocolate-coated fingers over Shaun's lips before rubbing them over his own neck, head tilting back as his robe fell open to his waist.

A bright eyed gaze watched him intently. Licking at his lips, Shaun drew in a deep breath and wallowed in the familiar sweet scent of his Master. The additional mixture of chocolate and spices heightened everything as his eyes followed each of Ashley's actions. He homed in immediately on Ashley's throat and followed the path of chocolate on his Master's skin.

"I need to find this stuff in syrup form." Ashley reached down and Shaun could hear him fumbling with the box. Then Ashley began drawing designs on his own chest, leaving a trail for Shaun to follow as he pleased.

Shaun grabbed for Ashley's hand and licked the chocolate from his Master's fingers before he attended to Ashley's chest. Once the chocolate was gone, he continued on, loving the underlying taste of Ashley beneath the chocolate. Every now and then, little sounds escaped Ashley—small gasps and moans, Shaun's pet name whispered on a breath.

The faint roughness of Shaun's tongue slowly scraped over Ashley's flesh, covering every bare inch of his Master's chest. His awareness was sharp and he caught the lingering taste of a slow simmering arousal in the chemicals in Ashley's skin. He wanted the taste, to learn Ashley's flavor, to always recognize even the minutest signals of his Master in the air.

Just as he had learned Ashley's scent, the differences in his Master's moods needed to be tasted and absorbed. It was a part of what tied them together. The pulsing note of

Shaun's purring rose and fell, and he reached Ashley's hand. Curling around it, his nails flexed into his Master's skin as Shaun shifted slightly, lowering his head. The strong scent of the clear drops leaking from Ashley's cock drew his attention. With the first touch of his tongue to the tip of his Master's cock, Shaun purred.

"Kitten." Ashley held onto his hand, their fingers twining together tightly.

Shaun could feel the slow tremor slide through his Master, just the barest ripple of pleasure. Slowly, his tongue circled the head of Ashley's shaft before probing at the small slit, taking the drops. It was an intoxicating flavor, and Shaun closed his mouth around the head.

"Oh. Kitten. So hot." Ashley squeezed Shaun's hand, his hips rocking slowly as he shivered and moaned. "My sweet, Kitten."

This was just the beginning. By the time Shaun was through, he'd know every inch of Ashley's body. He took in the rigid flesh, sucking gently on it. A low growl vibrated his throat as he began to establish his territory. Ashley was his Master. *His Master*. Nobody else's. The glide of his lips, teeth and tongue repeatedly slid over Ashley's cock, rapidly increasing in speed and strength. Now he wanted Ashley's acknowledgement of the territory he'd set.

"Kitten. Oh, God, don't stop." Ashley petted Shaun's head, stroking over his hair, his shoulders, caressing every inch of Shaun that he could reach. "My Kitten. *My Kitten*, and I am yours." With that, he came, heat pouring into Shaun's mouth as Ashley chanted 'my Kitten.'

As he held Ashley in his mouth, Shaun swallowed his Master's release. The saltiness was flavored by the unique chemical traces marking who Ashley was. When the last of the tremors faded from Ashley's body, Shaun released him. Lifting his head, he looked down at his Master, letting a low growl rumble deep.

"My Master."

"All yours, Kitten, in every way possible." Ashley

reached out and pulled Shaun down on top of him for a slow, sweet kiss. "My Kitten," he murmured on Shaun's lips, "and I am your Master. Always."

Part of the fierceness faded when Shaun gained the answer he wanted. Now he was more than happy to nestle in against Ashley, returning the soft kiss. The lingering taste of Ashley in his mouth was shared in the slow stroke of his tongue over Ashley's.

"Bedtime, Kitten. Petting time."

* * * *

Shaun heard the loud knock at the door. Pausing in the middle of his lunch, he got up to answer it. Before he reached it, another loud banging rattled the door. Opening the door, Shaun saw two men in suits and one in a white lab coat with a gun trained on him.

"Shaun Taylor?"

Recognizing the gun as a tranquilizer dart, Shaun stood frozen in the doorway. "Yeah."

"We're here to place you under detainment at the Institute. You need to come with us."

Shaun didn't resist when a hand grabbed his arm and pulled him out of the house. After one of the men shut the door behind them, they escorted him to the car. Aware of the gun on him, Shaun remained extremely passive, letting them shove him into the car. He tried to bite back the small sound trying to escape his throat. Scared half to death, Shaun wasn't fully sure was what happening.

Staring at the back of the driver's head, Shaun tried to keep himself calm. Minutes ticked by and nobody said a word to him. Looking briefly out the window Shaun saw the outside world going on as normal. They were in the business district and businessmen were returning to their offices from their lunch hour. Shaun sat in the car, becoming more and more terrified.

He knew Ashley worked not too far away and could barely still the urge to break out of the car to get to him. Even if he managed to get free, these men would hunt him down. When he saw the imposing façade of the Institute building coming closer, the fearful sound slipped free. He didn't want to go back there.

The large metal gates opened and the car continued along the drive up to the building. Shaun could see Dr. Longmuir waiting on the portico beside one of the columns. He hated that doctor. The few times Shaun had dealt with him, the patronizing tone and behavior of the good doctor always raised his hackles.

When the car stopped, Dr. Longmuir walked down the steps and opened the back door of the car. Smiling in a patently false way at Shaun, he held out his hand. "Hello, Shaun."

Staring at the doctor, then the hand, Shaun got out of the car without any help. When Dr. Longmuir motioned Shaun up the stairs, he turned to address the other men. "I'll handle him from here. Dr. Stanton wants you three in his office."

Shaun ignored all four of them and headed up the steps and into the Institute. The entrance was an airy, luxuriously appointed space that led to a series of equally well-decorated offices. Dominated by a five tier crystal chandelier, the two story lobby had been painted in hues of blue and cream. But deeper into the Institute the décor took on a depressing aura of grays and yellows. Nobody but the staff and inmates saw the Institute farther than its front offices.

Several comfortably upholstered chairs had been placed in front of the reception desk and quite a few buyers were already waiting. Every last one of them stared at Shaun when he walked past, and Shaun could hear the sound of whispers following him. When Dr. Longmuir caught up to Shaun, one of the men stood and intercepted the doctor.

"When will he be available, Longmuir?"

Before Shaun lowered his gaze, he saw the blatant lust and avarice staring at him from the man. His heart pounding, Shaun refused to show any signs of fear in front of either of them. It would be against the law to offer to sell him to anyone since Ashley already owned him. Yet there were those in the Institute who would try, and Shaun knew it.

"Sorry, Webster, this were is only here for testing. He already has an owner." The words cut short the conversation and Dr. Longmuir grabbed Shaun's arm, pulling him toward his office.

Ignoring the other man, Shaun kept pace with the doctor and entered his office. Shutting the door behind them, Dr. Longmuir motioned to the chair in front of his desk, then walked around to sit in his own seat. Shaun sat carefully down and watched the doctor, waiting for him to speak.

"You're here because you attacked a mortal in Lower Roth Park, Shaun. Because of the report your owner filed with the police, we can't outright destroy you. It does seem you may have had cause for the attack. But that aside, you still need to be tested. If we find any of your training has been bypassed, you will still be destroyed. Do you understand everything I've told you?"

The words struck a deeper fear in Shaun's heart, but he answered calmly, "Yes, Dr. Longmuir."

"Good." Opening one of the folders on his desk, the doctor continued, "You're scheduled for testing tomorrow afternoon. In the meantime, and afterwards, you will receive advanced training as well. I will be working with you personally during the testing and training. If I'm not satisfied with your progress in training, you will be retained until I am." Looking back up, he added, "Escape will do you no good this time. If you escape you will be hunted down and destroyed when found."

Not even blinking, Shaun nodded his head. "Will I be able to see my Master?"

"Not until everything is completed. If the testing and training prove satisfactory, you will be returned to your master. It really depends on you, Shaun. The fewer problems you give us, the better your grade will be. Now show me your mark."

Shaun knew better than to argue with the order. Bowing his head, he pulled the hair off the back of neck and turned in the seat to show it to the doctor. Taking a small knife and swab from the tray on his desk, Dr. Longmuir stood and moved to stand behind Shaun.

The cool, wet sensation of the swab was followed by the pressure of the blade to his skin, and Shaun didn't dare even move. A second later a flash of pain ran through Shaun with the cut of the knife.

"Very good, Shaun. The mark is authentic."

Grabbing a small piece of gauze from his desk, the doctor pressed it to the cut. "Hold it there until you stop bleeding."

\* \* \* \*

"Kitten?" Ashley closed the front door behind him and set his keys down. Something wasn't right; he could feel it in his bones. "Shaun?"

He went from room to room and when he didn't find Shaun, he picked up his keys and ran out the door. He made it to the police station in record time and paid no attention to anyone as he strode up to the officer behind the desk.

"I need to file a Missing Pet Report."

"Yes, sir. Name of your pet?"

Ashley watched as the officer pulled out a form. "Shaun Taylor, rare white tiger."

The officer's look set Ashley even more on edge. "Just a minute." The man stood and walked around the corner to poke his head into an office. A moment later, another officer came out.

"Mr. Winters?"

"Yes?"

"Hi, I'm Detective Shields. If you please…" The detective motioned toward his office.

Once inside, Ashley found he couldn't sit. He paced back and forth as the detective remained in that cool, calm, collected police demeanor.

"Mr. Winters, Shaun Taylor was picked up by the

Institute for attacking a human."

Ashley had to sit down then; he was going to throw up. "What?"

The detective gave him a weak smile. "I'm sorry, Mr. Winters. This is out of our hands."

Nodding, Ashley said, "I know. I know. When can I see him? When can he come home?"

"I can give you the number, but I'm afraid there's not much else I can do." The detective reached into a drawer in his desk. "However, there is one thing..." He pulled out a swab kit. "If Shaun is fully under your control, this will be the deciding factor in whether he lives or dies."

"I know."

When the detective stepped up to him, Ashley opened his mouth. The test was quick, a tiny bit of skin and saliva collected on the end of the wooden stick. It would be used to synthesize a chemical to test Shaun's reactions, to make sure he was firmly under Ashley's control. All he could think about was the terror his kitten was in.

By the time he got home, Ashley was shaking He knew the cops did what they had to do, but even knowing that didn't quite help. Detective Shields had been sympathetic, but there was nothing he could do. Ashley went into the kitchen, needing something to drink, to put out the raging fire inside him. The more he thought about it all, however, the worse it got. He threw his water glass into the dining room wall. In fact, he'd just left it there, too pissed to care. They'd taken his Kitten. Knowing how lost and scared Shaun would be didn't help matters at all. Unable to sleep in his bed, Ashley ended up stretching out on the couch, staring up at the ceiling. Minutes became hours, and he still hadn't moved. The silence was deafening.

* * * *

"Shaun, while your loyalty to your master is admirable, you will have many masters over your lifetime."

Shaun remained huddled in the corner of the room, sitting on the floor the whole time his trainer, Amelia, talked to him. Eric, the other trainer, continued where Amelia left off.

"Shaun, you are required to pass the advanced training, and the longer you take to cooperate the longer you will be in here."

Shifting to his hands and knees, Shaun crawled out of the corner toward them. The last time he'd escaped the Institute before they had begun advanced training on him. This time he didn't have that luxury, not if he wanted to go home to his master. All Shaun wanted to do was return to Ashley. The cold, sterile environment of the Institute had already started wearing down his spirit. Uncertain if he would be returned to his master, Shaun lived with the constant terror he would be forced to stay here, and even his nightmares echoed the very same fear.

"Very good, Shaun." Eric settled back in his armchair and motioned the were to come to him. Reluctantly Shaun moved closer to him before he stilled, kneeling obediently between Eric's legs.

"You are expected to serve us both, no matter what we ask you to do, Shaun. Whether the order is for our physical comfort or sexual needs, it is your place to provide what we demand of you. When I touch you again, you are not to pull away. The next time you do, we will end the session and disregard all of your previous training since yesterday. You will return here tomorrow morning and begin your training all over again." After Eric finished instructing Shaun, a slight gesture of his hand had Shaun straightening his position so Eric and Amelia could access him more easily.

The threat was a very real one. Shaun knew they would, without hesitation, stop their training and put him back to square one. When Eric's hand began stroking over the side of his neck, Shaun didn't move at all. All around the room, others were being trained as well, but Shaun had to remain focused on Eric and Amelia no matter what else was going on. Amelia's hand reached out, feeding Shaun a small treat as his reward for good behavior. When she smiled gently at him, Shaun carefully licked her fingers clean.

Several buyers had been allowed into the room to test the performance of the weres with their own marketability tests. Shaun had watched other weres undergo the examination the day before, but he hadn't been expected to participate. However, today it would be required of him. Though he wasn't to be sold after he left the Institute, the belief was that sometime in his lifetime he would be, and probably several times.

Amelia's hand lowered to the front of Shaun's chest, her nails parting his fur when they scratched lightly over him. "You really are a beautiful animal, Shaun. I have no doubt you will fill your proper place just as you should. You know what is expected when you are examined by the buyers, and your natural instinct will be to react. Don't try to control it or hold back. It will count against you if any of the buyers see that."

Yesterday he had let Amelia pet him and finally allowed her to touch him wherever she chose. Today Eric had been brought in to train him as well, and at first he had fought that, but now, he let Eric touch him also. Even when the trainer's hand moved slowly lower toward his genitals, Shaun didn't try to break free.

When a finger tip brushed against his cock, Shaun closed his eyes and bit at his lower lip. Every instinct wanted to get closer to the hands on him, yet Shaun wanted to fight against it.

"Shaun." Amelia's warning tone got his attention immediately and he quickly opened his eyes. Her hand lifted to his hair, fisting in the strands and forced his face closer to hers. At the same moment Eric's fingers circled his cock, rubbing his thumb firmly over the slit. A soft mewl rose in Shaun's throat before his hips jerked hard against Eric's hand.

Without a sound said, Shaun knew what Amelia

expected from her expression and his lips parted obediently for her. Aroused by the movement of Eric's hand, Shaun began to thrust against Eric's fist, and Amelia's tongue caressed inside his mouth. After a long moment both of them pulled back, leaving Shaun panting.

"Very good, Shaun." This time Eric fed him one of the shrimp treats, then patted him lightly on the head.

"Amelia, Shaun is next." One of the buyers walked over to them and handed the trainer a form to sign.

While Amelia signed the paper, Eric stood up. "Come on, Shaun. It's time for your examination."

Shaun nodded and moved to stand. For a moment, he tried to focus on Amelia and Eric and not on the strangers standing not too far away from them. He knew their hands would soon be on him and they would use him however they felt. He couldn't protest. He couldn't fight them. He had no choice but to allow them to do what they wished and give them the reaction they wanted.

Slowly facing them, he saw every pair of eyes on him. Two studied him with a casual detachment, but the third one frightened him. Several inches taller, Shaun had to look up at the man as he approached the group. A cruel twist of a smile hovered over the man's lips and he blatantly stared at Shaun, black eyes cold; fascinatingly handsome except for the fact that something more sinister obscured the pleasing lines of his face and body. The dark gaze flicked appraisingly over Shaun's body. When the man turned to look at the woman standing next to him, a veil of black hair momentarily obscured his features. Shaun couldn't even relax when the buyer stopped watching him. Something in his eyes had echoed down to a well of instinctive fear deep inside Shaun, something to be very frightened of.

A heavy hand landed on Shaun's shoulder, forcing him forward, and Shaun had no choice but to face the threat head on.

* * * *

Strapped to the table, Shaun mewled piteously. It had

only been two days, but he missed his Master and wanted nothing more than to go home. Already he hurt from the myriad of tests they had performed on him and he still remained tied to the table, waiting for another round. The needles, prodding, and man handling weren't at an end yet. He'd been left alone in the room, unable to move because of the body wrap holding him captive and Shaun could do nothing but turn his head. Staring at the ceiling, the sound in his throat rose and tears streamed from the corner of his eyes, wetting his fur. Shifting to human form was a punishable offense at the Institute.

When Dr. Longmuir entered, he moved to the table and began to examine Shaun with a clinical detachment.

"Please, can I go home, Dr. Longmuir?" Shaun couldn't help his whimper and the desperate need for the safety and security of his own home. The overwhelming longing for his master remained paramount in Shaun's mind.

The doctor ignored him and continued with the examination, fitting the strong straps to Shaun's limbs and making sure he was properly restrained before he began unwrapping him. Methodically he inserted small wires into Shaun's skin at various places over his body. The stinging pain made Shaun squirm against the table, but he couldn't escape the stabs of the wires. Closing his eyes tightly, more tears squeezed out from beneath the closed lids and he whispered hoarsely, "Please, I want to go home."

His request remained unanswered as Dr. Longmuir continued with his work. Finally after several long moments of affixing the wires to the skin beneath the fur, the doctor turned away and moved to the large machine dominating the entire wall of the room. Settling on a stool at the small desk next to the machine, he opened the folder and began recording his notes. "Subject: Shaun Taylor. I will begin the Demar Field test on a level of 120th sub par."

Pausing, he reached over and turned on the machine. Shaun gasped with the electric current shooting through him, then bit at his lower lip. Inside his mind, he tried to escape this place and what was happening. It didn't hurt, but it didn't feel comfortable, and Shaun knew it was only the beginning.

"Reaction noted, level 120 successfully found. Lowering the point scale point seven-three." After twisting one of the knobs, Dr. Longmuir said, "Shaun, turn your head to the left."

Shaun could feel a low burning sensation to the nape of his neck over his mark. Obediently he turned his head away from the doctor. Standing and moving back to the table, Dr. Longmuir's fingers rubbed over Shaun's fur against the grain to examine the skin beneath.

"Connection to the ownership mark observed in the red inflammation surrounding it. Change resonance to zero-three-two." As the doctor spoke, he flipped a switch on the console and Shaun felt a sharper stab of pain at the back of his neck. He clawed at the table beneath him, long talons making a hideous sound against the metal.

"Blue *nemmains* surround the mark bleeding through to the surface skin. No sign of any alteration to the neural responses."

As Shaun lay there in pain, a woman entered the room and approached the doctor. "Dr. Longmuir, here is the synthesized scent you requested." Pausing, she set the small vial on the pad by his hand, then turned to look over Shaun. "This is the one that escaped?"

"Yes. Increasing output to peak level par point eight."

Opening his eyes, Shaun looked up at her just as the current increased through his body. His body began to convulse and the other two peered intently at the black lines appearing on a nearby screen. Every part of his body felt like it was on fire, leaving Shaun desperately trying not to scream.

"See this line, Althea?" One finger traced over the upper line while Dr. Longmuir talked. "Completely unbroken. The neural lines haven't been bypassed, which is a very lucky thing for our subject. You can see it fully by his visible reaction to increasing the level to even the lowest denominator of zero one."

After twisting the knob slightly, they both stared at Shaun, watching him writhe against the table. Shaun's mind barely stayed in one piece to comprehend the physical sensation before it flooded him completely, tearing him apart. The feeling came from every part of his body, and the agony of it rushed through him relentlessly. A scream tore at his throat, but he couldn't escape it.

"Have you seen Dr. Raynor's report? He suggests bypassing the point scale to get the same accurate reading from the ownership signature. It would save on the amount of time needed for testing and lower the cost substantially." Althea spoke casually, watching the doctor finishing his report.

Shaun caught the tale end of their conversation when the flood of energy slowed in his body. It left every part of him aching, but at least the mindless pain was gone.

Dr. Longmuir shrugged slightly before he completely shut off the machine. "The few test trials we've run indicate too much mental damage occurs in the subjects. Not even training can fix the problem in three out of ten cases. I've not yet seen any figures to indicate if the savings in cost is greater than the lost revenue."

With a nod, he dismissed her to continue his testing. Aware and fully comprehending of what they talked about, Shaun didn't even move a muscle, not even when the doctor slowly approached him again. Without saying a word, Dr. Longmuir opened the vial in his hand and stuck it under Shaun's nose.

The minute Shaun caught the overwhelming scent of his master; a whimper escaped him, then quickly became a sharper pulse of need when his body reacted fully. His erect cock leaked as he tried to hump at the air. Instinct reacted instantly in Shaun, leaving him heavily panting.

The doctor observed Shaun's actions for several long moments before he spoke. "A brief introduction of the synthesized scent has induced immediate arousal in the subject, indicative of level five bonding with Ashley Winters."

Uncapping the vial again, Dr. Longmuir held it beneath Shaun's nose until Shaun had taken several breaths of it. Even tied down, Shaun's body strained from the table in frenetic movements. He could smell his master and need and longing coalesced inside him, making his body shudder repeatedly with the orgasm rocking through him. Shaun couldn't control the reaction and it left him crying out for his Master.

"Definite formation of the level eight bond noted in the subject. Control has been firmly established and confirmed by my observations. There have been no abnormalities seen within the neural or physical connection to Shaun's master."

Exhausted, Shaun closed his eyes tightly and more tears wet his fur. Beyond humiliated and still in physical pain, he did his best to attempt to stop the rising sobs. He badly wanted the safety and reassurance of his Master and refused to open his eyes because all he would see was the reality of where he was.

* * * *

Two days later, Ashley finally received a call from Detective Shields, letting him know the Institute was satisfied with the results of their testing. He could pick Shaun up from the police station later that afternoon. Barely making it through the rest of the day, he ended up going to the park to keep himself calm.

Right before four o'clock, he headed toward the precinct. Just before walking into the police station, he fought like hell to push away the screaming voice in his head. Then he opened the door.

As usual, the station was busy, everyone going on with their usual day-to-day routines. No one batted an eye when Ashley walked up to the desk. A few minutes later, he was led to a guarded room. Through the small window in the metal door, he could see Shaun. The guard let him in after confirmation of who he was. Ashley all but glared at the man as the door was closed behind him, leaving only himself and Shaun in the small detainment room.

"Kitten," he said, holding his arms open.

Shaun sprang from his chair and ran to him. His Kitten didn't say anything, just clung to him for dear life. Burying his face against Ashley's chest, Shaun kneaded his nails into Ashley's shirt. Before Ashley could say anything, the door opened. Then he was leading Shaun out of the station, his own mood finally settling to something resembling calm.

"Home, Kitten," he said after several minutes of walking. He never stopped petting.

It seemed Shaun couldn't get enough of the touch of Ashley's hand. He'd been scared the whole time. The institute testing had included reinforced training to insure his programming remained intact. They'd released him only after they'd been satisfied he hadn't bypassed his training and was sufficiently controlled by his Master. Every step he took nudged him up against Ashley's side.

As soon as they were home, Ashley locked the deadbolt on the front door, then pulled Shaun straight into the bedroom. He stopped beside the bed and undressed them both as quickly as possible. But instead of getting in bed, he began looking Shaun over, as if searching for any sign of physical harm.

Cupping Shaun's face gently in his hands, Ashley whispered, "I love you. More than life itself. You know that, right?"

"I'm just a pet, Master." Parts of Shaun's mind were confused; the reinforced Institute training had caused its own havoc. Humans could, in a matter of minutes, make his entire world fall apart. "They can take me away whenever they want, just because I defended you. I just wanted to come home."

"What have they done to you, Kitten?" Without another word, Ashley pulled Shaun into a kiss.

Shaun didn't cry. He'd cried almost nonstop at the institute, but he melted into Ashley, opening to his kiss.

MYCHAEL BLACK / SHAYNE CARMICHAEL

He badly needed reassurance everything was all right now. He'd blamed himself for being taken away, but he couldn't help the instinct to protect Ashley. Nestling as close as he could physically get, Shaun damn near tried to crawl into Ashley's skin.

Without breaking the kiss, Ashley got them both on the bed, him on his back as he held Shaun tightly against him. What started out as reassurance in the kiss, quickly turned to desperation as Ashley locked his legs and arms around Shaun's body.

As Shaun stretched against the feel of his Master, a small shudder ran through him. Pets weren't allowed to initiate sexual overtures, nor were they allowed to want what Shaun wanted. The ache ran through him with the arch of Ashley's body clinging to him, but he could do nothing about it. Remaining docile in the position, the press of his lips tightened to Ashley's as his tongue stroked quickly around his Master's.

Gasping into Shaun's mouth, Ashley rocked against him. "Please," Ashley begged, tugging Shaun closer. "I need you. So much. Show me I haven't lost you, Shaun."

Even as Shaun struggled with the notion of equality between them, he had to fight against his own indoctrination of who he was. Lifting his head, he stared down at Ashley, confused. His body wanted something his mind told him he couldn't have. It was something that normally would never have come into question between a Master and a pet. The determined rock of Ashley's body drew an instinctive nudge of his own hips, something Shaun couldn't stop.

Reaching for the bedside table, Ashley got a hold on the small bottle of lube. Keeping his eyes on Shaun's, he popped the cap on the bottle and somehow managed to pour some of the slick gel into his palm.

"I need you, Shaun," Ashley whispered. He slid his hand between them and wrapped his fingers around Shaun's cock, slicking it as he stroked. "In me…"

The feel of Ashley's hand sliding over his cock and

his words only emphasized the urge already awoken in Shaun. A small jerk of his hips followed the expert manipulation of the hand on him as a low sound escaped him. He slid his hand down to take hold of Ashley's hip as the shift of his own body pushed his cock in against Ashley. Whether or not he was supposed to, he had to; his body wanted it.

"Yes. Now. Please, Shaun…" Positioning Shaun's cock against his hole, all it took was a lift of Ashley's hips. His body arched, Shaun's name on his lips as Ashley impaled himself slowly.

Unused to this, Shaun's movements were crude, but he drove deeply into Ashley out of pure instinct to feel the heat around himself. Then he was hit with the more urgent need and he responded without real thought, thrusting forcefully into Ashley's body. His nails kept Ashley pinned where he wanted him, not allowing any other motion but to react to his thrusts. Hands finally settling on Shaun's arms, Ashley met every hard thrust, lifting his hips as his fingers dug into Shaun's biceps.

"Harder," Ashley panted, eyes locked onto Shaun's. "I won't break." Gripping tightly to Shaun's arms, Ashley jerked his hips up, crying out and shaking as the move drove Shaun deeper. "Yes!"

Given permission, Shaun didn't hold back. The powerful force of his thrusts jolted Ashley's body with every movement. A low growl began in his throat, the vibration rising in tone to a snarl as the movement of his hips quickened. With one hard shove, his body froze for an instant before violent shudders overtook him. He'd never felt anything like this, to be enveloped in the tight heat as his mind reeled with the strength of his release.

Ashley screamed his name, back bowing. Heat spread between them and for several minutes, Ashley stared wide-eyed at Shaun, body trembling.

Shaun stared down at Ashley. To know he had done this to his Master was an empowering feeling. He drank in the sight and sound as he held Ashley. The hard press of his hips kept him buried deeply in Ashley, his body refusing to relinquish him just yet.

"Shaun," Ashley whispered, moving his hand up to brush his fingers over Shaun's lips. "I am yours—body, heart, mind, and soul."

Not understanding all of it himself, Shaun just smiled down at Ashley. Raising his hand, the tip of his fingers grazed gently over the line of his Master's face.

# Chapter Nine

For several weeks, something had been troubling Shaun, yet he didn't say anything. The thoughts intruding in his mind were unwelcome. They had no part in any of what he had. He felt content in his home and in the relationship with his Master. Yet a part of what he couldn't have surfaced, and over the weeks became more frequent in his mind.

Sitting on the bank near the river, he drew his knees up, resting his chin on them. The sun had begun to set and the nearby park was quieting down. Kids were returning to their homes for dinner. Ashley had to work late, but he would be home soon.

"Kitten?" Settling behind him, Ashley slid his arms around Shaun's middle as he rested his chin on Shaun's shoulder. "Shaun. What's wrong?"

A soft purr rumbled with Ashley's closeness. "Nothing," Shaun said, turning his head just enough to lick Ashley's cheek.

Closing his eyes, Ashley smiled. "Something's been on your mind. I can feel it even when you don't say anything." Shifting to the side slightly, he looked at Shaun, smoothing a swath of white hair back, tucking it behind Shaun's ear just as a strand of black fell forward. "I was hoping you'd come to me about whatever is on your mind."

Shaun wasn't surprised Ashley had caught on to the occasional disquiet of his thoughts, and he sighed quietly. "It's just something I'm not supposed to think about, is all. It's not really important."

Brow wrinkling, Ashley slipped a finger beneath

Shaun's chin, tilting his head upward. "It's important to me, Shaun. Please tell me."

Twisting to reach Ashley, Shaun moved to his knees and slid his arms around Ashley's neck. "I'm happy with everything you give me." He hesitated then, afraid Ashley would either be shocked or angry. "You know, don't you? That you make me very happy."

"I know that," Ashley said, "but I also know when there's something on your mind. What is it, Shaun?"

"You'll be upset with me if I tell you." Lowering his eyes away from Ashley, Shaun looked over his Master's shoulder.

Turning his head back, Ashley looked into his eyes for a moment before speaking. "I love you, more than I think you understand, Shaun. Nothing will ever change that."

"You're my Master." Shaun had to swallow before he could continue. "I'm not supposed to want what I do." He lifted his hand to Ashley's face and touched the smooth, warm skin. An answering current ran through him, one of need and love. "I can't be human with you."

Ashley blinked. "Oh. Oh, Shaun." Cupping Shaun's face in his hands, Ashley held Shaun's gaze steadily. "I want you, in whatever form I can have you; but to be completely honest, I would love nothing more than to feel the man. I want to touch and taste and feel you as a human. I want to feel you surrounding me; I want to feel you inside me. Please."

Shaun stared at him in shock, not quite comprehending the words. He nudged his Master's hand, rubbing into its warmth as a source of comfort. It slowly dawned on him that Ashley seemed in no way angry and he began to relax. "You want me as human?"

"I want *you*. Human is preferable, although I'm certainly not opposed to you being half-shifted. But I would love nothing more than to play as two men. There's so much to explore, so much we still have to learn about each other: likes, dislikes, specific kinks. I'm not exactly the most conventional person in the world, if you haven't noticed. God knows you haven't seen my toy collection."

Tilting his head, Shaun studied Ashley. He had no clue what his Master was talking about; he was just very happy Ashley hadn't gotten angry at him. "You know I'm not allowed to be human with you, but I want to be."

Ashley chuckled and shook his head. "Shaun, in our home, you are allowed to do and be whatever you want. I'd keep it that way outside of our home, but unfortunately society would not take kindly to such things." He smiled slowly then and gave Shaun a wink. "Just imagine, Shaun. Your body held open by a plug as we go shopping, every move causing the toy to shift, keeping you on the edge and never letting you over it."

A shiver ran through Shaun as he remained intent on Ashley's voice and words. His eyes widened slightly. Shifting, he got slightly closer to Ashley, almost ending up in his Master's lap. "I know it is against the Institution, so it has to stay between us." After giving some thought to what Ashley said, he added, "I think I would really like that."

"Mm...and imagine what it would feel like to suck my cock while I fuck you with a toy." Sliding his arms back around Shaun's waist, Ashley pulled him the rest of the way onto his lap, rocking his hips up just enough to let Shaun feel his arousal. "And that's only the beginning of what we could do. There are so many possibilities to explore with toys, and even our hands."

Just the thought made Shaun squirm. A soft growl escaped his throat before he could stop it. He could almost feel what it could be like to have his Master do that to him. "I want you to do that."

Ashley pulled him in for a kiss, licking at Shaun's lips before sliding his tongue inside. With a slight shift of his body, he rolled Shaun onto his back, then hovered over him. Without breaking the kiss, he slid his hand down to press on Shaun's jeans just over his ass.

"Imagine me holding you," Ashley murmured on his

MYCHAEL BLACK / SHAYNE CARMICHAEL

lips, "right in the palm of my hand. Your body closing tight around my wrist, my hand buried inside you, making you insane with need."

With words alone, Ashley made Shaun's body tighten and he squirmed beneath his Master. Raising his head slightly, he opened to the teasing of Ashley's tongue. Small pulses of sound betrayed the arousal his Master brought out in him. "Please, Master, please." He wrapped his legs around Ashley, trying to keep Ashley pinned in position as his hips rocked against him.

"Say my name." Ashley moved down to Shaun's neck, licking and marking his skin.

Shaun turned his head toward Ashley, nuzzling against his Master's throat as he whispered, "I need you, Ashley."

Groaning, Ashley lifted his head and stared down into his eyes. "Home. Now. Otherwise, I'm going to give park goers one hell of a show."

Though they were shielded from most casual chance viewers, if they made too much of a noise, somebody would probably investigate. Reluctantly, Shaun let go of Ashley but couldn't resist one last grinding rock of his hips. It sent a sharp reminder through him of his own need, and how only Ashley could satisfy him. As Ashley moved off of him, Shaun stood and grabbed for his Master's hand. He wasn't about to let Ashley get too far away. Ashley hurried them home.

"Bedroom," Ashley said as he locked the front door. "Get naked and on the bed."

Obediently, Shaun went into the bedroom and stripped. He crawled onto the bed and remained on his hands and knees, watching as Ashley came in and went straight to the closet. A thrill of anticipation ran through him and Shaun could barely still it.

After pulling the plastic bin out of the closet, Ashley undressed and grinned at Shaun. "Ready?" He lifted the cover of the bin and stepped back, giving Shaun full view of the contents.

Leaning over, Shaun got a good eyeful. His eyes widened before he looked over at Ashley. Some of the things he recognized: the collar, whip and rope; the rest he could only imagine what uses his Master would have for them. Small glints of metal in the light had him curious and Shaun shifted closer, trying to nose around in the box.

"To say the least, I'm kinky," Ashley said. He crouched down beside the bin and started rummaging through it, setting on the bed a small plug, a fake cock, and a small, unlabeled container. When he was done, he closed the bin and crawled onto the bed, kneeling behind Shaun. "I want the man, Shaun. All of him."

Looking between the objects and Ashley, Shaun had to smile. Yes, his Master was very kinky. As Ashley came up behind him, Shaun looked back at him over his shoulder as the air hummed with the vibration of electricity as his half-form receded in a matter of seconds, leaving him completely human, except for his white and black striped hair.

"Beautiful," Ashley whispered, sliding his hands down Shaun's spine. "My God. Even your skin is soft." When he reached Shaun's ass, Ashley kneaded the round buttocks before spreading them open. "Fuck."

Just the idea of Ashley doing this to him in his human form was enough to make Shaun's body tighten. A soft hiss of breath escaped him with the sudden probe of Ashley's tongue into him. His head fell forward as he closed his eyes, moaning softly. He pressed slightly backward as his fingers kneaded into the covers.

Ashley pulled back just enough to lick around the outside, sucked lightly on the wrinkled skin, then plunged back in, sliding a finger alongside his tongue. Curling it forward, he kept licking as he stroked his fingertip over Shaun's gland. Shaun ground back, feeling the double penetration of tongue and finger. Moaning softly, his words wrapped within the sound.

"It feels good, Ashley."

He didn't want Ashley to ever stop. He wanted

Ashley to do anything and everything he wanted to him. He couldn't reach his Master so his fingers began to knead into the material of the covers as an outlet.

Ashley used his other hand to reach for the dildo and the small container. Popping the top off the container, he had to pull away to slick up the toy. He withdrew his fingers from Shaun and coated the dildo in the white grease. Then he pressed the head, which was a bit bigger in width than his own cock, to Shaun's hole and pushed it slowly inside.

"Oh, fuck, yes."

When he felt the internal stretch to accommodate the toy, Shaun whimpered softly. His Master's name became a hiss of breath. "Ashley." Raising his head, he tried to look over his shoulder at Ashley as his body shifted backward onto the toy. He wanted so badly for his Master to fuck him with it and to know his Master watched it all.

"So fucking good, Shaun."

Ashley pushed the toy deeper, then pulled it out. Setting up a slow, easy rhythm, he began fucking Shaun with it, twisting it just enough for the ridges along the dildo to rub every inch of Shaun on the inside. Shaun could see the fascinated expression on Ashley's face. It mirrored in his own with the sensations coursing in his body. He pushed back on his hands as the toy expanded him, letting his ass take in as much as he could. A slow tremor of excitement raced through him.

"Faster, please, Ashley."

Ashley started fucking Shaun harder and faster with the dildo, groaning loudly. The rubbing friction turned Shaun's insides into quivering jelly, and the rock of his body kept time until Ashley removed the toy.

"Turn over," Ashley said in a shaky, husky voice.

A soft mewl of disappointment sounded, but Shaun quickly shifted to his back. His legs spread open for Ashley as he slid his hands down his thighs to hold up his legs. The position gave Ashley the perfect view of what Shaun knew he wanted. His gaze held Ashley's, pleading silently as he called to his Master with a soft, needy purr. Ashley slid up his body and took his mouth in a kiss, sliding two fingers easily inside him. Deepening the kiss, his Master added a third finger.

It felt so good and Shaun arched, bearing down on Ashley's fingers, pulling them inside of him as his body squirmed. Opening to the kiss, pure hunger greeted Ashley as Shaun's tongue played quickly over his. He badly wanted every sensation his Master could give him.

Adding a fourth finger, Ashley licked at Shaun's lips, moving his fingers inside him, slowly spreading them open. "If you need me to slow down or stop or even come out entirely, then don't hesitate to tell me."

Shaking his head vigorously in answer, the sensation of fullness made Shaun's body tremble with the tension. "No, Ashley, stay there." His fingers tightened on his legs, keeping them held up for Ashley. He wanted more, though he really had no clue what his body was begging for. Each small movement drew a shaky breath from him.

"Shh," Ashley murmured. "Let me in, Shaun. Open for me."

Tucking his thumb against his palm, Ashley pushed gently, taking things slow. When the widest part of his hand started to go in, he twisted his hand slightly, then pushed one more time. Shaun's ass closed tight around his wrist, sucking Ashley's hand inside.

"Shaun. Oh, fuck."

The burning stretch of his body drew a tiny pained sound from Shaun as he felt the inner muscles protest. He tried to remain still and when his body drew Ashley's hand inside, a rush of feeling swept away all but the sensation itself. He could barely believe the fullness, and he shuddered in response. Closing his eyes, he felt himself, in a way, laid bare to his Master. The only sounds he could make were soft whimpers, calling to Ashley. Ashley gave him a kiss, then sat back up.

"Come on, babe," Ashley whispered. "Ride my hand. Come for me, Shaun." With a twist of his hand, Ashley started pumping it gently inside Shaun, his knuckles grazing over the smooth gland inside with every twist. "Come on, baby."

It took very little movement at all before powerful tremors shook Shaun's body, his mind suddenly adrift in the unbelievable sensations. "Ashley, Ashley." His Master's name became a chant until Shaun lost his breath as his entire body was flooded, his cock pulsing without a single touch. Everything was so strong, he felt like he would pass out.

"Oh, God… Shaun!"

Ashley's hand stilled inside him and his Master jerked, heat spilling onto Shaun's thigh as Ashley came. Panting, Ashley eased his hand out slowly, then leaned down to lick Shaun's cock clean. After wiping off his hand, Ashley slid up Shaun's body.

"Love you. God, I love you, Shaun."

All Shaun could do was let go of his legs. They were still shaky, in the same shape as his body. Staring up at Ashley, he slowly came down from the high his Master had given him.

"Rest, love. That would take a lot out of anyone." Ashley slid to the side and pulled Shaun close. "Next time you can do it to me. Did you enjoy it?"

Shaun curled up against Ashley, desperately needing the contact. Tipping his head back just enough to see Ashley, he whispered, "I don't think 'enjoy' is the word I would use." He could still feel the pressure inside him, leaving an echoing sensation of Ashley's hand.

Ashley smiled and kissed him softly. "I'll second that any day. I'd love to feel your hand inside me sometime." Entwining his fingers with Shaun's, he brought Shaun's hand up to kiss it.

Giving his Master an uncertain look, Shaun shook his head slightly. "I would like to, but I've never done that before." The idea of doing the same thing to Ashley had definite appeal, if he weren't afraid of accidentally hurting him.

"I'd coach you through it, but until then, I'm quite happy with anything else you can think of to put there."

Shaun had to laugh. Curling his hand around Ashley's, he said, "Being with you like this is…" He trailed off, trying to find the words, tears just on the verge of spilling.

Ashley reached up and caught a tear just as it escaped. "Like Heaven," he said quietly. "Being with you is Heaven to me. I could never live without you, Shaun."

Shaun understood exactly what Ashley meant. "Being with you is like every dream I've ever had, Ashley." Smiling, Ashley pulled him close for a kiss, both of them just relaxing into it. Ashley slid his fingers through Shaun's hair, stroking and petting. Heaven, indeed.

# Part Two

# Chapter One

There were only a few places that allowed pets to enter without being accompanied by their owners. Shaun could shop in the market if he had Ashley's permission. The owner of the store knew Ashley, so Shaun had been allowed to do their grocery shopping. Tonight he wanted to prepare a special dinner for his master.

He didn't exactly have Ashley's approval for this idea, but then it wouldn't be a surprise if he did. Since his master trusted him in all things, Shaun felt no qualms as he pushed the cart down the aisles, searching for what he wanted. He selected the lobster tails and the ingredients for the seafood salad he planned on making. As he passed by the candles, he hesitated. He definitely wanted something romantic for Ashley, and he paused for a long moment, eyeing row after row of candles. Finally, he settled on two slender red ones with ruby-colored crystal holders.

After picking out a good wine, Shaun took his purchases to the checkout. He put everything on the counter and patiently waited his turn. He knew the clerk by name and gave her a smile as she began ringing up his things.

"Something special tonight, Shaun?" Tina asked as she scanned his items. Most of the clerks knew him quite well and were generally friendly to him.

"Master's birthday." Shaun grinned at her. Spying a small box of Ashley's favorite chocolates, he picked it up and quickly added it to the pile. Most of the time Ashley always bought Shaun's favorite, and Shaun wanted to return the favor.

"Tell Ashley I said Happy Birthday."

"I will, Miss Tina." After he bagged everything, he took the receipt from her. In a good mood, he left the store and headed back to the house.

As he walked across the park, he spotted two enforcers walking toward him. Instead of passing him by, one of them stepped abruptly in front of Shaun. Forced to stop, Shaun stared down at the ground, waiting for one of them to speak.

"Your mark, were," the older man demanded as he grabbed Shaun's arm with bruising pressure.

Not daring to struggle or argue, Shaun bowed his head as the other man pulled back his hair. Shaun felt the press of the recorder to his neck as it scanned his tattoo.

"He belongs to Ashley Winters. He's clear."

"Pity. He'd be worth ten years' salary on the market." Disgruntled, the man raised his hand and gripped Shaun's chin, forcing Shaun to look at him.

Dread nearly made Shaun tremble as he saw the gleam of avarice in the man's eyes. With a shrug, the other man said, "He's legit. Nothing you can do."

Reminded of that fact, the enforcer released Shaun and moved to the side. "Get out of here, were."

Shaun didn't need to be told twice. He hurriedly walked away from them and maintained the pace until he safely reached home. Closing the door behind him, he leaned against it, trying to still the racing beat of his heart. After a few moments, he'd calmed enough to take the groceries into the kitchen.

Pulling out one of Ashley's cookbooks, Shaun followed the recipe to prepare the lobster tails. Once he finished that, he started making the seafood salad. It kept his mind from dwelling on the terrifying encounter in the park.

After he finished preparing the food, Shaun set the candles on the table, along with the vase of flowers he'd picked earlier. Wanting everything to be perfect, he carefully set their best cutlery and plates on the table.

Then, glancing up at the clock, he knew Ashley would be home soon.

Heading back to the bedroom, Shaun figured he'd have just enough time to get a shower. Knowing Ashley sometimes preferred him in his fully human state, Shaun shifted as he took off his loincloth. In the bathroom, he turned the hot water on and stepped in. The warmth eased away the last of his tension over the encounter with the enforcers. It had fed on his worst nightmare of being taken away from Ashley. That had already happened once, and Shaun remained on his best behavior, praying it wouldn't happen again.

As he lathered up the washcloth, his thoughts drifted to his master. It wasn't only Ashley's birthday, but also their first anniversary together. When Ashley had first forced Shaun to come home with him, Shaun couldn't have imagined the contentment he felt now. Ashley was something Shaun had never dared to dream of, yet his master gave everything of himself.

As he washed, Shaun smiled. Ashley spoiled him outrageously with chocolates and love. The truth of their relationship could never be known on the outside, but Shaun didn't care. He'd come to deeply love his master in a way he couldn't describe, even if his life depended on it.

Quickly washing his hair and rinsing off, Shaun finished his shower, then turned off the water. He grabbed for a towel hanging from the rack near the tub and dried off. Knowing it would please his master, Shaun returned to the bedroom and chose a pair of jeans and the black sweater Ashley had bought him for his birthday.

Quite often, Ashley wanted Shaun in his human form, something that could only be done in the privacy of their home. To the outside world, Shaun was nothing more than a pet, but it was something that no longer bothered him as it once did. He had found complete acceptance with Ashley. His master loved everything he was.

Combing through his white-and-black streaked hair,

Shaun looked at himself in the mirror. Being an extremely rare breed of tiger, his looks were noticed wherever he went. The attention rarely bothered him unless somebody wanted to buy him from Ashley. His master had received many offers, but Ashley had refused every one of them. Even in his human form, nobody could mistake Shaun for anything other than a were creature. The odd coloring of his hair betrayed what he was.

Setting the comb aside, he padded silently toward the kitchen. He took the pans out of the oven and placed lids on them before carrying them out to the dining room table. After lighting the candles, Shaun returned to the kitchen and got the chocolates and wine he'd bought. As he placed the box and bottle of wine next to Ashley's plate, he heard the front door opening.

Heart racing, he sprinted into the living room and waited for his master. Clasping his hands behind his back, he stood off to the side, waiting for Ashley to notice him as his master set his briefcase and keys down.

"Kitten, I'm…" Ashley's words trailed off as he caught sight of the dining room table. Then he spotted Shaun. The smile was immediate.

Bouncing on his heels, Shaun could barely restrain himself. The moment Ashley looked at him, he launched himself at his master. "Happy Birthday, and we've been together for a year."

Ashley whispered, "Happy Anniversary," right before cupping Shaun's face and kissing him softly but thoroughly.

A rumbling purr rose in Shaun's throat as he wrapped his arms around Ashley, hugging him tightly. After a moment, Shaun drew his head back. "I made a special dinner just for you."

A finger traced the line of Shaun's jaw and Ashley smiled. "Thank you, Kitten. Although I certainly remembered our anniversary, I managed to forget my own birthday," he chuckled. "So what sort of decadent feast did you make us?"

"Your favorites. What else?" Grinning, Shaun nestled happily against his master since Ashley didn't seem to be willing to let him go. "Lobster and seafood salad. I even bought a small present for you."

Ashley's rumble of pleasure was muffled as he kissed Shaun's neck. "One year," he whispered. "Little did I know, one year ago, that I'd find Heaven."

Content in Ashley's embrace, Shaun rubbed his cheek against Ashley's hair, listening to the soft whispers. He adored it when Ashley was in a romantic mood. Quite a few of their evenings had been spent that way, and Shaun always encouraged it. "I know at first I wasn't happy, but now I wouldn't change anything, Ashley."

Ashley nodded, kissed Shaun's neck again, and finally pulled back enough to look at him. "I love you, Shaun."

"Love you, too, master." Shaun pressed a soft kiss to Ashley's lips, then lowered his hand to take Ashley's. With a smile, he dragged Ashley toward the dining room table. As Ashley settled in his seat, Shaun poured them both glasses of wine and uncovered the dishes on the table.

"Oh." Ashley blinked, apparently lost for words. When he finally spoke, it was quiet and full of awe. "Shaun…it's…wonderful." Then he saw the box beside his plate. "Is this…what I think it is?"

Shaun sat in his own seat and grinned. "You're always buying my favorites. I figured you should have your own." Leaning forward, he ladled some of the seafood salad onto Ashley's plate, then put one of the lobster tails beside it. Once Ashley was served, he fixed his own plate.

"Thank you, love." Ashley opened the box and lifted the little paper cover. The aroma of gourmet chocolates filled the dining room and Ashley inhaled deeply. Picking out a dark chocolate truffle, he bit into it. His moan was deep and blissful, almost sensual.

Shaun's expression softened as he watched Ashley and a warm sensation spread through him, knowing he'd pleased his master. He'd been waiting anxiously all day for this. "I wanted to show you how much I love you."

Ashley opened his eyes and smiled. "You're perfect, Shaun. In everything you do." Leaning over a little, Ashley held the other half of the truffle up to Shaun's lips, the fine chocolate already beginning to melt on his fingers.

Leaning closer, Shaun took the piece of candy and carefully licked Ashley's fingers clean. Savoring the flavor, a smile softened his lips. "I think you would be the only one to think so, Ashley."

"No one else matters, Kitten. Just us." Ashley cupped Shaun's chin and pulled him close, licking a bit of dark chocolate from Shaun's lips. "Now, let's get to this fine feast you've slaved over."

"You're right. You're the only one that matters." In their time together, Shaun had entwined himself indivisibly from Ashley. Something he fully accepted and he wouldn't want it any other way. Spearing a piece of crab meat in the salad, Shaun began eating. With the first taste, he knew he had outdone himself in making it.

The second he took a bite of the salad, Ashley nearly sank down into the chair, moaning Shaun's name. "Oh. Perfect, love. Absolutely perfect. You, my dear Kitten, are a god."

Shaun laughed and laid his hand over Ashley's just for the contact. "I will definitely have to make this again."

Ashley nodded and turned his hand over, fingers lacing with Shaun's. "Yes. Most certainly."

Watching his master by the glow of the candles, Shaun sighed quietly. They finished their meal in companionable silence, and Shaun could tell from Ashley's expression his master had greatly enjoyed everything he'd prepared. When they finished, Shaun gathered the dishes and set them in the sink.

Ashley stepped up behind him, arms snaking around Shaun's waist. "I have something for you."

Figuring he would leave the dishes for later, Shaun turned to face Ashley, giving him a surprised look. "I didn't expect you to get anything for me, master."

"Why on Earth wouldn't I?" Ashley laughed and leaned in for a kiss, keeping it slow and easy. When he pulled away again, he took Shaun's hand and led him into the living room. Once Shaun seated himself on the couch, Ashley went to his briefcase and set it down to open it. He pulled out a rectangle wrapped in brown paper and handed it to Shaun.

Shaun relaxed on the couch as he took the package from Ashley. Uncertain of what it could be, he stared at it a moment before he started unwrapping it. When he first caught sight of the painting beneath, Shaun froze in amazement. The image of himself, painted as human, beside his master, stared back at him. It left Shaun speechless.

"Happy anniversary, Shaun."

Staring unblinkingly at the small, unframed painting, he noticed the signature at the bottom corner: 'To my dearest Kitten. Love, Ashley.' A knot formed in Shaun's throat and he looked quickly up at Ashley, blinking against the unshed tears. He didn't know what to say. Finally, he whispered, "You love me so much?"

Ashley crawled across the floor to kneel between Shaun's legs. "More than you realize. I haven't picked up a paintbrush in a long time, but now, with you, I feel like I could do anything. I wanted to give you something that was a part of us."

To say Ashley had completely surprised Shaun was an understatement. Reaching out, his hand pressed to Ashley's cheek in a loving touch. "I can't even tell you what I feel. Everything just grows stronger in me."

"You don't have to say it." Ashley took the painting and set it on the coffee table behind him. Then he rose up and kissed Shaun softly, whispering, "I can feel it every time you look at me, every time you touch me. Every breath I take is you."

"Sometimes I want to tell you, but you say everything better than I can." A small sound erupted from Shaun's throat, vocalizing his need to be close to his master. Turning his head slightly, he slowly rubbed his cheek against Ash's as the soft noise increased.

Ashley slid his hands under Shaun's sweater, moaning softly as he kissed a path down Shaun's neck. "Don't shift," he murmured, licking the sensitive spot just below Shaun's left ear.

Shaun pulled Ashley with him as he stretched out on the couch. "I'm not going to change. I know how much you like me to stay this way."

"Love you." The words were breathed across the hollow of Shaun's throat as Ashley nestled between Shaun's legs, hands still caressing Shaun beneath his shirt.

As Ashley nudged against him, Shaun relaxed fully, enjoying his master's touch. Raising his head, he nuzzled at the line of Ashley's throat. To him, the only thing that mattered was this. As Ashley slid in behind him, Shaun pushed back, spooning against his master. Reaching for the remote, Shaun turned on the TV then lowered the volume. This was their quiet time and he spent it cuddled tightly with Ashley.

# Chapter Two

Cain watched silently as Lord Élan entered the chamber. For a moment, the glimpse of the smooth, oiled body held him enthralled. A sense of barely restrained strength showed in the ripple of sculpted muscles. The werelord's golden eyes were fixed on the High Chamberlain Hapsus, who stood near Cain. Quickly lowering his gaze, Cain remained seated beside Élan's throne.

His lord was the chosen one of the Council of Eldest, and as such was the most respected and powerful werelion known to the assembly. When Cain had been brought to the Hall of the Eldest, he knew he would be the human server of Lord Élan. Cain had been handpicked by Hapsus for service, but Cain had no clue what that would entail.

Lord Élan had been chosen by Oiyan, God of the House of Fetters, and given the task of reuniting the Houses after they had been torn apart by the Wars of Division. Cain knew Élan's history very well.

"Have you found him?" Élan asked Hapsus as he sat on his throne, resting his hands on the lion heads that had been carved into the arms of the chair.

"Not yet, my lord. We are searching through the Noramerna Institute records. So far, we've found nothing to substantiate the rumors that have reached us."

Clearly displeased, Élan stared at him. "How is it the birth of an Imperial was not even noted in the records?"

"During the wars, we lost contact with only one of our lines, my lord. If the story is true, the cub would be the son of Lord Tyr-Set." With no change of expression,

Hapsus held the gaze narrowing on him.

Cain listened silently, unknowing of what they talked about until the mention of Lord Tyr-Set. Surprised, his gaze darted between them, but neither of them noticed. Many of the houses believed Lord Tyr-Set to have betrayed them during the Wars. Cain's blood was of the same line, though he wasn't a shifter. After the House of Mirra had renounced Tyr-Set, many of the family had faded away into the woodwork, only to rise out of the ashes, proclaiming another lineage. Cain had been one of them, claiming the last name of Wilhelm.

"I have always found Mirra's claims suspect," Élan spoke quietly, and the drumming of his nails punctuated his words. "Make sure none hear the same rumors that have come to my ears. If the boy exists, I want him brought to me."

Hapsus nodded then gestured toward Cain. "My lord, this is Cain Wilhelm. I have brought him to you as your human server. Do you accept charge of him?"

Instantly, Cain felt the lord's gaze resting on him, and he didn't dare look up. It took all of his effort to still the fine trembling of his limbs.

"Ah, yes. Cain." A finger slipped beneath Cain's chin, tilting his head up. "Yes."

Finding himself the subject of Élan's study, Cain daringly looked up. The glow of Élan's eyes warmed through him, and Cain found he couldn't look away. One of Élan's talons ran lightly against his skin, holding Cain's attention. "My lord."

"You are dismissed," Élan said to Hapsus without looking away from Cain.

"Thank you, my lord."

When the doors of the throne room closed once more, leaving them alone, Élan released Cain's chin and stood. "You are now my personal groom. You will attend me in my everyday matters." He started for the door off to the left of the dais. "You will draw a bath for me. There are oils to be used as well. Come along."

Cain scrambled from his position and followed behind Élan. His eyes fastened on Élan's back, trying to ignore the fact that the lord was only wearing a traditional style loincloth. As they entered the other room, Cain walked past him toward the bathing pool to prepare Élan's bath. A light tug on the chain suspended from the ceiling started the fall of scented water to fill the small pool.

Élan's loincloth dropped onto the stone bench beside the pool. "I trust you were paying attention to our discussion?"

Trying his best to keep his eyes averted, Cain nodded as he stood near Élan. "Yes, my lord."

"In private, you may look at me." Élan stepped around Cain and sank down into the heated water as Cain turned it off.

Kneeling beside the ledge, Cain reached for one of the bottles and a soft cloth. Fixing his gaze on Élan's face, he dipped the cloth into the water to wet it, then poured some of the gel onto the cloth. "Thank you, my lord."

Élan smiled and stood to allow Cain to wash him. "If the rumors prove to be true, then I will need someone close to me to find the young lord and bring him home."

After he stood with Élan, Cain gently ran the cloth over Élan's chest to cleanse his skin. Curious about the matter and desperately needing a distraction from the vision in front of his eyes, Cain asked, "Do you believe the rumors to be true, my lord?"

"I do not believe that Lord Tyr-Set betrayed us," Élan said with a sigh. "As for the rumors of his son... I do not know. I want to believe, but the chance of a lord's son having survived outside—in the human world—is very slim." He rumbled softly when Cain moved lower, washing his stomach. "You have good hands."

"You wish me to bring him home if the rumors are true?" Not daring to give his own opinion, Cain had to focus on Élan's body as he knelt again. Carefully, he washed downward over Élan's thighs, doing his best not to stare overtly at Élan's cock nestled in the triangle of golden curls. Gently cupping his genitals, he began washing them. Raising his eyes, Cain kept his gaze firmly on Élan's face.

Élan looked down at him. "I do. He belongs here. There is nothing in the human world for him."

Feeling the beginning hardness stirring beneath his hand, Cain quickly moved to Élan's hip. With a light pressure of his fingers, Élan turned around, and Cain began washing over the curves of his ass. Feeling the silkiness of the skin beneath his fingers, Cain couldn't help the slow caress of his hand as it smoothed the soap over Élan. "I will do as you wish, my lord."

"Very good," Élan murmured. He reached up and gripped the spout above his head. Moaning, he stretched, the firm muscles moving beneath slick skin. "When you are done, I would like the patchouli oil for my massage."

Cain bit at his lower lip, fixated on the sight of Élan's body as he finished washing him. He wasn't sure if the gods were intent on punishing him or making his wildest dreams come true. Once he was done, Cain stepped back to grab a towel and waited for Élan to rinse off. The thought of massaging the male form in front of him did a number on Cain's insides, yet he ignored it because it wasn't his place.

When he was rinsed, Élan stepped out and up to Cain, smiling down at him as Cain began drying him off. "Tell me about yourself."

Clearing his throat, Cain drew in a deep breath to still any wayward sound. "I served in the House of the Sun until your Chamberlain brought me here, my lord." After drying Élan off, Cain laid the towel on the stone bench then moved toward the massage table. "I worked in Lord Ason's home as a house server." Though he didn't openly question things, Cain did wonder why he had been brought here.

Élan stretched out on the table, face down. Hands resting up above his head and legs parted slightly, he relaxed with a rumbling purr of contentment. "Then you do not know why you are here?"

"I know I am to serve you, my lord." Reaching for the red bottle on the small counter near him, Cain opened it and poured some of the oil onto his hand. After putting the bottle down, he rubbed his hands together to warm the oil before he began smoothing it over Élan's back. The pressure of his hands kneaded the muscles beneath in firm strokes. Listening to the soft sound, Cain could feel it vibrate over his senses.

Élan's purr grew deeper. "I chose you."

"My lord?" Uncertain of what Élan meant, Cain's hands faltered slightly before he recalled the task at hand. Using his thumbs, he applied a gentle pressure along Élan's spine, running down to the small of his back. The deepening sound made Cain shiver, and this time he couldn't still the reaction. It pulsed through him in a way he couldn't explain. Though he had served other weres, he'd never had a noticeable response to them.

"That feels good, Cain," Élan whispered. Turning his head, his golden eyes almost seemed to glow in the dim light. "I've known about you for quite a while."

Sliding his hands further down, Cain massaged the firm flesh of Élan's ass as he stared unblinkingly at him. He wasn't sure how to take the words other than Élan had seen and approved of him, seeing him in service. "I didn't realize that, my lord."

Élan's eyes sparkled for a moment, then returned to their normal color. "What sort of services did you provide to your former lords?"

"I was in charge of one of Lord Ason's public rooms. He had a large collection, and I maintained a small portion of it." As he spoke, Cain continued the slow massage, working to relax Élan's body.

"I requested you to act as my personal attendant. You will bathe me, massage me, stay at my side throughout the day. Have you been with anyone yet?"

"No, I have never personally attended any lord. I have always been a house server." While not quite true that'd he always been a servant, part of the prevarication was true. Lowering his eyes from Élan, Cain disliked hiding the truth from him.

Élan rolled over carefully onto his back and gripped Cain's chin, firmly but gently. "I sense there is more you wish to tell me."

"No, my lord." Startled, Cain's eyes briefly met Élan's before he shook his head. What was it about the werelion that made him want to confess the truth? He could see a gentle understanding in the depths of the golden eyes, yet Cain had learned the hard way not to trust.

"Very well," Élan said. He released Cain's chin and settled. "You may continue."

Breathing a quiet sigh of relief, Cain poured more of the oil and warmed it with his hand before he began an efficient massage, starting at Élan's chest. Keeping his eyes trained on his work, the glide of his hands eased any tension within the groups of muscles.

Élan closed his eyes and let out another soft purr. "I am assuming, then, that you are untouched?"

Surprised by the question, Cain glanced quickly at Élan's face. "No, my lord, I am not a virgin."

"Then you know about pleasure—in its many forms." It was not a question, but it was obvious Élan expected an answer.

"I have had a male and a female lover, though they were not weres, my lord." Though he found the subject of their conversation odd, Cain didn't show it. Élan was allowed to ask whatever he wanted, and Cain knew it. "I am not the most experienced, but I've known the pleasures of both."

"So you have never been with a were." Élan nodded and opened his eyes, staring up at Cain. "What role have you played?"

"With Terin, I received." His words were a soft murmur as he focused on massaging the oil into Élan's skin. He didn't look up as he answered the question.

"Did you enjoy it?"

Though his face flushed red, Cain answered him. "Yes, I did, my lord. Terin was a very patient teacher."

"Did he tell you who his teacher was?"

"No, my lord, he didn't." It wasn't unusual for ones like Cain to take lovers of their own. Their lives weren't that strictly regulated by the weres they served. And just as the others, Cain had chosen to be a server to those closest to the gods.

"I taught him."

Cain's eyes widened as he stared into Élan's. He opened his mouth to say something, but wasn't certain of what to say. "I didn't know that, my lord."

"You were just a child when I first saw you. Your father served Lord Tyr-Set. Do you remember living in his home?"

Fear made Cain take an abrupt step back as he stammered, "My family is Wilhelm, my lord."

Élan sat up and held a hand out to Cain. "Please. I did not mean to startle you, Cain. I knew your father — before the Wars. You have nothing to fear with me."

Staring at him uncertainly, Cain finally fell to his knees, pressing his head to the floor. "Forgive me, my lord. I could tell no one the truth. They would kill me."

"Cain." The name was whispered as Élan crouched down in front of Cain. "You are safe with me." He lifted Cain's head until their eyes met. "And when we are alone, I am Élan."

In hindsight, Cain realized Élan had been testing him before, to encourage him to tell the truth. When his eyes met Élan's, he whispered, "You wanted me to tell you earlier."

"I did." Élan urged Cain to sit up. "I brought you here for your safety, though I will admit to having my own reasons beyond that."

Surprised when Élan drew him from his position, the werelord's close proximity made Cain shiver. "I am sorry. I didn't mean to disappoint you. The House of Mirra still hunts those who served Lord Tyr-Set."

Élan rested his hand on Cain's shoulder. "You didn't disappoint me, and you are safe in my house, Cain. Just as any of Tyr-Set's line would be. When it became necessary for your line to flee, I ensured they found safe haven."

Cain didn't dare question him, but he couldn't understand why Élan would have done such a thing. The werelord risked a great deal. Though the House of Mirra wasn't as prominent as it had been at the end of the wars, it still held considerable power. They probably wouldn't be able to bring down Élan's house, but Mirra could start another war. It would be the one way Mirra would divide the houses once again, and set them at each other's throats. The name Tyr-Set would make an excellent wedge, and Cain realized it.

"Come, I will show you to your room, and you can settle in."

Standing, Cain followed behind Élan toward one of the doors. When Élan opened the door, and Cain stepped inside, he realized the room connected to Élan's. Instead of the normal server's quarters, the luxury of the room rivaled Élan's. The bed was covered in sumptuous cream silk and velvet draperies were tied back against ornately carved mahogany posts. The light cream and dark brown echoed in the walls and furnishings. Cain could see it wasn't a server's room, but then little the werelord did made sense to Cain. As Élan turned back to his own room, Cain stared at him, trying to decipher the strange behavior of his lord.

# Chapter Three

In full form, Shaun lazed in the backyard near the pond Ashley had built. Though his master had stocked it with fish, Shaun had a very hard time trying not to get the golden fish as they swam by the paw he dangled in the water.

Knowing he would probably get in trouble if Ashley came home from work and found him with wet paws, Shaun backed up slowly, trying to ignore the lure of the flashes dancing beneath the surface. Sometimes he became antsy within the confines of the house and spent time prowling and pacing the back yard. The large, surrounding fence insured their privacy from the homes behind theirs. Instead of ignoring the fish as he should, their mesmerizing darts across the pond had Shaun fixated on them.

"I counted those fish when I put them in, Kitten."

Shaun's whiskers twitched in reaction to his master's voice. Ashley had named every blasted one of them as well. A fact Shaun couldn't figure out at all. Why give your food names? Settling back on his haunches, he chuffed his disagreement to his master.

One corner of Ashley's mouth twitched slightly. He stepped off the back porch and walked over to the pond. After making a show of counting each and every of the twenty-two fish, he reached out to scratch Shaun's head.

Lifting his paw, Shaun lazily licked the incriminating wetness away, giving his master a bland, harmless 'I'm not guilty of anything' look. A quick dart of his eyes back at the pond had the cat plotting each of those twenty-two fishes' demises. He let his body shift to his half form since his master seemed to prefer it the most when he took Shaun out for walks.

"Can we go for a run before dinner?"

Ashley turned to face him and pulled Shaun close. "Once I have my kiss."

A rolling purr rumbled from Shaun's throat as he lifted his face to Ashley's. This was their daily ritual, as familiar to Shaun as his own name. One teasing lick against his master's lips encouraged one of the lingering passionate kisses Shaun loved. Arms sliding around Shaun, Ashley opened to him, humming happily as their tongues met. The kiss was leisurely, playful, full of promises. When Ashley broke the kiss slowly, he smiled and stroked Shaun's cheek.

"Love you, Kitten. Ready to go play for a while?"

Shaun knew very well about the promises that would come later, and it made him reluctant to end the kiss. Still purring, he leaned forward to nuzzle against Ashley's throat. "In a minute."

Ashley's chuckle faded into a low moan, his head tilting to give Shaun more room. "Kitten." The name was whispered, Ashley's fingers threading through Shaun's hair.

Light nips of his teeth grazed Ashley's skin, tasting the unique flavor Shaun adored. The tilt of his head pressed against his master's hand as he pulled his head back. "I put a roast in the oven, and it should be done by the time we get back from the park."

"That sounds wonderful." Ashley smiled and took his hand. "Come on, Kitten. Let's get dinner started and then we'll play."

"Just need to put the potatoes and carrots in before we go." Shaun wrinkled his nose at the thought of the vegetables. He just fixed them because Ashley liked them. Tugging at Ashley's hand, he pulled him back into the house and toward the kitchen.

Ashley laughed and shook his head. "Don't you know vegetables can be fun, Kitten?"

# KITTEN

Giving Ashley a doubtful look, Shaun let go of his hand to get the roast from the oven. There was already a bowl of peeled potatoes and carrots soaking in water on the counter, and Shaun set the covered pan next to it.

Leaning back against the counter, Ashley plucked a carrot from the water. He watched Shaun as he flicked his tongue over the end of the vegetable. Then he pushed the carrot slowly into his mouth, teeth barely grazing the orange flesh.

Picking up a pot holder, Shaun took the lid off the roast and tried his best to ignore his master. Unfortunately, he wasn't clothed and his arousal was more than apparent as his cock started to harden. Casting a side glance at Ashley, Shaun's tongue darted out and wet his own lips. He simply couldn't bite back the small, pained sound that escaped him. Determinedly, he began scooping out the potatoes and carrots and dumping them in the pot.

Ashley lowered a hand to the front of his slacks and kneaded his cock through the thin, khaki fabric. "What's wrong, Kitten?" He swirled his tongue around the end of the carrot and let out a soft groan, pushing his palm harder against his pants.

Shaun's sex drive had become ever present since his master had awoken it in him. Something Shaun found nearly impossible to disregard. His body wanted what it wanted, and it wanted to be possessed by his master. Dropping his gaze to Ashley's hand, he watched its movement, fascinated. Not daring to touch his own cock or his master's, Shaun's eyes lifted back to Ashley, silently begging both in look and the unconscious arch of his body towards Ashley.

Carrot forgotten, Ashley tossed the vegetable into the sink and dropped to his knees. Wrapping a hand around Shaun's cock, he flicked the tip with his tongue, licking away the clear drops before sucking the head into his mouth. His other hand curled around Shaun's hip, encouraging Shaun to take what he needed.

The instinctive need for the heat and feel of Ashley's mouth edged at Shaun's senses, and his hips reacted instantly with a forward push. Pulses of sound bubbled up from Shaun, interspersed with purrs of deep pleasure. Each slow thrust into Ashley's mouth set Shaun's nerves on a fine trembling edge. He had no vocalizations for this other than the sounds spilling from his throat.

Ashley's eyes rolled up and pinned Shaun with an intent gaze. "Come for me, Kitten. Let me taste you."

Shaun wouldn't come without Ashley's permission, and once given, the drive of his thrusts quickened. With the glide of teeth and mouth around his cock, the sensations sent Shaun over that edge. Small convulsions rushed through him with his orgasm, pumping his come deep into Ashley's mouth. The sound of his cry rose sharply with the release.

Ashley licked him clean and stood, pulling Shaun into a kiss. He pressed against Shaun, thighs bracketing Shaun's leg. Ashley broke from the kiss, his breath quickened as he rocked harder. "Kitten…"

Shaun's thigh held tightly to the pressure of Ashley's body and when Ashley ended the kiss, Shaun quickly dropped to his knees in front of his master. He wanted and demanded the same taste. Unfastening Ashley's pants, Shaun's mouth quickly enveloped the hard flesh, suckling on it before his head moved back, partially releasing it. With the next slide into his mouth, his throat relaxed to take the full length in, encouraging his master to come.

"Kitten." Ashley gasped and his fingers tangled in Shaun's hair. He rocked and thrust, sliding his cock over Shaun's tongue and when Shaun swallowed, Ashley shouted his name, prick throbbing as he shot.

Shaun eagerly drank every drop, and the vibration of a low purr encompassed Ashley's cock. Finally, with one last lick, Shaun settled back on his heels, looking distinctly pleased with himself. "I love making you lose it."

Ashley laughed breathlessly and slumped against the counter. "Love, you will never hear me complain." He looked down at Shaun and grinned slowly. "However…there's a lot to be said about a certain Kitten, trussed to the bed, spread out and needing."

Grinning mischievously, Shaun got back on his feet and began putting the rest of the carrots and potatoes in with the roast. His master's words sent a distinct tingling through him and he murmured, "That's for later. And since you said it, it's a promise."

Ashley stepped up behind him and brushed Shaun's hair to the side. Leaning in, he gave Shaun's throat a quick nip with his teeth and whispered, "I can guarantee it, my Kitten." With that, Ashley walked away and into the bedroom.

Hearing the distinct promise in Ashley's voice, Shaun didn't bother to suppress the shiver. Terribly distracted, he still managed to finish adding the vegetables then put the lid back on the roaster and slid it into the oven. Padding silently out to the living room, Shaun got his loincloth from the chair where he'd left it and refastened it around his hips as he waited for his master to return.

"On your knees, Kitten," Ashley said as he returned to the living room. There was no doubt it was a command. "And bend over for me."

Even though surprised, Shaun quickly fell to his knees and bent forward, placing his hands flat on the floor. Looking up at Ashley, the earlier tingling over his senses increased sharply as he waited on his master's pleasure.

Ashley walked around and knelt behind Shaun, running one hand over the curve of his ass. "I'm upping the stakes," he explained. He popped the top on the lube. "We will go play…" He worked two fingers slowly into Shaun, stretching him gently, twisting slightly to stroke over his gland. "…but you will be full."

Since Ashley had actually never done that, Shaun was very surprised, but he obediently raised his ass for his master, feeling the rubbing of the fingers deep inside. Another small pulse of sound came from him with the teasing of his ass. "Yes, master."

The fingers disappeared and then something larger began pushing slowly in. "Relax, Kitten," Ashley coaxed, working the plug in a little at a time.

Drawing in a deep breath helped Shaun prepare, and he felt the hard metal ease into his ass then pop into place. The air from his lungs exhaled with a soft, mewling sound and the bow of his back kept his ass arched in place for Ashley. They had played with vibrators and plugs before, but Ashley had never required Shaun to wear one in public.

"So beautiful, my Kitten," Ashley whispered. He traced the flared bottom of the plug, caressing the sensitive skin stretched around it. "Full and ready for me."

The simple touch made Shaun tremble and his awareness centered on the feeling of fullness in his ass. His nails kneaded into the floor, focusing on the sharper desire that occupied his thoughts now. A soft purr answered Ashley as Shaun turned his head to look back at his master. Seeing how pleased Ashley looked warmed him.

"Let's go play, Shaun." Ashley smiled and stood, then offered Shaun a hand up. When Shaun stood, Ashley slipped the collar around Shaun's neck and buckled it, making sure it wasn't too tight. Then he hooked the leash to the ring on it. "One of these days, I'll find us a collar that will be special, just for us."

Gingerly, Shaun shifted finding it near impossible to ignore the sensation in his ass. Smoothing down the back of the loin cloth, he looked quizzically at Ashley, unsure of what his master meant. As he moved for the front door, he asked, "Another collar?"

"Yes." Ashley opened the front and waved Shaun out. He caught Shaun just before he could walk out, though, and pulled him close. "My collar, Kitten. Not as your owner...but as your Master."

When Ashley talked like that, Shaun never knew what to say. Something like that could be only between humans. There was a world of distinction in what he was, and in what Ashley talked about. Shaun ducked his head, rubbing against Ashley's chest as a rumbling purr rose in his throat.

"For your safety, no one would know," Ashley whispered. "But I will know, and you will know. That's all that matters."

Shaun lifted his head and nodded slightly. Drawing back, he started out the door. The odd sensation in his ass aroused him, and it was extremely hard not to notice his own sensitivity.

Ashley locked the door and followed behind him. Just before they stepped out onto the sidewalk, he slipped his hand down and tapped the base of the plug. "Run for me, Kitten."

Given the go ahead, Shaun set off in a sprint towards the park. Try as he might, he couldn't ignore the friction rubbing inside him. Still he continued, racing ahead of Ashley. When he headed towards a group of trees, he paused. Tightening the muscles of his ass, he noticed it only strengthened what he already felt. Ashley caught up with him, then passed him by, flashing Shaun a look over his shoulder before heading toward the river.

Other owners and their pets were playing in the park, most of the humans talking to one another while their pets—all in animal form—milled about lazily. The sun was setting, dropping everything into a dull, golden-red haze. Ashley stopped at the riverbank and dropped to the ground, panting from the run. He started to pull out his cigarettes, then stopped. Shaun glanced warily at the others in the park. He wanted to attack his master, wanted the plug out and his master's cock in his ass. Stepping slowly toward Ashley, Shaun's demeanor became distinctly more stalking. Each step he took increased the internal agitation. A low growl bubbled up from his throat even as he tried to still it.

Without looking back, Ashley pulled his hair out of its ponytail and shook his head, letting the length fall down over his back. He'd thought about cutting it months ago, but Shaun had begged him not to. Then he reached into his pants pocket.

Before he reached Ashley, Shaun managed to get himself back under control. At least, he showed he could control himself. Slipping down to the ground, he knelt behind his master then almost jumped when he felt the sudden vibration of the plug in his ass. His eyes widened as his body squirmed then forced himself to settle again. A plaintive mew sounded from him before he could stop it.

Ashley glanced over his shoulder at Shaun and grinned. "What are you thinking about right now, Kitten?"

"Master." The same tone infected his voice. Shaun plastered himself against Ashley's back.

"Yes?" Ashley leaned back against Shaun. "I asked a question, Kitten. I am waiting for an answer."

The vibration in his ass distracted Shaun as he rested his forehead against Ashley's shoulder, and he needed a moment to try to clear his thoughts. He blurted out the only thing he could think about. "I want you in my ass, master. Not this toy. I want you."

Ashley hummed, the sound happy, satisfied. "Very good, Kitten. In that case…" He turned off the vibrator. "When you are ready, we will go home. You will feed me, then I will give you everything you need."

The intensity died off and Shaun relaxed slightly. The toy had a high impact on him, but then he was always acutely aware of his master, and his own need for Ashley was never far from the surface. Nuzzling against the nape of Ashley's neck, Shaun peppered the skin with kisses. "I wanted a run, but now maybe we should just go back home."

Moaning softly, Ashley tilted his head, giving Shaun more room. "Soon, Kitten. Harder…"

Clamping his teeth lightly to Ashley's skin, Shaun growled softly as his arms wrapped around his master. His scent filled Shaun's senses with each breath.

Ashley gasped and reached back, wrapping one hand behind Shaun's neck. "Shaun…Kitten…" he shivered in

Shaun's arms, another moan slipping free.

Now it was his turn to tease his master, and Shaun took full advantage. His claws dragged down the front of Ashley's shirt but didn't tear the fabric, though he wanted to. He left a trail of soft kisses over Ashley's skin before he bit more sharply into him.

"Shaun!" Ashley's fist tightened in Shaun's hair. "Fuck. Kitten." His chest rose and fell quickly, heart pounding.

From the tone of Ashley's voice, Shaun knew he couldn't push it any farther. He released Ashley and quickly jumped up, taking off in the direction of the small lake. If he didn't start running now, it was doubtful he'd get any exercise. Ashley's laughter followed him, his Master moving slower. The sun had set and with the exception of a few others, they were alone in the darkening park. Ashley finally took off in a run, letting Shaun stay ahead but not by much. Shaun ran without any notion of where he was going; he simply needed the exercise. He stayed away from the others who were still in the park and lengthened his stride once he reached the larger clearing near the lake.

By the time Ashley had nearly caught up with him, it was fully dark. The moon sparkled on the water, the smooth surface marred only by the occasional fish. Ashley dropped to the ground, breathless, and sprawled out on his back. "Okay, you win," he panted. "I'm quitting the cigarettes."

Turning to watch Ashley, Shaun had to laugh. He wasn't even winded but had greatly enjoyed his romp. "I told you so." Padding silently across the grass, he moved back to Ashley and quickly straddled him. A slightly downward grind of Shaun's hips signaled his mood hadn't fully changed yet.

"Smart ass," Ashley grunted. His hands curled on Shaun's hips, the look in his eyes hungry and determined as he rocked his hips up, pulling Shaun down at the same time.

"Need you, master." Shaun groaned low in his throat as he stared back at Ashley. The feelings pulsing through him strengthened with the heat of Ashley's look.

"Home." Ashley lifted Shaun off of him. "Now."

Eager to comply, Shaun jumped up and grabbed his master's hand, helping him up. At a quickened pace, they returned to the house. Shaun had already exercised his early restlessness and only his hunger for Ashley remained. After opening the front door, he stepped inside then stilled, waiting for Ashley to decide if he wanted dinner first or his pet.

Not releasing Shaun's hand, Ashley started for the bedroom. When they neared the bed, he turned and tugged Shaun into a kiss, pulling the loincloth off in one split second. "Bed," he growled against Shaun's lips. "I want you spread out for me."

After nipping at the lips so close to his own, Shaun grinned then obeyed his master. He scrambled onto the bed, taking care to display his ass to its best advantage, wanting Ashley's full attention on him. Looking at Ashley from over his shoulder, Shaun parted his legs further, giving Ashley a view of the plug still firmly lodged in his ass.

"Turn over."

Once Shaun had rolled over and was on his back, Ashley spread Shaun's legs apart. He looked up into Shaun's eyes as he took hold of the plug, jostling it a little. Shaun's hips lifted and a plaintive sound spilled from his lips. He went instantly from teasing to badly wanting with very little effort on Ashley's part. He didn't try to reach for Ashley, though, since his master would determined the play.

"What do you want, Kitten?" Ashley pulled the plug out a little, then let Shaun's body suck it back in. "How do you want it?"

Twitching in reaction, Shaun gasped in a breath before he tried to answer Ashley. He squirmed down slightly then raised his legs, wanting to drape them over

Ashley's shoulder. "Deep and hard, master. Please use me."

Ashley undressed quickly and hovered over Shaun, his breath warming Shaun's ear as he whispered, "as you wish." The plug was pulled out suddenly and Ashley thrust in, giving Shaun no time to catch his breath before capturing his lips in a hard kiss.

The sudden pressure inside Shaun made his hips push hard into the movement, forcing Ashley deeper inside him. Both hands grabbed for Ashley's arms, clawing into them as his body writhed beneath his master. The edge of his teeth bit into Ashley's lip to draw blood then his tongue tasted the tiny drops. Shifting, Ashley grabbed Shaun's legs and draped them over his shoulders, practically bending Shaun in half. The angle drove him deeper, his cock grazing Shaun's gland with every deep, forceful thrust.

"Ashley!" His master's name was torn from him in a sharp cry. With each shove inside him, the buck of Shaun's body rocked against Ashley. Ashley owned him body and soul, and Shaun gave into that each and every time they joined as one. Need spiraled well beyond Shaun's control, leaving his body trembling.

Breaking the kiss, Ashley stared down into Shaun's eyes as his hand wrapped around Shaun's cock. "Come, Kitten. Now."

There was no way Shaun could refuse the command in Ashley's voice. The trembling turned quickly to hard shudders as the pulses of his orgasm raced like lightning through his body. At first deeply internal, a few seconds later come spurted from his cock, slicking Ashley's hand. Sharp growls escaped Shaun, reacting to the intense wash of pleasure.

"Shaun." Ashley groaned and a bruising pressure assaulted Shaun's lips, Ashley's tongue forcing its way in as he jerked, filling Shaun with his release.

Clinging tightly to his master, Shaun held on through the onslaught overtaking both of them. As Shaun came down, he could barely move. He was lost in the feelings that swept through him. Tears wet his fur, but he barely noticed them.

"Shh," Ashley murmured, kissing the soft black and white fur. He pulled out slowly and rolled onto his side, pulling Shaun to him. "I didn't hurt you, did I?"

Instinctively craving the close contact, Shaun snuggled against his master. Tucking his head to Ashley's chest, he mumbled, "Just need you, master. Don't want to let you go."

"I'm here." Ashley kissed Shaun's head softly, smoothing his hand over Shaun's hair. "I love you, Shaun, and I will never let you go."

# Chapter Four

Élan sat in his private study, staring up at the two portraits hanging on his wall. They both were of Tyr-Set, one in human and the other in wereform. Tyr-Set had been a proud man, one Élan had called his friend. The two had been close for most of their lives. The thought Aldar Tyr-Set might have had a son sparked hope in Élan.

Over twenty-one years ago, Aldar and his new wife had disappeared after the accusations of treason made by Lord Nostra. Élan had been suspicious of Nostra's claims at the time, especially since the House of Mirra stood to gain the most. Élan had had no success tracking down Tyr-Set. Three years later, Nostra had brought the bodies of Aldar and Misha to the city, claiming he had found them both dead. Élan didn't fully believe it.

Élan believed Nostra's attempts had been funded by Noramerna to bring Ausafca to its knees and provide Noramerna with an unending supply of wereslaves. It had almost succeeded. In Euroas, the were lines had been forced underground. The division between the houses of Ausafca had almost brought the were lines down as well. Élan had, through sheer force, brought the houses back together, something he wasn't proud of.

If Aldar had had a son, Élan wasn't sure how the child would have escaped Nostra's notice, or how the child might have ended up in Noramerna. Élan had a sneaking suspicion, however it happened, one of Aldar's most trusted servants would have had to have been behind it. Only one name came to mind. David Tyr-Set had been Aldar's Chamberlain. Élan knew the man hadn't returned to the city until a few months after the deaths of

Aldar and Misha. David had changed his name, and Élan had backed his application for service to Lord Ressur. The missing time would have been more than enough to have taken a child to Noramerna.

When Hapsus and Cain entered, Élan motioned Cain to stand near him as he addressed Hapsus. "Find Rath Wilhelm for me. I want him brought here. Make sure none see him enter the hall."

"I believe he serves in the House of Grace, my lord." After bowing his head to Élan, Hapsus left the room to carry out his orders.

Turning to face Cain, Élan smiled when he saw Cain staring at the two portraits. "We were very close. Like brothers."

"I barely remember him. My father served as his right hand and was killed with him. I remember one night several men came to our home. My mother was in tears, insisting my sister and I go with them. I never saw my parents after that."

"Your father and mother both insisted on staying with Lord Tyr-Set and his wife. The men were mine. I sent them to bring your family to safety. Afterwards, I could find no trace of Tyr-Set or the others." Élan placed his hand on Cain's shoulder. "I believe Aldar was brought down by House of Mirra for their own gain. It has taken me many years to find the truth, and soon I will prove it, Cain. Your family name will be restored to you."

"The House of Light was destroyed, my lord." Sadness haunted the dark eyes turned on Élan.

"But I believe it will be reborn." Élan could say no more of his own plans.

The door to the study opened and Hapsus entered with another man. "My lord, here is Rath Wilhelm."

Bowing his head, Rath greeted Élan. "My lord."

Élan returned to his chair and Hapsus stood silently beside him. Carefully watching Rath, Élan noticed the man showed no emotion when he saw the portraits. Deliberately he used Rath's real name. "Please sit with me,

David Tyr-Set."

Pretending to be puzzled, Rath's voice contained none of his fear, but Élan could sense it. "My lord?"

Élan decided to come right to the point. "I brought you here to question you about Aldar's son. Rumors have reached me of a white weretiger in Noramerna, and I need to know what you know of the matter."

"Son?" To his credit, David showed absolutely no reaction to Élan's words.

Calmly regarding him, Élan spoke quietly. "The time for subterfuge has passed, David. If the young cub is the child of Aldar, he needs to be returned to his rightful place."

"There is no child, and what you suggest is impossible. All know Lord Tyr-Set was a traitor."

"David, I am not testing you. I am speaking the truth. Mirra will pay for its deceit and the truth will be known. If by some miracle Aldar's child has survived captivity in Noramerna, I will make sure he is brought here and kept safe in my house."

The man seemed to weigh Élan's words carefully before he spoke. "I left the child with my sister, Amelia, and I have had no contact with them since that night. My only desire was to keep Shaun safe. Lady Misha entrusted me with his care, and I promised her I would take him to a place where no one could get to him."

Though Noramerna wouldn't have been the ideal place, it would have been the one place nobody would have looked if knowledge of the child's birth had become public. "That was very well done of you, David. Oddly, there would have been no place safer for him. What is the name he would have been registered under?"

"Shaun Fields, my lord. My sister agreed to raise Shaun as her own. She had planned on keeping his true nature a secret when it became his time to shift."

"Lady Misha gave birth to him in human form." Given the circumstances, Élan wasn't surprised. It would have been nearly impossible to smuggle a werecub out of

Ausafca, but a mortal child would have been easier. Addressing his Chamberlain, Élan said, "Find what you can on Shaun Fields, Hapsus. I want the information immediately."

"Yes, my lord." Hapsus moved toward Élan's desk and sat down in front of the computer.

Glancing at Cain, Élan smiled as he introduced him to David. "You might be interested to meet Cain Tyr-Set, David. I believe you know who he is."

Startled, David glanced at Cain, then smiled. "I worked with your parents. They were both very brave."

Tears welled in Cain's eyes before he blinked them back. "Thank you."

"Cain now lives in my household, David. I had him brought here for my own reasons."

Before David could reply, Hapsus interrupted the conversation. "I have the information you want, my lord."

Sliding from his chair, Élan stood behind Hapsus. "Tell me what you've found."

"Shaun Fields was registered to Miss Amelia Fields shortly after Lord Tyr-Set's death. She died less than a year later, and the child was adopted by Mr. and Mrs. Jeremiah Taylor. The records show Shaun was placed at the Noramerna Institute shortly before his eighteenth birthday by his adopted parents. It doesn't seem anyone was aware of Shaun's true line."

Frowning heavily, Élan began to pace. "Where is he now?"

"His records state over a year ago, he escaped the Institute and was captured by Ashley Winters a few months later. About a month after that, Shaun was taken back to the Institute for an attack on a mortal. After being given advanced Institute training, he was released back to his owner. Apparently they determined the attack had been provoked and didn't destroy him."

The thought of any were held captive to human slavery dismayed Élan. Turning away from Hapsus, Élan spoke to Cain. "I want you prepared to travel to

Noramerna as soon as possible. Hapsus will give you the list of our agents, but I want them kept in the dark as to exactly what you are doing."

"I understand, my lord."

"Whatever resources it takes, I want Shaun brought back to where he belongs." Facing David, Élan continued, "I need not tell you to mention nothing of what we have spoken about."

David shook his head. "No, my lord. I have kept Shaun's existence secret for all of these years. I will never speak of it."

Cain took Élan's hand to still the agitation. "I will bring him home, my lord. No matter what it takes."

"For now, come." Élan nodded once to David and Hapsus, then led Cain out the door.

Without glancing at the others, Cain followed beside Élan down the long hall, sharply conscious of the werelord near him. As Élan drew him into his private quarters, Cain was surprised when they didn't stop near the bathing pool. Casting a quick side glance at Élan, Cain went with him out into the sanctuary garden. Normally no one but Élan entered the garden since it was his private sanctuary. Parting the gauze curtains with his other hand, Élan closed his eyes as they stepped out into the garden. The sun was just beginning to set, but the last of its rays were shining through the slender windows of the garden's walls.

"I like to come out here to relax," Élan said. "At night, there is just enough light to read by."

"Do you read much, Élan?"

Élan smiled wistfully. "When I have the time. I miss being able to, really. What about you? What do you do to relax?"

"I like to play card games. Unfortunately partners are hard to find." Cain stood beside Élan, looking up at him. The werelord topped him by several inches.

"And if I offered?"

Cain's brow rose in surprise. "I have to warn you, I'm good. And being an important werelord won't stop me from kicking your ass," Cain teased.

"Promise?" Élan's grin was purely wicked.

Bowing his head politely, Cain murmured, "You can rely on it, my lord." Eyeing Élan from beneath the strands of hair that had fallen across his face, a teasing smile curved Cain's lips.

Élan bent and whispered near Cain's ear, "I'm looking forward to it."

Cain's breath caught in his throat when he felt the heat against his skin. Before a visible reaction might betray him, he quickly scrambled for a distraction. "Besides reading and cards, do you enjoy anything else?"

"Quite a few things, though…" Trailing off, Élan shook his head and smiled. "Your company is enough for me."

"Thank you, my lord."

As Cain moved away from Élan, he approached a row of towering blue flowers. The fragrances perfuming the air were actually relaxing to the senses. Coming up behind Cain, Élan reached around him and plucked one of the flowers.

"These are some of my favorites."

Cain followed the movement of Élan's hand with more interest than he should have. Not even the sweet odor of the flowers could overcome the scent of the werelord so close. Cain knew if he took a small step back, he could lean against Élan. A slow, even breath drew on the unique scent of Élan. He'd gotten into the habit of doing that far too often. "They are beautiful. I remember my old home had a very small garden with a fountain. It was my garden."

"Do you miss it?" Élan asked, not moving from where he stood. He drew his hand back, letting the petals of the flower brush lightly over Cain's left cheek.

Closing his eyes, Cain reacted to the light touch with the turn of his head. "Sometimes. I remember bits and pieces about my parents. Mostly I remember how happy I was. I haven't felt that since it was all taken."

"Would you like to feel it again?" The words were whispered, Élan's breath warm again on Cain's ear, the werelord's body just barely brushing Cain's.

The question was something Cain hadn't expected and he wasn't sure how to answer. "Sometimes I would, but then sometimes I know how easily it can be taken."

"I would never take it from you," Élan said. "I would protect it for you." Wrapping his other arm around Cain, Élan took Cain's left hand and placed the flower on his palm, then curled Cain's fingers over it gently. "It's yours. I need someone to help me care for it."

Cain understood the words the moment they were spoken. It was something that hadn't occurred to him because he'd thought Élan merely meant him to be a server. "Do you truly mean that, Élan?" Looking down at their hands for a moment, Cain turned, unable to resist raising his gaze to Élan. The golden glow within Élan's eyes captivated him, leaving him speechless.

"I do." Élan's gaze drifted lower, then back up to Cain's eyes. "It is yours."

Élan's words only puzzled Cain. Cain thought he'd understood what the werelord had meant, and now he wasn't so sure.

A strand of dark hair escaped from Cain's braid and Élan reached out, tucking it behind Cain's ear. "I want to gain your trust, Cain. Even if I can never have you."

Élan confused him completely, and Cain stared at him, trying to understand the meaning behind the words. "But I am your server, my lord. My life is to serve you."

Giving him a soft smile, Élan leaned forward and kissed Cain's forehead, whispering, "I don't want a server. I want you."

Feeling the warmth of Élan's lips touching his skin, a gasp of surprise escaped Cain. It took him a moment to comprehend what he was being told. "But why? I am not even of royal blood. You are the most powerful of the chosen."

Élan cupped Cain's cheek and his thumb brushed

across Cain's lips. "You have been my chosen for a very long time."

Bemused, Cain couldn't believe what Élan said. It made no sense to him. If any suspected who Cain really was, not even Élan could stop the uproar that would arise. "My lord, my lineage is of Tyr-Set, though I am not a shifter. You know nothing about me." Even though Cain argued with Élan, the press of his face leaned into the gentle touch, feeling the warmth of it flow over him.

"I knew your father." Élan pressed a soft but chaste kiss to Cain's lips. "And I've known you since you were born."

A sound came from Cain's throat with the brush of Élan's lips. The werelord attracted him beyond reason, and Cain could sense the gentleness behind Élan's actions. Before he could stop himself, he answered the light pressure with his own. Then just as quickly, he drew back before it could become anything more. He bowed his head. "My lord, if you took me as your lover and any of the others discovered who I am, they would be enraged."

"That is my concern. There are those who support me, and there are those who do not. As for you being my lover, then it will be at your discretion. I will not force you if you do not want me in that respect."

Looking up, Cain stared into those golden eyes. Who would not be attracted to the handsome werelord? Many would have accepted Élan simply for the prestige they would receive. Cain knew many would vie heatedly for the position, but he wasn't like that. His expression reflected his uncertainty, and he spoke hesitantly, "Many would wish to be your lover, Élan, to gain whatever they could for themselves. I am not the same as they are. I've only had two lovers in my life, and I loved both of them."

"This is not a matter of position, or gain."

They returned to the bedroom, Élan heading toward a dark wood counter filled with food. He plucked a grape from the bunch sitting on a silver platter, and chewed it slowly.

# KITTEN

"I've had many lovers over my lifetime, Cain. I'm older than many—even my own kind—are aware. I've loved those I was with, though not all of them loved me. Some considered me crude, rash—too used to speaking my mind. I've lost much in the way of companionship, because of that; but I can't change who I am."

"It isn't you. I have only been shown kindness since I came here a month ago. I sense gentleness in you that I've never seen in any other except Terin." Moving to stand beside Élan, Cain asked, "May I eat as well?"

Élan blinked at him, the look almost comical on the otherwise stoic features. "Of course you may. You are free to do whatever you wish. I hold no contract on you, Cain." He picked another grape and held it to Cain's lips, whispering, "I never signed one."

Astonished, Cain's eyes widened and he hesitated before taking the grape. After chewing and swallowing, he asked, "Do the others know that?"

"A few trusted souls, but the majority does not. I'm not the most trusting man in the world."

"Why would you do all of this, Élan?" Cain tried his best to understand why the revered werelord would go to so much trouble on his behalf. "Do you have feelings for me?"

Élan studied him in silence for a moment before speaking. "Yes. I do."

"I really don't understand why." Looking down at the table, Cain took a slice of orange. "It would be hard to argue with you since you are the one who brought me here, and I am not under contract to you."

"Whether you want me is up to you. I've been yours longer than you know."

Leveling a pensive stare on Élan, Cain helped himself to several more pieces of the fruit. For some strange reason, he once again found himself the sole focus of those golden eyes. Most times, Élan confused him, and the confusion only seemed to grow the longer Cain remained in the were's presence.

# Chapter Five

When Shaun woke up, he found himself strapped down to a metal table. A doctor was bent over him, examining him from head to toe. Shaun closed his eyes, trying to block out the nightmare as intrusive fingers poked and probed him everywhere. Shaun couldn't think clearly with the fog clouding his mind. He opened his eyes again, but everything had the feel of a nightmare to him.

Another man entered the room and stood near the doctor. Immediately Shaun recognized the newcomer as the same trader who had made him so fearful when he'd been imprisoned in the Institute for attacking a mortal.

"Your best bet is to breed him with a female white, Sam," the doctor said. "There would be a sixty percent chance that at least one in the litter would be white. If you use a golden, the odds decrease substantially. Eventually you would probably get a white, but it might take several litters to produce one."

Shaun's thoughts cleared slightly. The last thing he remembered was opening the front door when someone knocked, then the sting of a dart. Fear enveloped him as he realized the trader must have kidnapped him.

"There is also an increased chance that a white might crop up at a later point even with a golden from a litter sired by this one." Lightly, the trader—Sam—patted Shaun's head.

"Most times the gene would be dormant. It's true it could come out further down the line, but there are no guarantees on it. We can increase the odds, but there are defects that will show up in the cubs. A golden from the line of a white were like Shaun would fetch a good enough price, so I wouldn't advise tinkering in that direction."

"I'll take your suggestion into consideration, Jamison." Sam grinned down at Shaun. "Mr. Takito's white will be coming into heat in two months. I just want you to make sure he's healthy."

Their comments barely registered through the fog clouding Shaun's head. He wanted to struggle but found his limbs wouldn't cooperate.

Doctor Jamison smirked as he patted Shaun's leg. "He's healthy, and once you put him in the breeding kennel with a female in heat, he'll do his duty. You'll be able to breed him as often as you like."

"The sales will be under the market since Shaun has already been reported as stolen. Eventually I'll lay out enough money to fix the records." Shrugging uncaringly, Sam studied Shaun. "I had wanted to buy this creature, but his owner wouldn't sell. It worked out better this way as far as I'm concerned."

When another man came into the room, the doctor began unfastening the straps around Shaun. "Take him back to his cell for now, Jimmy. Make sure he's fed and watered. I added a special vitamin to his diet. Make sure he takes three pills a day."

"I will, Dr. Jamison." Jimmy took hold of Shaun's leash as Shaun sat up. "Come on, Shaun. Let's get you fed, then you can head out to the exercise area."

"Sam, I have a new medicine you can use when you're ready to breed him. It'll ensure he remains in proper form for breeding." Moving toward the counter, the doctor picked up a folder and began writing his notes in it.

"Lay me in a supply for the rest of my animals as well. It's a bitch when you can't control them during the mating."

The door closed, cutting off the conversation, and Jimmy led Shaun down the hall and out of the small building. Shaun followed in a haze. He hated the feeling of his mind and body being disconnected, but he could do nothing about it until the drug wore off.

When they reached his cell, Shaun prowled the cramped quarters, trying to ease the rubbery feeling in his legs.

"Don't leave this cell, Shaun." Jimmy disappeared further down the hall, then returned a few minutes later with two bowls. After placing them on the ground, Jimmy petted Shaun's head as Shaun knelt. "There you go. When you're done, I'll take you out for a run."

The food would make Shaun feel better, and he knew it. Moving to all fours, he ate from the bowl. After finishing part of the nearly tasteless meal, he lapped at the tepid water in the other bowl.

"Don't worry, Shaun. The feeling will wear off once you've had some exercise. But if you don't behave yourself, Doc will give you another dose to keep you obedient."

Settling back on his haunches, Shaun looked up at Jimmy. "Where's my master?"

"Sam Holliway is your master." With a shrug, Jimmy gestured toward the open door of the cell and tugged on Shaun's leash. "You'll be fed three times and let out once a day to exercise in the yard after your dinner."

With the tug, Shaun stood and let Jimmy lead him through the building to the outside. The exercise area was no more than twenty feet wide, and a white fence outlined its perimeters. "Don't go past the fence, Shaun. If you do, you'll be punished."

Warily, Shaun stepped onto the dirt and looked around the compound. He could see a guard patrolling above him along an outer wall. A rifle was slung over the man's back and another weapon was holstered at his belt. When Shaun walked out into the open, another guard appeared overhead and leaned against the wall, watching him. The guard pulled a rifle from his back, resting it on the railing.

After unfastening the leash, Jimmy stepped back. Glancing between Jimmy and the guard above his head,

Shaun hesitated. His first instinct was to escape, but the situation made him cautious.

With a bored look, Jimmy leaned against the wall behind him. "Go ahead, Shaun. If you try to get out, they'll only dart you again, and Mr. Holliway will beat you and keep you drugged for the next week as punishment. It's up to you."

Shaun nodded abruptly, then began walking on the path in the dirt. It ran in a circular form bordering the white fence. After a moment, Shaun started running in the circle. Every move he made was watched by the guard above him.

Pulling in a deep breath, Shaun caught the scents of a farm nearby. He definitely wasn't in the city anymore, but he still had no clue exactly where he was. He wanted his master and tried desperately not to break down in tears as he ran. Glancing up at the wall, Shaun tried to calculate his odds of being able to climb it quickly enough to get to the guard before the man could dart him.

After a quick study of the outer wall, Shaun noticed three other guards besides the one watching him. The odds were most definitely one of them would dart him before he could even reach the wall itself. While he could run fast, he couldn't outrun a tranquilizer gun. For the moment, Shaun could do nothing but run laps in the dirt courtyard.

"Shaun, time's up." Jimmy called out to him, pushing away from the wall.

Reluctantly, Shaun stopped and moved toward him. After refastening the leash, Jimmy pulled Shaun back inside and down the hall to his cell.

"If you behave for the next few days, you'll be taken out of this cell and allowed to stay with the other animals." Jimmy undid the leash and stepped out of the cell. The clang of the metal door made Shaun jump as Jimmy slammed it shut. "See you tomorrow, Shaun."

Shaun watched as Jimmy turned the key in the lock, then placed the key ring back on a peg in the wall across from the cell. It was too far for Shaun to reach. Besides the half empty dishes of food and water, the only other thing in the cell was a thin blanket folded on the floor.

Moving toward the barred window, Shaun could see the sun low in the sky. Curling his fingers around the bars, he tried with all his strength to pull on them. When they didn't budge, Shaun tried to get the bars to turn in their concrete housing. Finally, with a sigh, Shaun left the window and went to the blanket. It was only large enough for him to either lay on it or cover up with it. Since the evening was mild, Shaun laid it on the floor and curled up.

\* \* \* \*

"Where is he?" Ashley slammed his hands on the detective's desk, staring the man down.

The detective looked up at him, one eyebrow raised. "Mr. Winters, I'm sorry. We're doing the best we can. However, I'd greatly appreciate it if you would calm yourself. There's no need for shouting."

Ashley grit his teeth and spun around, stalking out of the man's office and slamming the door behind him. He'd reported Shaun missing—stolen—the second Shaun hadn't come home. Fear and rage boiled inside Ashley, twisting everything into one tightly-wound knot. No one could tell him a damn thing.

He reached their home without entirely remembering the trip there. In a daze, he closed the front door, the silence deafening. No Kitten came rushing for him. There were no kisses, no strong arms to wrap around him.

Defeat weighed on his heart and Ashley slid down to the floor, crumbling under it all.

\* \* \* \*

It had taken Cain two weeks to reach Noramerna via the underground smugglers' routes from Ausafca to Sevilla, Spain. He'd been in New Roth for only a day, and he already hated the place. All around him he saw the denigration of weres as they were paraded around by leash by their fashionable owners. In the market place, he watched the proceedings of the sales and had to hold back his anger. It hadn't taken him long to realize weres were not allowed in public in their human form. To him, Noramernians were an abomination to all Cain held dear. He'd heard stories of how they treated weres, but it wasn't the same as seeing it.

When he'd arrived, he'd notified agents of his presence and started watching Ashley Winter's house, but he had yet to see any sign of Shaun. Each time Cain caught a glimpse of Ashley, he had to restrain his own urge to kill the man. How could such a thing be allowed to exist? The culture shock to Cain's system was too far beyond what he could absorb. All he could think about was getting to Shaun and insuring the were was freed and taken to where he belonged.

On the second night of his watch, Cain waited until dark to approach the back of the house. Ashley hadn't come home yet, and Cain didn't want to waste the opportunity. No doubt the madman had Shaun caged somewhere in his house. It could be the only explanation for why Cain had caught no sign of the were.

Using a towel he'd brought along, Cain covered one of the back windows and quickly shattered it with his fist. The cloth protected his hand and muffled the sound of breaking glass. He let the towel drop to the floor and hurriedly undid the latch for the window, then climbed in.

The house was dark, but Cain had the natural ability to see well within darkness. He caught the strong scent of a were all over the house. Systematically, he searched each room, looking for Shaun. A mess of broken glass and debris littered the living room and several other places. Cain wasn't certain of what to make of the mess, or of the lack of any cage or restraining chains.

Once he'd thoroughly searched the house and found no evidence of Shaun, Cain quickly returned to the back window and slipped outside. What in the hell was going on? Had Shaun been sold to another master? He made his way back to his car and got in. Before he started it, he stared over at Ashley's house and debated waiting for Ashley. Cain doubted he'd have any problem getting the information he wanted from the human.

After a moment, he temporarily discarded the notion. He needed to return to the hotel and get in contact with Élan. Starting the car, Cain made the five-minute drive to his room. When he parked the car in front of his hotel room, he noticed somebody standing near his door. As he got out, the man approached him.

"Cain Wilhelm?" Holding out his hand, the man showed him the small mark on his palm. "I'm Robert Finchley. Élan sent me with a message."

With a nod, Cain moved toward his door and unlocked it, then motioned Robert inside. After shutting the door, Robert turned to face him.

"The were you are looking for has probably been taken to a small compound ten miles outside the city."

"Give me the address, and I will take care of it." Cain reached for the pad and pen on the table near the door and slid it toward Robert.

"I also have a letter for you." After pulling it out of his pocket, Robert handed it to him, then picked up the pen to write out the address.

Taking the envelope from him, Cain noted the seal hadn't been broken. Using his thumbnail, he broke it open and began reading the letter.

*Word has reached me of a trader offering the breeding services of an unusual were on the black market. Since I doubt there are two of the same kind, Ashley Winter must have sold Shaun, or Sam Holliway kidnapped him. The most likely place he'd keep Shaun is at his compound right outside the small town of North Falls. Robert will fill you in on the agents we have in that area.*

*Keep the others in the dark as much as you can. I'm trusting you to do what you must to bring Shaun home to me. And I want you home safely as well.*

*É*

Stuffing the note into his pocket, Cain took the notepad as well once Robert finished writing out the address.

"The area is a farming community, and you'll find refuge on the Willows farm. I wrote their address down as well. If you want, I can draw you a general map there."

With a nod, Cain said, "Please. I would appreciate it." Returning the pad to him, Cain stepped away to begin piling his clothes haphazardly back into his suitcase. "I'll be leaving as soon as I'm done packing."

Pulling the two sheets from the pad, Robert gave them to Cain. "Good luck, Cain. If you need to return to New Roth, tell them to let me know."

"I will." Politely, Cain shook the man's hand before Robert turned and walked out. Then he finished his packing and loaded his suitcase into the car. It wouldn't take him long to reach his destination. Once there, he would have to scout out the area to figure out the best way to free Shaun.

\* \* \* \*

"Chester, please," Ashley begged his friend. "Please help me."

"I will, I will." Chester crouched down in front of him, laying a hand on Ashley's shoulder. "I'll see what I can dig up in the system, okay?"

Ashley nodded, the tears still stinging his eyes. "I can't live without him. Shaun is my reason for being."

"He's a lucky man," Chester said, giving him a soft smile.

Ashley returned the smile as best he could. "We both are."

Patting Ashley's shoulder, Chester stood and went into the kitchen. "You thirsty?"

"Yes, actually."

"What would you like? Water, juice, milk, soda, coffee..." Chester's head appeared around the door frame. "Beer?"

Ashley laughed for the first time in a good while. "Water is fine. Thank you."

"Coming up." Chester disappeared again, but continued talking. "Any word from the police yet on fingerprints or anything like that?"

"There were none," Ashley said dryly.

Chester returned a moment later and handed him a glass of ice water. "Hmm..." Sitting in the chair across from Ashley, Chester sipped on a beer, brow wrinkling in deep thought.

"What?"

"Just kinda weird that it's taking so long."

"The police aren't known for caring much about weres," Ashley said dryly.

"Unless, of course, the owner is a politician or has tons of money."

"Neither of which applies to me." Ashley finished his water and sat back.

"You're welcome to stay here, ya know. I have a spare room."

The thought of going back home — of sleeping on the couch because he couldn't sleep in the bed — was enough to convince Ashley to accept the offer. He nodded. "Thanks, Chester. It means a lot."

* * * *

A week went by before Shaun was allowed to leave his cell. His new surroundings weren't much better, but he did have more than a ten by ten space in which to move around. The other two weres he lived with frightened Shaun. Not because they were mean or violent, but because they appeared so broken. Their confinement and the usage to which they'd been put had aged them beyond their years.

Sadly, Shaun watched them as he sat on his blanket. The oppressive feel surrounding him made him want to claw through the stone wall of the room just to escape. The panther raised his head and stared back at Shaun. Carefully, he crept toward Shaun with a soft whimper.

The werelion watched them for a moment, then ignored both of them as he rolled over onto his side, facing the wall. It took no more than Shaun's upraised hand to encourage Siah to get closer.

Very quickly the panther wedged his body against Shaun's side, and Shaun held him close. Resting his cheek against the cold of the stone, Shaun closed his eyes. A wave of need rushed through him, and he nearly cried out with it. He wanted his master, the safety of Ashley's love, and their home. During his imprisonment, Shaun struggled with the depression threatening to overwhelm him. He knew if he couldn't get free, eventually he'd become like Siah and Nathan.

Knowing what Sam Holliway planned to use him for would, sooner or later, drive Shaun insane. Whether or not Shaun ever had children had never bothered him. But knowing his children would be used as he was would be more than he could bear.

Swallowing against the knot of tears in his throat, Shaun turned his head slightly, rubbing his cheek against Siah's black fur. He prayed Ashley found him soon. His faith in his master was unshakable. Just the thought of Ashley was enough to ease the black despair and keep it at bay. Maybe Ashley could help Sian and Nathan, too. Shaun had only been housed with the other two for three days, but in that time, Siah had attached himself to Shaun. Shaun could sense the underlying need for simple contact from both of them. Siah had just been quicker and more open about showing it.

"Tell me about your master, Shaun."

While Shaun hadn't spoken about Ashley coming to save him, he had talked about his master. Smiling at Siah, Shaun said, "Ashley is special."

Before Shaun could continue, Nathan spoke from his corner in a disgruntled tone. "No master is special. They are all the same."

"You're wrong, Nathan." A confident tone rang in Shaun's voice. "My master treated me very special. He liked spoiling me with chocolate and treats, and he never hit me. He never even put me in a cage like they did at the institute. I slept in his bed." Though Shaun couldn't tell them that Ashley treated him the same as a human, he could describe the things Ashley did for him.

Siah regarded Shaun in wide-eyed wonder, and Nathan rolled over on his back, shooting a disbelieving look at him. "You're full of shit."

Shaun sighed quietly. "No, I'm not, Nathan. I want to go back home to him so much, it hurts."

The lack of vehement argument from Shaun and his expression made the disbelief on Nathan's fade slightly. Instead of saying anything, Nathan abruptly rolled back on his side, going back to staring at the wall.

"The only master I've had is Mr. Holliway." Siah rested his head on Shaun's shoulder as he spoke. "I was born and raised at the Institute in Chicago. When I was old enough, Mr. Holliway bought me."

"How long have you been here, Siah?" Shaun asked quietly.

"I've been here for four years, and Nathan has been here six." Glancing over at Nathan, Siah lowered his voice to a whisper. "He's from Euroas."

Unsure why Siah spoke in a whisper, Shaun gave him a puzzled look.

"I was born free." The tone of Nathan's voice rose sharply.

"Born free?" Shaun had never heard of the term.

"Yeah. Some areas in Euroas, like Italy, aren't like Noramerna. I wasn't born a pet. When I was fifteen, traders captured me in a raid on our town. Holliway bought me when I was put on the market."

"I didn't know there were any places like that." Though Shaun didn't press Nathan, he hoped the werelion would tell him more

"Shaun, I came from a world where ones like us run things. The humans don't keep us as pets. Special houses, headed by a werelord, used to be all over Euroas. But the war destroyed many of them and forced the others to hide. In Italy, we were still free. Ausafca is the only continent were the were houses still rule. Or that's how it was when I was taken. I don't know if it's like that anymore."

Studying Nathan thoughtfully, Shaun couldn't miss the initial tone of pride, nor did he miss it when it faltered over the last sentence. He didn't say it out loud, but the thought took hold to ask Ashley if they could go to Italy or Ausafca. He couldn't still the wishful hope that Siah and Nathan could go with them.

# Chapter Six

Settled at the bar, Cain sipped his soda as he waited for Jimmy to show up. One of the agents at Willows farm, Stacy, had told him Jimmy Asarin was Holliway's handler and always stopped by the bar every night after work. She'd given him a pretty good description of Jimmy, and Cain figured he would try to pump the guy for information.

Ignoring the creeping dismay of seeing several were waiters and waitresses being obnoxiously fondled by the patrons, Cain focused on the front door, praying Jimmy would show up soon so he could get the hell out of there. He couldn't do anything about the poor creatures who served in this place, but that didn't stop him from wishing he could free them.

Half an hour into his ordeal, Cain spotted Jimmy coming into the bar. A couple of the people called out, "Hey, Jimmy," as the man approached the bar counter.

Turning to face him, Cain smiled as he asked, "You wouldn't happen to be Jimmy Asarin, would you?"

Surprised, Jimmy turned slightly to look at him. "Yeah, why?"

"I'm Steve Tennant. My cousin told me Holliway might be hiring, and I should go talk to you at Holliway's place right outside of town. I was planning on heading there since I'm looking for a job." The lie spilled smoothly from Cain's lips.

After he ordered his drink, Jimmy nodded to Cain. "In about two weeks, Sam'll be looking to hire two more trainers. He's getting a shipment of weres in on the thirtieth."

"Is he good to work for?" Cain asked casually, probing for information.

Jimmy shrugged. "He's a cheap bastard, but he pays regularly. The job isn't that hard. Mostly grunt work. Feeding and exercising the weres. If any new ones are untrained, you give them a crash course."

"Doesn't sound too hard," Cain commented before he took a drink of his Pepsi.

"Nah, it isn't. The three I have now are pretty well-behaved. Sam's had two of them for several years. And even the new one isn't hard to handle. If you got hired, you'd take over their handling and I'd get a break until the new group arrives. Usually Sam has a full stable, but he sold off some of his stock because the price was right. If you're qualified, there's a good chance you'll be hired. The last four handlers we had weren't worth shit, and Sam won't rehire them."

"What exactly does the job entail?" Cain had to bite back a lot of what he wanted to say concerning Jimmy's bored attitude about the atrocities mentioned.

"The routine is pretty easy to learn. The weres eat three times a day. Nine AM, one and five PM. You prepare their food. After the evening meal, they get their exercise—fifteen minutes in the yard—then they're bedded down for the night. Most of the time I work in the main building, taking care of the breeding paperwork. Every three days, around nine in the evening, a truck comes in with supplies and the handlers take turns unloading it. Usually, after the weres get their exercise, you can leave. Unless it's a truck night. Then you have to stay late to check the incoming inventory and help the driver unload."

Since it was Monday, Cain knew the truck would deliver supplies tomorrow night and he planned on watching the compound. Another one wouldn't be due until Friday and that would be the night he would free Shaun. He'd need that much time to execute the plan he had in mind.

"I'll stop by probably next Monday," Cain said, not wanting to arouse suspicion. "Would around eleven o'clock be good?"

"That'll be fine. I'll be in my office then. Normally we only handle the male weres, but occasionally a client wants a pregnant female taken care of until she births. With the new stock coming in, I'll definitely be needing the help." Jimmy had described everything with appalling casualness.

"Thanks for filling me in." Cain couldn't even imagine a life like that, but he kept his expression from showing his disgust as he nodded to Jimmy. He finished his soda quickly and stood. "See you Monday at eleven."

* * * *

Situated near an outcropping of rocks, Cain stretched out on his stomach in the grass and trained his binoculars on the compound at the bottom of the foothills. He could see four guards patrolling the outside wall. He knew a truck from one of the nearby farms would arrive later in the evening at the compound to deliver a supply of food. He could see no sign of Shaun as yet, but Jimmy had told him the weres generally were exercised after their evening meal. There were several squat buildings of gray stone— all of them longer than they were wider, except for a two-story one near the center of the compound.

Other than the four guards, there were no others moving in the compound. Each of the guards appeared well-armed. When he focused back on a small fenced-in area, a door opened and Cain saw a flash of black and white fur. Focusing on Shaun, Cain watched as the young werecat began running on a small, circular path. When he looked down at his watch, Cain noted the time.

As he looked back at Shaun, Cain felt a deep wave of relief. He'd found the son of Lord Tyr-Set. It wouldn't be long before they both could get the hell out of there. Cain couldn't take much more of being in this country, and he missed his lord far more than he thought possible. A pang of longing for Élan rose in him with just the simple thought of the werelion. Every moment Cain hadn't been occupied with the plans to set Shaun free, every thought had been of his werelord. Pushing down the unaccountable feelings, Cain scanned the compound one more time before he set his sights on the handler leaning against the wall near Shaun. It was Jimmy.

Normally the agents at Willows left Holliway alone because the compound was too well-guarded. Since none of them mentioned any rumors about white tigers, Cain figured they had no clue Shaun was there, and Cain hadn't filled them in.

About fifteen minutes later, Jimmy motioned to Shaun and the were walked over to him. He leashed Shaun and took him back into the building. Five minutes later, the door opened again and a werepanther walked out. Cain observed the routine patiently as a werelion was also brought out for his exercise. After they headed back in, Jimmy came out about ten minutes later, walked to another one of the buildings, and went inside.

There was no other movement in the compound except the guards. Cain settled in for a long wait, watching the sunset on the horizon. Once twilight descended, lights on the outer walls lit up the area right outside the compound, but the inner area remained unlit. When Cain saw the lights of a truck driving toward the compound, he watched as it stopped at the gate. As the gate opened, lights in the yard came on and the truck drove slowly toward the building next to the one where the weres were kept. A large bay door opened and the truck drove inside. Cain could see no other people inside the building before the door closed.

A few moments later, a small door opened and the driver walked out. He headed toward a larger building to the right and disappeared inside. Cain knew the driver would be going over the inventory list with Jimmy. It was more than twenty minutes before they both came out and headed toward the building housing the truck. After they went inside, Cain waited patiently for another fifteen minutes before the large bay doors opened again.

As the truck pulled out, Jimmy walked out as well and waved to the driver before heading to his car. Standing up, Cain brushed the grass off of his clothes and walked back to his own car. He felt satisfied that the plan he'd worked out in his head could be accomplished.

\* \* \* \*

After laying out a small fortune in gold, Cain was able to bribe one of the loaders at the supply barn to let him work on the truck in the middle of the night. It also insured Cain would go unnoticed when he returned to hide in the truck before it went on its round to Holliway's compound. Cain had to still his bursts of impatience as he waited for Friday to arrive.

Once he had Shaun and the truck returned from its delivery, he and Shaun would make their way to his car. After that, it would be a straight shot to Charleston on the coast. A flight had been scheduled to take them to Sevilla in southern Spain. It would be the closest they could get to Ausafca without rousing the suspicions of authorities. From there, black market smugglers would take them south to one of the ports where they would board a ship to Ausafca.

After leaving his car in a small clearing near the road, Cain tracked down a path worn into the grass. Thankfully, he did have the ability to see well in the dark. He was only a few minutes walk from the farm. As he headed toward a row of trees bordering the property, he paused and took a quick look around. Nobody was visible from his vantage point. With the cover of darkness, he ran from the trees to the back of the large warehouse. Flattening himself against the wall, he listened carefully. When he heard no sounds from within, he pulled the tarp covering the doorway slightly to the side and peered inside. He could see the truck, but nobody was nearby.

Slipping inside, he went to the back of the truck and knelt down to crawl underneath it. Once he was positioned, he unfastened the harnessing he'd rigged to the bottom and angled his body back into it. There was plenty of room for him and Shaun in the large contraption that covered a good portion of the bottom of the truck. They would be high enough to be safe from the road, and positioned so that nobody could see them beneath the truck. It wasn't the most comfortable place in the world, but, it would do for the short time it took to get back to the farm.

He knew the truck had already been loaded, and he only needed to wait for the driver. The loader, Chris, had told him they generally loaded the truck, then ate dinner and played a round of cards before the truck pulled out.

No more than ten minutes later, Cain heard a voice as a door opened.

"You better get going and get 'er out of here, Lex. Jimmy is waiting to go home."

A deep voice answered, "I'll be there in a second, Chris. Don't forget—when I get back, you owe me another round. Where in the hell are the keys, dammit?"

"Right here, you idiot." The jingle of keys followed, then Cain heard the approaching footsteps of the driver.

The driver got in, started the truck, and pulled out of the warehouse. As they headed down the dirt driveway toward the road, the number of ruts reminded Cain of how damn uncomfortable his position was. Once the truck pulled out onto the pavement, the ride became considerably smoother.

Mentally, Cain reviewed the equipment he had put together. He'd brought a small tranquilizer gun to use if necessary. He didn't want to take the chance of anybody raising an alarm. If necessary, he had another, milder form of tranquilizer gun to use on mortals. He also carried a vial of poison on him to use if he was caught. It had been a failsafe method that he'd purposely not discussed with Élan.

The truck slowed to a stop, then a moment later the driver accelerated. When the truck stopped again and the driver shut it off, Cain waited until he heard the closing of the bay door and the driver leaving the building. He really didn't have much time to find Shaun and get him out.

Unfastening the harness, he got out of it and quietly crawled to the end of the truck. After a quick look, he moved out from under the truck and stood. He opened the small door a fraction and looked out, waiting for the guard on the upper wall to pass by. Then he waited for another few seconds. He knew he had less than a minute to get to the door of the other building before the next guard came around. Opening the door further, he ran as fast he could to the building he'd seen Shaun come out of days before. When he turned the door handle, he discovered, to his relief, that it wasn't locked.

Entering the building, Cain paused for a few more seconds, listening carefully for any sounds within. Hurrying down the small hall, he passed several empty cells. When he reached the fourth cell, he saw three forms huddled inside. He recognized Shaun instantly. Reaching for the key on the peg near him, Cain held tightly to it to stop it from making any noise. All three weres seemed fast asleep, and Cain wasn't sure how easily they could be woken.

Very slowly, he unlocked the barred door and pulled it open. Shaun was the furthest one from him, and Cain cautiously stepped into the cell and approached the sleeping were. Crouching down, he laid his hand on Shaun's shoulder and gently shook him. The weretiger stirred restlessly, then opened his eyes, yawning widely. Before Shaun could say anything, Cain held his finger to Shaun's lips to keep him quiet. Leaning over, he bent down to whisper in Shaun's ear.

"I'm here to free you."

As he drew back, Cain saw the excited look in Shaun's eyes as the were whispered back, "My master sent you."

Choosing not to answer, Cain stood and motioned for Shaun to follow him. When he got up, Shaun looked over at the other two weres and shook his head.

"I can't leave them. Please."

Hesitating, Cain was about to explain they couldn't. There was plenty of room in the harness for him and Shaun, but he wasn't sure about the other two. Looking into Shaun's eyes, Cain found he had no resistance to the pleading look Shaun gave him. With a swiftly whispered mental pray, Cain nodded and said quietly, "Wake them up."

Not giving Cain a chance to change his mind, Shaun moved to the werelion and shook him as he said, "Don't say anything, Nathan."

The were grumbled as he rolled to his back, and the moment he saw Cain, his eyes widened. After doing the same to Siah, and getting the same reaction from the werepanther, all three of them stood. The other two looked at Shaun, waiting for an explanation.

"He's freeing us," Shaun explained quietly. Clearly stunned, Siah and Nathan just blinked uncomprehendingly at Shaun.

"We have to hurry. We don't have much time." Cain's words galvanized them into action, and they followed him as he led the way back to the outer door. "We're going to the building next to this one. Just follow behind me and don't make any noise."

After they nodded their agreement, Cain opened the door a little and watched for the guard to pass. Nobody made a sound behind him, though they were crowded up against him and each other.

"Time to go," Cain whispered a few seconds after the guard passed. As he ran toward the other building, the other three quickly followed. After getting into the building, Cain led them to the truck and motioned for them to get on the floor. "There's a harness under the truck where we'll hide."

After saying another prayer there would be enough room for them and that the harness would hold, Cain slid to the floor and under the truck. Quickly, he unfastened more of the harness before motioning to Shaun to crawl in.

When the weretiger had wriggled to the very edge of the side strapping, Cain gestured for Siah to get in. Once the werepanther was safely in, there still appeared to be just enough room for Nathan and him.

It took the lion a bit longer to shove his body in beside the panther, then edge as close as he could get to the other side of the strapping. Cain drew a deep breath, then exhaled it before he squirmed and wriggled his way into the remaining space. After a few minutes of pushing, Cain managed to clear the outer frame and reached up over it, refastening the snaps. Unfortunately, he had to keep his arms in that position since there wasn't room for him to bring them down to his sides.

A few moments after they had settled, the outside door opened and Cain heard Lex's voice. "Let's get this done so we can get out of here, Jimmy."

For the next fifteen minutes, all four of them remained completely silent, listening to the other two men joking around as they unloaded the truck.

Finally Jimmy said, "This is the part of the job I hate the most. God, my back hurts now."

"You're getting old, Jimmy," Lex laughed. "At least you get to drink it off at the bar. I've got two more hours before my day is done."

"Shit, all you and Chris do is play cards anyway, Lex. Now get your ass out of here so I can get home."

After Lex got into the truck, the bay doors opened as he started the truck. "See ya Monday, Jimmy."

As the truck pulled out of the building and up to the gate, Cain hoped no one would notice the weres were gone until the next morning. By then, they'd already be on their way to Spain. Glancing over at Shaun, Cain saw the weretiger grinning and he winked at him.

Several moments later, the truck pulled into the farm warehouse and the driver shut it off. As he climbed out, Chris called out, "Get your ass in here, Lex, and get the cards dealt. I wanna get a round in before we load up for the next trip."

"In a minute, in a minute," Lex muttered as he moved toward the front office. "Truck is driving funny. Need to take a look at it."

Cain hid his dismay, and he could feel the tension in the bodies near his.

"You can do that after the next load, if it's still driving funny. Now get your ass in here."

"All right. Chris, give an old man a minute, damn."

When the door closed, Cain quickly undid the snaps. Crawling out of the harness was considerably easier than getting into it had been. In short order, the other three climbed out as well. After Shaun crawled out from under the truck, Cain pointed toward the tarp that covered the back door. Silently, the three weres followed behind Cain as they made their way out of the building and to the path back to the car. Once all of them were safely inside the car, Cain felt free to speak.

"You guys can relax now. I'm taking you out of here and to safety."

"You're taking me to my master," Shaun said happily.

"Shaun, I need to take all three of you to Ausafca." Starting the car, Cain drove across the grass and onto the road.

"Ausafca?" Three voices repeated the name all at once in a questioning manner.

"It's the safest place to take you," Cain answered them calmly.

Instantly, Shaun objected. "No, I have to go to my master. You have to take me to him."

Glancing over at him, Cain frowned. He'd been afraid this might happen. "Are you sure that's where you want to go?" As he opened the small cooler next to him, Cain waited for Shaun's answer. He'd been wise enough for a contingency plan if Shaun proved stubborn.

"Yes. I want to go back home. You have to take me to New Roth."

Cain hated to lie, but he was given no choice. "All right, Shaun, I'll take you back there. What about you two?"

Siah and Nathan looked at each other briefly before both said, "Ausafca."

With a nod, Cain reached into the cooler. "I brought along some food in case you'd be hungry." Picking up one of the sodas, Cain handed it to Shaun. When Shaun took it, he grabbed the soda that had been meant for him and passed it back to Siah.

"There are burgers, fries, and a bunch of snacks as well. Help yourself, guys."

It didn't seem to matter to any of them the fast food was cold. They wolfed it down, then started on the chips and Twinkies Cain had bought. After drinking part of his soda, Shaun rested the cup between his legs. Blinking blurrily at Cain, he half smiled as he rested back against the head rest.

In a quick side glance, Cain noticed when Shaun drifted off. Looking up in the rear view mirror, he spoke quietly, "I'm Cain Wilhelm. I work for the House of Fetters, and the werelord Élan. We're going to Ausafca. Noramerna is not safe for any of you."

Nathan met his gaze and nodded. "I know. I was hoping you could take care of Shaun's resistance to the idea."

Cain relaxed in his seat with the realization that neither the lion nor panther would take exception to him drugging Shaun. "Glad we see eye to eye."

Nathan replied gruffly, "He's a soft-hearted cub."

Chuckling, Cain smiled. "Just like his father was."

\* \* \* \*

"It pays to have friends in low places," Chester said as Ashley sat down. "Shaun's been taken to Ausafca."

"What?"

Chester pulled out a map and pointed to the continent. "Ausafca."

"I know what it is," Ashley grumbled. "What I need to know is why...and how the fuck do I get to him."

"Ash," Chest said as he rolled the map up once more,

"there is no safe route to Aufasca. Chances are, whoever took Shaun got here and back through the underground trader routes."

Ashley just stared at him.

"The black market."

"How do I do it?"

Chester sighed. "You got enough cash, you can find a trader who'll take you anywhere."

"Good." Ashley stood and after a moment, pulled Chester into a tight hug. "Thank you. For everything."

"Thank me when you find him, Ashley."

# Chapter Seven

If anyone came to check on him, Élan never noticed. His paws sank into the rain-soaked ground of his garden as he paced restlessly. The note Hapsus brought him still lay on the stone bench, wrinkled from Élan crumpling it tightly in his fist. Someone had attacked Cain and Shaun on their return home. Élan didn't know who, but they were a day late. Other servers and members of the household avoided him at all costs. It seemed Hapsus was the only one brave enough to stare down a fully shifted, rather pissed off lion.

The bedroom door opened and Hapsus stepped inside, calling out, "My lord?"

Seconds later, Cain nearly pushed him out of the way as he entered the room. "I told you I could tell him myself, Hapsus."

Stalking across the room, Cain halted at the sight of Élan in full form. He'd never seen the werelord in anything other than his mortal form. Awestruck, Cain remained frozen in his spot, staring at the magnificent animal prowling the garden.

Élan stopped abruptly and seemed to smile, baring razor-sharp teeth. A moment later, he padded across the floor and began sniffing and looking Cain over. When he found a wound on Cain's left side, however, a low growl rumbled free. Catching the bandage in his teeth, Élan carefully pulled it away, letting the bloodied cloth drop to the floor. Then he began licking at the cut, cleaning away the small bit of blood and speeding the healing process.

The sensation against the wound made Cain wince, but he made no sound. Dropping to his knees in front of

Élan, Cain could only stare at the beautiful lion. The golden eyes mesmerized him, the sight of them so familiar. His voice was a soft whisper. "My lord."

A deep purr answered Cain and Élan nuzzled up against him, licking at Cain's neck. *I know you can hear me.*

Cain couldn't resist, he wrapped his arms around Élan, shivering with the scratching from the rough tongue. Élan's voice in his head brought a smile to Cain's lips. Burying his face in Élan's thick fur, he answered, "Yes, Élan."

Élan pulled back and a moment later, knelt half-shifted before Cain. "Are you all right?"

Drawing his head back, Cain's smile widened. His lord in all forms was truly an impressive sight. In half-form, Élan retained the lengthened claws, and fur covered the muscular body, tapering to finer fur below his stomach. Golden hair surrounded Élan's face. The sight was fascinating.

Cain ran his fingers over the golden fur at Élan's throat in a gentle caress before he answered. "I'm fine. One of the Euroas underground groups attacked our camp, believing we were slavers. But as soon as they saw Shaun and talked to the smugglers, they realized who we were and helped us."

Élan nodded and let out a long sigh. "I suppose I should thank them before I eat them," he grumbled.

Laughing, Cain shook his head. "You can't eat them. They helped us." Pausing, he eyed Élan silently, his expression softening. "I missed you, Élan. I couldn't think of anything else but getting away from that awful place and returning home to you."

Élan smiled and cupped Cain's neck, letting one claw trace over the delicate skin without breaking it. "Hapsus is annoyed with me, I think. He says I was moody and insufferable waiting for you to come home."

"Is that your way of saying you missed me, too?" Unable to control his own reaction, Cain shivered. The smile became a mischievous grin as he continued running his hand along Élan's fur, its silky texture irresistible.

Rising up on his knees, Élan shifted closer to Cain, staring down at him. "You could say that." Then Élan kissed Cain softly, the touch chaste but lingering.

Cain craved the familiar sense of Élan's presence. Without protest, his lips parted to the werelord in a need he wasn't fully sure he understood. So much had happened in his time away, and he badly needed the contact to restore his own mental balance. Big hands cupped Cain's face and Élan's tongue swept through his mouth, a deep, rumbling purr filling the kiss. A soft moan escaped with Cain's breath before he shifted closer to Élan, the tip of his tongue circling slowly over Élan's. The vibration of sound spilled over Cain's senses, and he gave into his own instincts.

Breaking the kiss slowly, Élan rested his forehead against Cain's and closed his eyes, simply letting them both settle back into something resembling normal. "Are you hungry?" Élan asked after a few moments of silence.

Cain nodded, trying to steel his nerve to explain everything to Élan. "That place, my lord—it was a horror. I never want to go back there." Cain's tone took on a vehement edge, then lowered as he added, "I had to drug Shaun because he wanted to go back to his owner." He hesitated to explain the rest. Drawing a deep breath, Cain finally continued, "Shaun wanted me to help the two weres that were imprisoned with him. I couldn't turn him down. I told Hapsus to put them in one of your upper rooms. Those bastards nearly destroyed Siah and Nathan. Their spirits have been broken." The revulsion Cain felt filled him as he lifted his gaze to Élan's.

Élan pulled Cain to him, holding him close. "I know," he whispered. "I've been there. And you did the right thing in bringing the others. Thank you so much, love."

Relief flooded Cain with Élan's words, and he snaked his arms around the were, seeking the comfort of his lord. "I prayed you'd want to help them, Élan. I don't know if they can be, but I had to bring them here."

"I'll do everything in my power to. That I promise you." Élan hugged him tighter and kissed Cain's hair. "I want you by my side, Cain."

"I wanted to ask if you would let me stay here with you tonight, my lord. I need..." Trailing off, Cain wasn't certain of exactly what he did need, but he knew only Élan could give it to him.

"That is something you need never ask." Élan tilted Cain's head up. "I am here when you need me—anytime."

As Élan stood, he pulled Cain up with him and drew him toward a tabled loaded with food. Standing near Élan, Cain picked out several pieces of fruit and placed them on a plate. Knowing Élan loved grapes, he picked up several handfuls and added them to his dish. Élan moved to the bed and slid back to rest against the headboard. Very quickly, Cain joined him, sitting on the bed beside him.

"I swear, Élan, the whole time I was there, the only thing I could think about was getting home. I hate those people and their ways. It's against everything I believe in—everything I hold dear."

"It is," Élan said with a nod, urging Cain to come closer. "It's a terrifying, filthy place. I've been there more times than I care to remember to rescue others."

"I would return if I had to—if you wanted me to—but it wouldn't be easy." Sighing quietly, Cain took an apple from the plate and offered some of the fruit to Élan as he stretched out beside the were.

"I hope that time never comes." Élan picked up a handful of grapes, popping one into his mouth. "I'm just relieved to have you home."

Taking a bite of the apple, Cain chewed on the sweet flesh. "When Shaun wakes up, you'll have some explaining to do to him, Élan. I didn't want to drug him, but I don't think he would have come willingly with me. He's been too conditioned."

Élan nodded. "I was afraid of that. Aside from all of that, how are you? How's your side?"

"Before I got your message about the trader, I broke

into Winters' house. I thought maybe the man was keeping Shaun locked up or something. I searched his house, but I didn't find any cage or even any chains. Which was odd." After he reached over and set the plate down on the stand, he continued, "My side doesn't hurt anymore." Glancing down at the wound, Cain noticed it had already closed again and no longer bled.

"Odd indeed," Élan mused, chewing on another grape. "And I'm glad your side isn't hurting now. It was a nasty cut. Thankfully, the blade wasn't poisoned. It's not uncommon for the more militant groups to resort to such things. I will speak with Shaun in the morning. As for the other two, Hapsus will look after them. He's one of my best healers, even though he can be downright annoying at times."

After finishing the apple, Cain tossed the core to the plate and licked his fingers. "I was told some of the groups were in dire straits. Some of them are trying to force their way into above ground status, and there are growing pockets of them."

"They are." Élan finished off his grapes and caught Cain's hand. With a sly smile, he began licking Cain's fingers. "Taste good."

Intently watching Élan, Cain chuckled as the werelord licked the stickiness from his fingers. Laying his head against Élan's chest, he rubbed his cheek against the silky fur with a contented sigh. "I dreamed of being home, dreamed of you."

Resting their hands on his chest, Élan shifted until they were both lying down. With his other hand, he pulled the blankets up over them. "Dreamed of me?"

Nestled comfortably against Élan, Cain wiggled deeper into the bed and relaxed. Not looking up at Élan, he nodded slightly. "It kept me sane, my lord."

Élan slipped his hand beneath Cain's chin and tipped Cain's head up to see his face. "When I said I wanted you by my side, I didn't just mean this, Cain."

He'd thought about Élan nearly the whole time he'd

been away. About the position he held with the werelord, and his own hopes. Looking up into Élan's eyes, Cain asked, "Then what did you mean?"

"I want you as my consort, Cain. My Chosen."

A ripple of shock ran through Cain, since that wasn't the answer he'd really expected. "There are others more suitable than I am," he whispered as he closed his eyes and turned his head slightly, taking a deep breath of Élan's scent.

"Not for me."

"I'm beginning to think that, as long as I can remain with you, I don't care in what position I serve. I need to be here." Cain had a lot of time to examine his own thoughts and emotions about Élan. Most he really couldn't understand, but it no longer bothered him. Things were simply as they were for him.

"I'm not about to disagree." Élan kissed him, licking softly at Cain's lips.

In answer, Cain's lips parted in a clear invitation as he wedged himself tightly against Élan's side. One of Élan's hands cupped the back of Cain's head and Élan deepened the kiss, his rough tongue leaving no part of Cain's mouth untasted.

* * * *

It was hard to believe Tyr-Set's son had been found. Élan marveled at how closely Shaun resembled Lord Tyr-Set—his build, his markings, and, judging from what Cain had told him, even Shaun's personality mirrored his father's. Élan smiled but resisted the urge to touch the silky black-and-white hair on Shaun's head. Just like his father, Shaun Tyr-Set was a beautiful creature to behold.

A small twitching jerk of Shaun's hand and the movement beneath his eyelids told Élan that Shaun would wake soon. When Shaun opened his eyes and Élan saw the luminous gold shading, he was struck anew by the familial resemblance.

Blinking rapidly, Shaun tried to focus on him, then a confused expression descended over the young were's features. "Who are you? Where am I?"

"Shh…" Élan smiled, hoping it would ease Shaun's nervousness. "You're safe. You are on the continent of Ausafca. I am Lord Élan, of the House of Fetters."

Instead of calming him, the words only agitated Shaun. The sudden tension of his body became visible even beneath the covers. "Where's my master? Where's Ashley?"

"You no longer have to worry about a master, Shaun. Whatever hold or mark Ashley Winters has on you can and will be broken. You will never have to worry about serving anyone ever again."

That wasn't something Shaun wanted to hear. One hand tore the covers off before Shaun leapt up from the bed. A piteous growl rose in his throat as he looked wildly around the room.

"Shaun." Élan stood and went to Shaun. He cupped Shaun's face, forcing Shaun to look at him. "It's okay. You're safe now. Trust me. Please."

Staring back at him wild-eyed, the weretiger only seemed to grow more agitated and upset. Shaun growled. "I want Ashley! You have no right to keep me away from him."

Sighing, Élan nodded. "I will have a message sent to Ashley. Will that help?"

The words at least calmed Shaun somewhat, though he eyed Élan with a suspicious look. "You promise?"

"I am a man of my word," Élan said. "I promise. But you have to trust me, Shaun."

With Élan's assurance, the mood abruptly melted away from Shaun. Nodding, Shaun smiled. "I did want to come here with him. Nathan told me a little about Ausafca. Ashley will like a place like this."

Élan kept his own opinions of that to himself. "Are you hungry? I can have a bath drawn for you as well, if you'd like."

Nodding to Élan, Shaun said, "I am hungry and could probably use a bath." Pausing, Shaun gave him a curious look before asking, "Do you always rescue weres like you did us?"

"When it is possible, yes. You, however, are special, Shaun. Once you are settled in and comfortable, I'd like to tell you about your family."

"My family?" Puzzled, Shaun followed Élan to a table. When Élan pulled out a chair, Shaun sat and stared at the variety of food laid out on plates in front of him. A grumbling sound in his stomach reminded him of his hunger and he pulled one of the plates, laden with a steak, toward him.

"Yes." Élan sat in a chair on the other side and leaned back, watching him. "Your father was Lord Tyr-Set, one of the great werelords."

Tilting his head, Shaun listened intently to Élan as he cut a few pieces from the steak. For a moment, Shaun remained silent. "I used to wish that Jeremiah Taylor wasn't my father. He wasn't, was he?"

"No, he was not. Your father—Lord Tyr-Set—and your mother—Misha—were betrayed by the House of Mirra during the Wars. The House of Mirra accused your father of betrayal to the other Houses, and to ensure your safety you were taken by a trusted server to live with his sister. When she passed away, you were adopted—as a human—by the Taylor family. Your heritage, your true nature—your identity—have been kept secret all this time."

As he ate, he continued to listen to Élan and reason things out in his own mind. "Élan, I grew up mortal. Always thought I was mortal. It wasn't until right before my eighteenth birthday that I shifted. My parents sold me to the Institute days later." Drawing a deep breath, Shaun tried to gather his thoughts to explain better. After eating a few bites of his steak, he continued, "At first, I couldn't accept being a were. Not until Ashley took me in. He taught me to accept myself just the way I am."

Élan's expression remained neutral. "You should be proud for who and what you are. I have had human lovers, Shaun. However, I have never been, nor will I ever be, a pet. Your days of being such are over. You are free."

"I was never a pet to Ashley. He loves me." Quickly, he finished the steak, then reached for an orange and began to peel it. He did have a sweet tooth for fruit, though he still didn't like vegetables all that much. Looking up at Élan, he smiled. "You knew my real father. What was he like?"

"Lord Tyr-Set was a close friend." Élan's expression turned wistful and he smiled. "He was always helping those without, no matter the circumstances. He never raised his voice or resorted to violence, yet his commands were followed loyally. He had a heart of gold, much like you, and could sweet-talk even the most hardened frown into a smile."

"I can tell you liked him very much. I wish I could have known him. The place I lived had a lot of bad people. Nathan said they weren't like that here." Shaun had no problem in settling into the notion that weres weren't pets, and thus he wasn't either. Ashley had already taught him that.

"I cared greatly for your father, considered him a brother, of sorts." Élan reached for a bunch of grapes and began plucking them off the stems, popping them into his mouth one after another. "Here, we run things, Shaun. We live in equality with humans. I daresay, sixty percent of the businesses — private and public — are run by weres. We make the laws, but we do it fairly — working with both sides of the population."

"It sounds wonderful, Élan." After making short work of his orange, he turned to face Élan. "Ashley and I both dreamed about a place like this. But I never knew it existed. Nobody taught me."

Finishing off his grapes, Élan said, "that is what I intend to change. I want to teach you, Shaun — about your heritage, our history, and what I hope for us to accomplish now that you are here."

Instinct told Shaun that Élan probably didn't believe

him about Ashley. The fact that Élan never directly commented about anything he said about Ashley reinforced the feeling. Watching the werelord unblinkingly, Shaun decided not to say anything more about it. Once Ashley arrived, Shaun knew Élan would change his mind.

Standing up, Shaun stretched, the movement gracefully feline. "I want to learn everything. Especially about my real parents."

"Excellent." Élan stood as well and started for the door. "Come with me. I have something for you."

"I should have asked what you hope to accomplish because I'm here." Grinning at Élan, Shaun followed behind him. "And where are Siah and Nathan? Can I see them soon?"

Élan laughed as he led Shaun down the hall. "Siah and Nathan are quite all right. You may see them anytime you wish. As for what I hope to accomplish..." Élan stopped in front of a door and opened it, gesturing for Shaun to enter. "I hope to restore the House of Tyr-Set back into its former position of power," he said after closing the door behind him.

"With me?" Shaun barely got the words before he saw the two life-sized paintings on the wall. Instantly he recognized himself and stared unblinkingly at the weretiger in the pictures as he slowly approached them. Reaching up, he hesitantly touched one, whispering in an awestruck tone, "That's my father."

The first thing Shaun noticed besides the uncanny resemblance was the proud carriage of his father's body. As his eyes traveled upward, they fastened on his father's face. Staring into those eyes, Shaun could almost feel the emotion in the softened lines of his father's face. The kindness in his eyes was unmistakable.

"It is. That is Lord Tyr-Set. As majestic as he always was." Élan stood beside Shaun. "I want you to take your place as the new Lord Tyr-Set, Shaun. Follow in your father's footsteps. I can help you."

Shaun didn't hear Élan at first. He continued staring at both portraits of his father, enthralled by the likeness to himself. For the first time, he saw someone the same as him. When Élan's words finally sank into Shaun's brain, he turned to look at the werelord in disbelief. "You want me to take my father's place?"

"I do."

As he worked through his thoughts, his brow creased. Glancing back at his father, Shaun wasn't so certain of himself. He had the feeling he'd have one hell of a big pair of shoes to try to fit into. Ashley had always had more faith in Shaun than Shaun had in himself. That thought alone made Shaun realize he might have found something really worth trying for. "I'd like to try."

Élan put his hand on Shaun's left shoulder, giving it a reassuring squeeze. "Then know I will be here to help you, Shaun."

\* \* \* \*

In the end, he'd sold everything. All Ashley had to his name now were a few suitcases and the painting he'd done for Shaun. Now here he was, waiting for the trader's boat to dock at a nondescript Ausafca port. The second the gangplank was down, Ashley hurried down it. His suitcases were unloaded and as they dropped with a heavy *thud* to the wooden dock platform, he winced, thanking all the gods he knew of that he'd not packed anything breakable. He only hoped the painting survived the trip. He had no idea anymore what day it was. Being out at sea had turned the days into a blur, and he hardly remembered anything of the trip. He'd stayed in his cabin for most of the voyage, coming out only to grab a quick bite to eat, ignoring the traders just as they pretty much ignored him.

After collecting his things, he started looking for someone — *anyone* — to take him to wherever Shaun was. He finally found the port authority and went in, manhandling his suitcases up to the counter before dropping them to the concrete floor.

# KITTEN

The attendant glanced up over the rims of his glasses, perched low on his nose, and regarded Ashley with a touch of curiosity mixed with a good bit of visible disdain.

"Can I help you?"

"I have a problem," Ashley said, not quite knowing how to ask what he needed to ask. One gray eyebrow rose, and when the man didn't answer, Ashley continued. "I'm looking for someone. His name is Shaun Taylor. He was taken from Noramerna and brought here, I was told."

"A were then, I assume?"

Ashley nodded. "Yes. Black and white striped tiger."

Dark brown eyes went impossibly wide. "Just a minute."

Before Ashley could say a word, the man disappeared. A moment later, he returned, followed by a woman. The man whispered something to the woman, and the woman glanced over at Ashley, giving him an obvious once-over. Then she shocked the hell out of him.

"Ashley Winters?"

Ashley's mouth dropped open. "Y-yes..."

"Come with me, please."

A buzz sounded and the door to Ashley's left clicked open. The woman waited while he gathered his suitcases, then she led him down a long hallway.

"Shaun was brought through here," she said. "Lord Élan has him." She stopped at a door and pointed into the room where several workers busied themselves by going through bags and packages of all sorts.

"Leave your things here."

Ashley dragged his suitcases into the room and a worker took them. "When will I get them back?"

"Whenever Lord Élan is satisfied that they are intact," the woman answered. "Now come with me. You must have a physical before you can enter into the city."

Ashley groaned, even though he understood the reasoning. He followed the woman into another room with a paper-covered table. She gestured him inside, then closed the door without another word. Before he had a chance to become uncomfortable, another door—one he hadn't noticed—opened and a man in a white coat walked in.

"Good afternoon, Mr. Winters," the man said. He offered Ashley a hand and, surprisingly, a smile. "I'm Dr. Richmonds. I see you're on your way to Lord Élan. Very well, let's have a look at you. Take off your clothes, please."

As the doctor turned to the cabinet and snapped on a pair of exam gloves, Ashley stripped down to his underwear. Having been through physicals with regular doctors, he steeled himself for whatever this one had planned. When the doctor turned around, he scrutinized Ashley.

"Everything, please."

*Oh, gods...* Ashley stood and shoved his underwear to the floor, tossing them onto his clothes. Okay, so maybe that flush was a bit more than irritation at being delayed. The doctor stepped up and started poking and prodding Ashley's neck, checking his lymph nodes. Then he opened Ashley's mouth and took out a tongue depressor. Forcing Ashley's tongue down, Dr. Richmonds examined Ashley's mouth and throat, then patted the table.

"Lie down for on your back, please."

Ashley got on the table and stretched out, eyes closing as he rested his arms at his sides. The cold circle of a stethescope pressed over several points on his chest and stomach. Then came the usual poking and pushing against his sides and belly. He bit his tongue when his cock and balls were handled, balls rolled and pressed, cockhead squeezed and examined closely. He let out a breath when that was over.

"Turn over, please."

Shit.

Rolling over, Ashley buried his face against the table as those hands started pressing along his back and sides. Then his ass cheeks were spread apart and he was shocked when a slick finger pushed inside him. Instincts were strong, but he kept his hips flat on the table. Then the finger was gone and a slender tube was inserted. After three impossibly long minutes, it was removed.

"Everything is normal," Dr. Richmonds announced finally, snapping off his gloves. "You may dress. Your luggage will be inspected and taken to Lord Élan's palace. Welcome to Ausafca, Mr. Winters."

"Thank you," Ashley grumbled.

He waited until the doctor was out before sitting up. Gods, he felt like hell. He dressed as quickly as possible, then opened the door he'd come in through. The woman from before was waiting for him. He followed her further down the hall and she stopped, opened a door, and smiled for the first time.

"Welcome, and enjoy your stay."

Ashley just nodded and stepped out into the afternoon hustle and bustle of the city. The palace loomed over it all — tall and majestic. Ashley didn't really see it, though. Shaun was in there...somewhere. Jaw set firmly, Ashley strode straight for the building, determination holding a firm grip on him.

# Chapter Eight

When he reached the palace gates, two guards stepped in his way.

"I'm Ashley Winters."

That seemed to be enough, and one of the men turned and led Ashley up the steps and into the main entry hall. "Lord Élan is holding court this afternoon. Go." The guard pointed to a set of huge double doors.

Taking a deep breath, Ashley pushed the doors open. Lord Élan was seated on a large throne, and even from the distance between the dais and the doors, Ashley could feel the werelord's stern gaze fall directly on him. He walked in, the doors closing behind him.

"Lord Élan," he said as he walked forward. Stopping just at the dais, he gave a slight, reluctant bow. "I've come for Shaun Taylor."

"I'm sorry, Mr. Winters," the werelord said calmly, fingers steepled in front of him, "but Shaun is here to stay."

"What?" Ashley laughed and shook his head. "I didn't come this damn far to be told—"

"Mr. Winters. Shaun no longer belongs to you."

Ashley's mouth hung open. "Excuse me? Belong? He never belonged to me! Where is he?"

"Mr. Winters, I do not think you understand."

"Then explain it to me so I can," Ashley said through his teeth. "How else am I supposed to react when my lover is taken from me?" Flashes of memories raced through his mind suddenly—images of Shaun's torture at the Institute. Without thought, he advanced on Élan. "I swear to the fucking gods, if you harm a single hair on him—"

The werelord lifted his hand regally. "He is perfectly

safe, I assure you. However, he is no longer bound by the rules and trappings of your society."

"He was never my servant," Ashley said dryly.

"Nonetheless, whatever…*ownership*…you possessed over him is now gone."

The Lord's pronouncement hit Ashley like a ton of bricks.

"Kitten…" He stared up into Élan's golden eyes, praying the werelord would understand. "Shaun does not fare well in captivity."

"He is not a captive here." Élan clapped his hands once and the doors at the far end of the throne room opened.

Ashley turned and relief and heartache flooded through him in equal measure. "Shaun…"

"Ashley?" The werecat froze in the doorway, shock registering on his features. A split second later, he raced across the marble floor to tackle Ashley. The force of the collision sent Ashley sprawling on his back, and Shaun quickly scrambled over him, lavishing licks on every spare space of skin he could find.

Ashley gripped Shaun's head and kissed him hard, the desperation overwhelming. When he broke the kiss, the questions started pouring out of Ashley nonstop. "Are you okay? Have they hurt you? What happened, Shaun? Who did this?"

"I'm fine, Ashley. Nobody hurt me. Lord Élan brought me here so I would be safe." With the mention of the werelord, Shaun quickly looked up over at Élan and gave him a sheepish smile. Sliding off, Shaun helped Ashley stand and pulled him closer to Élan.

Ashley refused to let go, keeping one arm protectively around Shaun's waist. "We've met."

Eyeing Ashley questioningly, Shaun lowered his voice, "Is something wrong, Ashley?"

Ashley tore his gaze away from Élan and looked at Shaun. "The sooner I know what the hell is going on, the better." His expression softened and he turned them until they were facing each other, arm still around Shaun's waist. Ashley cupped Shaun's cheek and sighed. "I brought your painting. I couldn't bear to leave it behind when I left home. It was all I had…"

"Shaun," Élan intervened quietly, "why don't you take Ashley to your room where you can talk in private. You have a lot to explain to him."

Shaun pressed a soft kiss to Ashley's lips, then turned to nod to the werelord. "I'll talk to you later, Élan."

Taking Ashley's hand, Shaun led him out of the main room and back into the central hall. His fingers tightened around Ashley's as they walked up one of the staircases, then down another hall to his room. Once they were inside, Shaun quickly shut the door and pulled Ashley toward the two portraits on his wall. "That's Aldar, my father, Ashley. My real father."

Ashley stared at the male were. Although the portraits were of the same man, one was human, while the other was in were form. In both forms, the resemblance to Shaun was striking, undeniable. "You look like him," Ashley said quietly.

"I had thought the man that sent me to the Institute was my father. But they adopted me, Ashley. And this is my mother, she's so beautiful. Her name was Misha." Shaun drew him closer to the small miniature of a young woman. Her expression of peaceful serenity seemed to visibly soothe something inside of Shaun.

"She is." Ashley looked around the lavishly decorated room. "You seem…happy here."

"They don't want to hurt me here, Ashley. My father was a Lord of Ausafca, and Élan told me another lord betrayed and murdered both of my parents. He wants me to remain here and take my rightful place." Turning to face Ashley, Shaun's eyes begged him to understand.

Ashley's shoulders sagged and he dropped down onto the chair behind him. He stared at the floor for several seconds, then closed his eyes. "I…" He swallowed hard and squeezed his eyes shut tighter. "Shaun…"

Shaun dropped to his knees in front of him and nudged in between Ashley's legs. "What, master? What's wrong? Aren't you happy for me?"

"Kitten." Ashley opened his eyes. "I am happy for you. It's all I've ever wanted for you—to be happy." He reached out and cupped Shaun's face. "But I don't want to lose you, Shaun."

"Lose me?" Shaun stared blankly at Ashley until he realized Ashley might not want to stay with him. The whole time he'd believed his master would want to stay with him. Tears began forming in his eyes and slipped down his cheeks, wetting his skin. "I don't want you to leave me."

"Shaun. No." Ashley slid off the chair and caught Shaun's face in both hands. "I can't live without you. I'd never leave you. I promise." Without giving Shaun a chance to respond, Ashley kissed him.

The trembling of Shaun's body stilled as he lost himself in Ashley. A soft, pulsing purr began to rise in his throat as his arms tightly encircled his master. His own desperate need answered Ashley's eagerly, and it was a long moment later before Shaun could pull back. "Ashley, Élan told me you could remain with me as long as you understood that I'm not a pet. I tried to tell him that that wasn't how you saw me, but I'm not sure he believed me."

Ashley's sigh was ragged as he rested his forehead to Shaun's. "Thank the gods," he whispered. "Though I'd defy the gods themselves to stay with you. I need you, Shaun. I need you too much to ever let you go."

"Are you really sure you want to stay here? We can't leave Ausafca. You know how they would treat me if we did. There was a trader who kidnapped me. He wanted to use me for breeding. Then Cain got me out of there and brought me here."

"I know," Ashley sighed. "Élan explained what happened." He sat back against the chair, pulling Shaun close. "You are my life, Shaun. I have no one else to miss me. If you wish to remain here, then here is where we will stay." He reached up and stroked the mark on Shaun's neck. "How did he do it?"

"He told me the mark wasn't a part of our nature, and that kind of bond was meant to happen naturally. I didn't want him to do it, but Élan told me if the relationship with you lasted, we would have our own bond, not one manufactured by others." He arched his neck into Ashley's touch and whispered, "I so much want everything to be as it should be between us."

Ashley smiled. Leaning in, he moved Shaun's hair and brushed his lips over the tattoo, breath warm against the skin. "Then it will be."

A soft purr rolled from Shaun with the press of Ashley's lips. "He explained to me that he's had relationships with mortals. There is nothing wrong with it here. But the relationship must be between two equals." Raising his face to look at Ashley, he smiled as he added, "I thought that's what you always wanted between us."

"Yes." Ashley shifted and pulled Shaun to straddle his lap. "Gods, yes. No more pet, no more bullshit, Shaun. You are my lover, my partner."

Draping his arms over Ashley's shoulders, Shaun nestled as close as he could. "You are still the master of my body and heart, Ashley. Nothing will ever change that. But I am not a pet anymore. I am a man and a were, and proud to be both."

Ashley smiled. "You have every right to be, Shaun. And you don't know how happy I am to hear you say that."

"Élan taught me a lot. About myself and my family. We weren't meant to be slaves to men. We are the closest to the gods and meant to share our lives as equals with humans. I never knew any of it. But now I want to share everything with you." Resting his head on Ashley's shoulder, Shaun sighed quietly. "I don't think I could ever go back to living in a place where I am nothing but a pet. I want us both to stay here."

Ashley nodded, hands moving up and down Shaun's

back in an errant caress. "Everything I have is here. Everything I want. It is what I fought for so long with Illian, and what I will die fighting for with you, Shaun."

"I knew you would come. Élan didn't believe you would, but I did. He'll accept you because I do, and I think, given a bit of time, he'll believe in you like I do. This time, both of us will fight for it, not just you alone."

"He infuriates me," Ashley admitted ruefully, "but I respect him."

"Right now, he's one of the few who can help me. He wants to restore my family's house and he wants me to take my father's place. He really did think that if you showed up, you were going to demand I be returned to you as your pet—that you'd try to make me go back."

Ashley buried his face in Shaun's hair. "I sold everything to find you. I had no intention of going back, regardless."

"You did what?" Pulling his head back, Shaun stared at Ashley, then he smiled. "I can't believe you did that."

Shrugging, Ashley grinned slightly. "All I have now are three suitcases full of clothes and your painting. Hell, as much as I hated to, I sold your collar. I needed the extra money to make the trip to find you. We can always get a new collar, though it sure as hell won't be for a pet."

"That must be why I adore you. You'd do anything for me." Lowering his head, Shaun nuzzled Ashley's throat. The rising sound of his purr wove between them as he nipped gently at Ashley's skin. "We will get a new collar for me, but one of our own design."

Ashley shivered and groaned softly. "Anything in this world. Gods, Shaun…"

A sharper bite followed the first one, then Shaun slowly turned his head, his lips catching Ashley's, the push of his tongue demanding entry. Every other thought scattered to the pure taste and feel of Ashley.

Ashley opened to him immediately, moaning as he sucked on Shaun's tongue. He barely got out the words "need you" before he dove back into the kiss. The low purr became a deeper growl of sound as Shaun's fingers kneaded against the front of Ashley's shirt, then abruptly popped all the buttons with one sharp tug of his hand. After sliding off the shirt, Shaun's nails raked downward over Ashley's back. In one motion, Shaun moved from Ashley's lap and pushed Ashley down to the floor. A heated flare lit the golden eyes as Shaun stared down at him. A determined yank unfastened Ashley's pants, and Shaun swiftly got rid of them then began on his own clothes. Once they were both bare, Shaun quickly straddled Ashley and slid upward until the head of his cock pushed against Ashley's lips.

Hunger and surprise colored Ashley's features and he gripped the base of Shaun's cock, flicking the tip with his tongue as he kept his gaze locked onto Shaun's. "Come on, Kitten," he whispered, painting his lips with the slick drops leaking from the slit. "Take it."

A shudder rolled through Shaun as he insistently pushed his cock into Ashley's mouth. His tone and attitude took on an aggressive demeanor as he growled, "Make me ready so I can fuck you."

"Fuck yes." Ashley's lips sealed around the head and he sucked Shaun down, humming softly as he gripped Shaun's hip, encouraging movement.

Shaun grabbed Ashley's hair, pulling his lover into the thrust of his hips. Thanks to the wet, heat surrounding his cock, it didn't take long for Shaun to near the edge. He pulled back, and with a motion of his hand, gestured for Ashley to get on his hands and knees. One eyebrow rose and Ashley smiled slowly. Without a word, he turned over. Bracing himself on one hand, Ashley sucked a finger into his mouth. Then he reached under himself, pushing the finger deep inside as he shot Shaun a come-hither stare over his shoulder.

"Fuck me."

As Shaun knelt behind Ashley, he drew the tips of his nails slowly over the curve of Ashley's ass, the scratches leaving tiny, red marks. His thumbs kneaded at the crease of Ashley's ass, nudging slowly towards the hole as he watched Ashley fuck himself. He'd dreamed of this too many times while they'd been separated. Leaning down, Shaun's tongue joined the finger, slicking the tight passage and savoring the musky taste he adored. Without giving Ashley time to move the finger, Shaun straightened and in one thrust, nailed Ashley, pushing in along side his lover's finger.

"Shaun!" Ashley's back bowed, but he didn't pull his hand away. He rocked back hard against Shaun, pushing another finger in alongside Shaun's cock. "Oh, fuck," he panted. "Shaun."

The push of Shaun's hips became relentless, and he buried himself in the enticing heat of Ashley's body. A feral growl erupted as Shaun became lost in the consuming need surging through him. The rhythm of the hard slaps of their bodies came faster, and the near painful grip of Shaun's hands forced Ashley back against every forward snap of his hips. One hand slid up over Ashley's back and yanked him up by the shoulder. Lowering his head, Shaun bit down, driving his slightly-elongated canines into Ashley's shoulder, drawing blood, pinning Ashley in place. Even in a human body, the animalistic need rose beyond control, and Shaun gave into it completely.

Ashley jerked in his arms, Shaun's name forced out on a scream. Pulling his fingers out, Ashley reached up and twisted his fingers in Shaun's hair, encouraging more. "Keep going. Gods, can't stop, Shaun."

Fully controlling Ashley's movement, Shaun had become nearly savage. His teeth held firmly to Ashley, tasting the sweetness of his lover's blood. One of the hands at Ashley's hip glided across to Ashley's cock, beginning a demanding rhythm with the tight curl of Shaun's fingers to the hard, heated flesh. Fully laying his own claim, Shaun wasn't about to allow Ashley to get away from him. A hard shudder rushed through Ashley and he cried out Shaun's name as he shot. Shaun followed quickly behind him, keeping Ashley in place as he spilled deep inside Ashley's ass. After letting go of Ashley's shoulder, Shaun's sharp cry echoed in the room.

Ashley slumped back against Shaun, his breathing ragged. He eased his grip on Shaun's hair, but didn't let go completely. "Bed, Kitten," he said in-between breaths. "I'm getting too old for this floor stuff."

Chuckling, Shaun playfully slapped Ashley on the ass before he reluctantly let go. Slowly he drew back, then stood and helped Ashley up. "I didn't hurt you, did I?"

Ashley laughed as he stood on shaky legs. "Hell, no." He tugged Shaun over to the bed, collapsing down onto it and pulling Shaun with him. "No idea what got into you, but fuck…" He smiled at Shaun. "Whatever it was, don't stop."

* * * *

Ashley was far from happy as he followed the man — the were? — named Hapsus down the hall. All he'd been told when Hapsus had woken him up was that Lord Élan wanted to see him. Ashley didn't like the werelord. Shaun might think Élan helpful and nice and only the gods knew what else; but Ashley had his own choice words to describe the arrogant, proud asshole. And that was him being nice about it.

Hapsus stopped in front of a wooden door and knocked. Without any audible answer, he opened the door and stepped to the side, ushering Ashley into the room with a clipped gesture. Ashley bit his tongue and walked in, the door closing behind him. Élan was seated behind an ornate desk made of dark-stained wood. Thousands of lions crawled up the sides and front, and on the top was painted a majestic representation of the king of the jungle. At least Élan knew art when he saw it.

"Thank you. I'm quite fond of my desk."

Ashley's gaze snapped up at the werelord. "Stay out of my head."

Élan didn't seem phased and simply motioned for Ashley to sit in a nearby chair. "Please, Mr. Winters, have a seat."

Still glaring at Élan, Ashley sat down, though he was far from relaxed. "Why, might I ask, was I awakened from much-needed sleep?"

The werelord sat back in his overstuffed chair and steepled his fingers in front of him. Pompous prick. "Your belongings have been brought up."

Something about that statement didn't settle well. "And…?"

"They were searched, of course," Élan said, nodding as if it was perfectly reasonable.

Ashley blinked, but before he could speak, a slight lift of Élan's hand stopped him.

"It is procedure, Mr. Winters. Nothing against you personally. You came from Noramerna, therefore it had to be done."

"I trust my things are intact," Ashley snapped.

Élan inclined his head in a nod. "They are. However, there is one item I found most intriguing." The werelord stood and walked over to an easel sitting beside the desk. With a casual flick of his wrist, the cloth was whisked away, revealing the painting Ashley had done for Shaun. "I find this very…interesting."

Ashley clenched his teeth together hard enough to cause pain. "It was a gift, from me to Shaun."

"Ahh." Élan nodded slowly. "And you painted this?"

"I did."

"While living in Noramerna," Élan added, not sounding exactly believing.

"It was a gift," Ashley repeated—almost growled, really. He was growing tired of this game quicker by the second.

"I see." Élan covered the painting once more, then returned to his seat. "You will tell me of your relationship with Lord Tyr-Set's son."

"Excuse me? What exactly do you want? You know I came here for him. Isn't that enough?"

Élan's answer was short and no-nonsense: "No." He

settled back into the chair, apparently expecting a long, detailed story. "How soon after you found him did you put your mark on him?"

Swallowing the growl, Ashley forced his tongue to do something other than lash out. "One day."

"And how long thereafter did you wait before taking him?"

"Before taking him?"

"Sex, Mr. Winters. How long did you wait before mounting him like an animal?"

Ashley shot up out of his chair, glaring at the werelord with nothing short of rage. "That is none of your business!"

"On the contrary, Mr. Winters," Élan said with infuriating calm, "it is."

"Several months. Happy?"

"And did you force him in this?"

It took every ounce of willpower Ashley had to keep from crawling over that damned desk. "I did not."

"Very good. Do you consider yourself his Master?"

That one caught Ashley off-guard, if only because of their playing. "Define 'Master.'"

One of Élan's eyebrows rose slightly. "Do you consider him a pet, Mr. Winters? Your sexual trysts, so long as they do not bring harm to him, are none of my concern."

"No, I do not. He calls me Master when we play. Outside of that, he calls me Ashley, as I've always wanted him to."

"You are dismissed," Élan said without anything further.

"My painting?" Ashley asked, gesturing to the covered easel.

"I will return it to you in time."

Resisting the urge to hurl the nearest blunt object at Élan, Ashley spun on his heel and stormed out of the room, slamming the door behind him.

# Chapter Nine

When Cain awoke, he was alone. The space near him still held the warmth of Élan's body. Sighing, he burrowed his face in Élan's pillow, taking a deep breath. Gods, he loved the unique scent of his werelord. Rubbing his cheek in the softness, Cain reveled in the scents surrounding him. At first, he'd been hesitant about his interactions with Élan. When he'd moved into the House of Fetters, Cain had absolutely no clue how much he'd come to feel for the werelion.

Hidden beneath Élan's gruff exterior lay a heart of gold. In the past, Cain had heard about Élan's ruthlessness in forcing the Houses to remain intact. Many still feared him. Élan was quick to anger, but he also cared deeply about the people of Ausafca. Cain had seen Élan's anger a few times when the werelord dealt with too many of the petty concerns between the Houses. Yet behind closed doors, all Cain ever saw was the gentleness and affection Élan shared with him. He'd never witnessed Élan taking out any of his anger on those in service to him, though quite a few refused to approach the werelord when he was enraged.

Rolling over to his back, Cain stretched lazily. He knew he needed to get out of bed, but it required several more moments of trying to rouse himself to achieve it. After washing up, Cain dressed in a dark pair of pants and a vest. He picked up the brush, running it through the tangled mess of his hair, then efficiently braided it. In no hurry, he left the room and wandered downstairs to Élan's council room. The moment he entered, he saw Élan was already in a bad mood. It didn't bode well for the men standing in front of the throne.

Stifling his sigh, Cain silently made his way to Élan and settled on the cushioned stool beside the werelord. Élan reached over and rested his hand against Cain's cheek. With a slight turn of his head, Cain pressed a kiss to his lord's palm. A calmer smile from Élan was Cain's reward before they both looked at the other three men.

"Now tell me, do I have the support of your Houses?"

"Élan, you have proven the traitorous behavior of the House of Mirra. Yet, while the House has declined in power, some of us still fear them," Jareth answered.

"Do any of you believe it will still stand when I am through?" A deceptive calm in Élan's golden eyes regarded each of them in turn. Uneasily, the three men shifted from foot to foot, none of them able to hold that gaze. "Hapsus, bring Shaun in."

Bowing to Élan, Hapsus turned and headed to one of the inner doors. Not once did Élan look away from them as Hapsus opened the door and motioned for Shaun to come in. The moment the young white tiger cub entered, the others froze in total shock. With his distinctive white-and-black hair, markings, and features, none could mistake Shaun's family linage. Ashley followed behind Shaun, then moved to his side as they approached Élan.

Smiling confidently, Élan announced, "Lords of Ausfaca, may I present Lord Shaun Tyr-Set, House of Light." Turning his head the slightest bit, he winked at Shaun before his voice took on a silky softness when he addressed the other three. "Now, Lords, do I have your support?"

Bolder than the others, the youngest were walked to Shaun. "Simon, House of Trial, will back the House of Light."

A moment later, the other two stepped forward as well.

"Jareth, House of Earth, will back the House of Light." With a bow to Shaun, he took one step to the side.

"Talon, House of Nine, will back the House of Light."

# KITTEN

Shaun stood to the side of Élan, studying the other weres with a great deal of interest. "Thank you. I know you all knew my father."

"You look much like him, Shaun." Smiling, Talon took Shaun's hand and squeezed it gently.

Grateful for the words, Shaun smiled back at him. "Thank you, Talon."

"You have our full support, Élan," Simon said to Élan, smiling. "If you had told us before of your plans to restore the House of Light, we would have backed you earlier."

Élan smiled and shrugged. "I have my reasons. Shaun's presence is still a secret, and I expect it to remain as such until further notice."

"You can be assured none of us will speak of it," Jareth spoke for them all. With a smile at Shaun, he turned to leave, and the other two followed.

"Shall we?" Élan asked, giving a sweeping gesture toward the breakfast room off to the right of the main throne room doors.

As Élan stood, Cain rose with him and they led the way into the breakfast room. Shaun took hold of Ashley's hand, tugging him along. At the table, Cain sat next to Élan, and Shaun and Ashley settled on the other side of the table. Their servers silently began offering each of them food on silver trays. Looking over the selection, Shaun helped himself to several pieces of bacon and sausage, then took some of the scrambled eggs.

"I trust Shaun has filled you in." Élan leaned back in his seat. He nibbled on a piece of bacon, waiting for Ashley's response.

"He has." Ashley looked up at him before starting on his own breakfast.

"Shaun, have you any questions? It's been a while since we've been able to sit down and talk in relative peace," Élan said.

"I'm just curious about what you are going to do next, Élan. Will everybody support us?" Shaun had no problem asking the forthright questions.

"We will meet with the other Houses. The Lords you met earlier obviously support us, and they will convince others to do the same." Bacon gone, Élan started on a bowl of grapes that had been set beside his plate. "After that, I plan—"

"What exactly is in it for you?" Ashley interrupted him.

As Cain stared at Ashley in shock, Shaun had to lift his hand to hide his grin. He knew his master all too well. Not daring to look at Ashley or he'd start laughing, Shaun fixed his gaze on his plate, fastidiously eating his food.

Élan just chewed a few grapes as if considering Ashley's question. "Peace of mind, Mr. Winters."

"Have you gone insane?" Ashley leaned forward, pointing his fork in Élan's direction. "You are calling for the equivalent of a revolution, and all you can say is 'peace of mind'?"

Even Shaun realized that not all of the Houses would agree and there was a chance of serious division arising. He'd spent some time in the library, reading about the previous wars, and his father's "supposed" activities. "I've been concerned myself about the chances of a strong opposition, Élan."

Discreetly, Cain lowered his hand beneath the table and rested it on Élan's thighs. He didn't interfere in the conversation, but he kept directing side glances at the werelion.

Élan smiled and covered Cain's hand with his own. "Our biggest opposition is House of Mirra. While their power has declined considerably in recent years, they are still a force to be reckoned with."

"And you plan on dealing with them how?" Ashley glared at Élan, his food forgotten. "Do you think they'll just let you waltz right in or whatever, declaring the restoration of Tyr-Set?"

"No, Mr. Winters," Élan answered calmly. "Shaun will do it."

"What?" Ashley's fork clattered to his plate. "You

really have lost your mind."

This time it was Shaun's hand reaching for Ashley's shoulder, and a quiet voice calling for calm. "What do you mean by that, Élan?"

Ashley fell silent, looking toward Élan expectantly. Cain watched each of the others pensively, and his hand turned within Élan's, fingers clasping around his lord's.

One dark gold eyebrow rose in curiosity before Élan answered. "The only way to establish you as Lord of Tyr-Set is for you to do just that: make it clear to everyone that you are the new lord and things are changing. The House of Mirra will be dealt with, I assure you."

"For the sake of a new world order, you put the man I love at risk," Ashley grumbled.

Élan was silent for a moment, then nodded. "He is quite capable." Élan looked to Shaun and smiled. "And I will be there with him every step of the way."

"Get in line," Ashley muttered under his breath.

A questioning cast settled on Shaun's features, but he didn't say anything. Nodding to Élan in understanding, Shaun then turned back to Ashley. "You've always had more faith in me than I have in myself, Ashley. I think Élan might be right."

Ashley sighed and nodded. "I trust your judgment, Kitten. Above all else."

With a smile, Shaun leaned over to press a kiss to Ashley's lips. "I know."

Élan watched them quietly. "Your things have been taken to your room, Mr. Winters. Everything is there."

Ashley glanced over at Élan and gave him a curt nod, muttering a "Thank you." Turning to Shaun, he asked, "You done eating?"

"Yeah, I need to head to the library, though. Cain promised to find some of the books I wanted to read."

"Whenever you're ready, Shaun," Cain said as he stood.

Standing as well, Shaun leaned over for another quick kiss. "I'll see you in an hour or so."

Élan remained silent when Ashley got up and walked out after them without another word. Élan finished his breakfast, waving away the server who offered him more water. He had to admit, albeit grudgingly, that Ashley Winters was not quite what he'd expected. When Shaun had essentially quieted Ashley, Élan had expected…something. What he had not expected, however, was Ashley falling relatively silent. A master would have disciplined a pet right then and there, but Ashley Winters did nothing of the sort.

"Maybe there's more to him after all," Élan mused quietly.

The throne room was blessedly empty for once and when he was done, Élan headed down the hall toward his chambers. There was much to be done, much to be discussed, but with Cain and Shaun busy in the library, Élan decided to make the best of the temporary peace. Ashley Winters' arrival had thrown everyone into a perpetual state of watchfulness. No one trusted Shaun's human, though Élan figured the man deserved the benefit of a doubt.

Just as he rounded the corner, Élan caught sight of movement. The door to Shaun's room was open and Élan stopped, his curiosity taking precedence as he watched Ashley pull off his shirt. Dark scars crisscrossed the man's back and shoulders.

"Those are trader scars."

Ashley stiffened immediately. "Yes," he said, not looking at Élan.

"What happened?"

"I was defending someone." Ashley leaned forward and braced himself on the dresser, finally meeting Élan's gaze in the mirror. Haunted eyes told Élan a good deal more than Ashley's words did.

"You were defending a were."

Ashley sighed and looked away abruptly. "I was. Illian was my lover."

"And not your pet," Élan finished for him. Ashley

nodded. "They found out, didn't they?"

"They did. He was taken from me." When Ashley's eyes met his, Élan could see the heartache still there, though buried deep. "I couldn't stop them."

"Do you love Shaun?"

"More than you could possibly know."

Élan nodded. "Come with me. I want to take you somewhere. Shaun can't go until his presence here has come out publicly, but you can. And, I think, this is something you need to do on your own."

Ashley put his shirt back on and met Élan in the doorway. "Why?"

Turning to lead the way down the hall, in the opposite direction of his room, Élan waited until they stepped out into the inner courtyard of the palace before answering. "The House of Illumina is where the spirits of weres go when they've left this world."

"So it's a house of ghosts?"

Élan shook his head. "No, no. Consider it…a pit stop on the way to another incarnation, if you will. It's a sacred place, and when grieving, it is necessary, if only for the solace it provides."

Ashley stopped and turned a dubious stare on Élan. "Why are you taking me there? I am not a were."

Élan turned to face Ashley, keeping his expression neutral. "No, but you are lover to one. Shaun cannot leave Ausafca, so if you intend on staying with him, then you should be aware of our practices."

"All right," Ashley said with a sweeping gesture of his hand. "Lead on."

They continued on in silence for the better part of twenty minutes. Élan kept them on his private path, though there was a public entrance. When the white marble building came into view around a corner, Élan smiled. Aside from his garden, the House of Illumina was a favorite place for him to relax, to remember the former Lord Tyr-Set and himself when they were both cubs.

"There is a public entrance, but this is my private

room for prayer." Élan unlocked a nondescript door and stepped aside. "You may use this room for as long as you wish."

Ashley looked tentative, then finally nodded. "Thank you," he said after a moment. Then he surprised Élan with a smile before disappearing into the dark room, the door closing behind him.

* * * *

It took a few minutes for his eyes to adjust, but once they did, Ashley found that he was in a chapel of sorts. There was a small marble altar with two white candles, a bowl, and an urn full of water. He went to the small kneeling pad before the altar and got down on his knees. Eyes closed, he simply let the images come back to him, images he'd pushed to the back of his mind so long ago.

*"Illian!" Ashley struggled against his binds, terror turning the world a dark shade of red. "Stop!"*

*"You were warned, Winters," one of the guards sneered. A bloodied whip hung from the guard's right hand. Then the guard turned his head and shouted, "Do it already, will ya!"*

*Snarling and snapping at the men who held him, Illian was hauled out before Ashley. Terrified eyes bore through Ashley's soul, tearing him apart. Tears wet Illian's fur and then he howled pitifully. The next few seconds seemed like forever and Ashley watched helplessly as his beloved wolf's throat was slit right in front of his eyes.*

"Illian!"

Ashley snapped back into the present, his own scream startling him. Tears streaked his face, though he couldn't remember crying. He crumpled forward, face pressed to the cold marble altar, and let himself finally grieve. He lost track of time, caught somewhere between the present and Illian's death. Something brushed his shoulder and blinking away the tears, Ashley looked behind him.

"I'm so sorry," he whispered.

The spirit smiled, those eyes so familiar and loved. "It

177

wasn't your fault, Ashley."

"I tried. Oh, God, Illian, I tried."

"Shh…" A transparent hand reached out and Ashley felt a breeze blow gently across his cheek. "You're safe now. You both are. I love you."

The words stuck in Ashley's throat and he watched Illian's spirit fade away. Despite the tears, it felt as if a weight had finally been lifted from his soul.

* * * *

"Your Ashley impresses me, Shaun." Cain grinned as he set three books on the reading table.

Shaun grinned back at him before he reached for one of the books higher on the shelf. "He grows on you. When he first took me to his home, I didn't trust him at all. But…" Shaun paused, trying to think of the words to describe his master. Then he laughed. "He's Ashley."

"Though Élan won't admit it, I think Ashley impresses him, too." Cain sat down at the table as Shaun joined him.

Laying the book down on top of the others, Shaun sat down. "I know neither of you believed me about Ashley when I first came here, but he has always treated me as human. Though we couldn't behave like that outside of our home. Still, he is the one who helped me accept myself as a were, and he helped me to realize I wasn't just a pet to him."

Resting his elbows on the table, Cain relaxed in his seat. "For a Noramernian, Ashley is very unusual."

Meeting Cain's gaze, Shaun shrugged. "I'm not so sure about that. There are a lot of them who are interested in helping weres. Not all of them agree with the bad way weres are treated. I used to work with my next door neighbor quite a lot before I was taken to the Institute. Chester was a member of the CPG. They tried to protect weres, and Chester didn't like Ashley at first, either. He thought Ashley was going to treat me like a pet."

"When I was there, I saw the worst side, Shaun. Something I never want to see again if I can help it. But I'll take your word that there are some who aren't like that."

"The ones like me and Ashley probably hide in their homes like we did." Deciding to change the subject, Shaun asked, "What about you and Élan? You two are close, aren't you?"

Cain hesitated for a moment before answering. "Élan wants me as his consort."

Eying him with a puzzled look, Shaun leaned back in his chair. "Isn't that good?"

"Yes and no. I've come to love my lord, but I am not the most appropriate one to be his consort."

"Would you consider a Noramernian to be a proper consort for me?"

"No, but it would be your choice to make, Shaun. And Ashley is unique."

"Just so, Cain."

Cain's eyes widened. "I hadn't thought of it that way." His voice softened, matching the expression of his face. "Élan is most adamant that I am the one for him. Maybe he is right."

"He thinks he is always right," Shaun laughed.

Cain's lip twitched before he said anything. "That he does. What about you and Ashley? Are you thinking of the unification ceremony?"

"Unification ceremony? You mean like getting married?"

Cain shook his head. "Marriage is a Noramerna concept. The partners are not considered equal within the relationship. Nor do all within the species have access to marriage. It is no more than an excuse for one of their kind to dominate over another. The unification ceremony is for all, no matter their status, gender, or species. Both partners are equally important within the relationship and within society."

"A unification ceremony sounds perfect for me and Ashley." It wasn't something Shaun had to think too long and hard about. The two of them were perfect together. Shaun shot a shrewd look at Cain. "And for you and Élan."

Though Cain tried to appear dignified, the staid expression dissolved into a mischievous one. "I will be talking to him about it."

# Chapter Ten

Shaun knocked on the door of Élan's study and waited for permission to enter. A moment later the door opened and Élan smiled, seeing him.

"Come on in, Shaun. I was just about to go look for you." As Élan stepped back, Shaun walked in and shut the door behind him.

"I wanted to talk to you."

Taking Shaun's arm, Élan guided him toward the couch where they could be comfortable. "About what?" When they sat down, Élan uncapped the bottle of wine and poured them both a glass.

"I would like to start a program, Élan. To help an organization in Noramerna called CPG."

After handing a glass to Shaun, Élan nodded. "I've heard of them."

"I worked with one of their members. Chester was my neighbor when I lived with the Taylors. One time he told me and Ashley that there were quite a few enforcers and judges that sympathized over the mistreatment of weres. Chester and a couple more of my neighbors tried to petition the Institute to get me back when I was sent there." Shaun had thought considerably about what he wanted to do. "Not all Noramernians are uncaring about weres."

"I'm not sure it would do much good, Shaun. Sad to say, I think Noramerna is too well entrenched in the slavery of weres."

"I don't believe that, Élan. There are a number of organizations that do try to fight. They just don't have enough people or money, but they still reach others. They need our help. It's nice we have freedom here, but I'm not sure if that's enough." The passion Shaun felt about it echoed in his words.

"You have a good heart. Just like your father." Élan smiled as he rested his hand on Shaun's. "You want to help the world."

"That's not a bad thing." Smiling back at Élan, Shaun twisted his hand, squeezing the werelord's.

"No, no, it's not. I suggest you work out a proposal of your ideas, Shaun. You'll probably face some opposition to the idea when you're ready to present it to the Assembly, but know that I will support you."

Shaun shifted closer, resting his head on Élan's shoulder. "Thank you for bringing me here and returning me to my family, Élan. And thank you for letting Ashley come here, too."

A soft sound rumbled in Élan's chest as his arm slipped around Shaun's shoulders. "I have told you before how much like your father you are. Each day I spend with you only increases my belief in you. You are very much his son. He would be as proud of you as I am."

For several long moments, they both enjoyed the quiet silence of their growing friendship. Shaun had learned to trust the werelord, sensing the deep integrity that ran beneath Élan's actions and words. Shaun knew he would rely on Élan's wisdom and help for a long time to come. It was something Élan seemed to have no problem giving him.

As Shaun lifted his head, Élan smiled at him and Shaun leaned over to press a soft kiss to the werelord's cheek. "Thank you for everything."

"I will always be here when you need me, Shaun."

Standing up, Shaun stared down at Élan for a long moment of silence. Before he turned to leave, he whispered, "I will live up to my father." Élan didn't need to say anything, the warmth of his expression showed it all.

Thoughtfully, Shaun headed down the corridor

toward the private section of the house. When he saw Cain, he waved to him but didn't stop. There was much he wanted to talk to Ashley about. Pausing at his bedroom door, his hand rested on the knob for a moment before turning it to open the door. As he closed it behind him, his expression softened, seeing Ashley napping on the bed. To him, Ashley was the most perfect person in the world. Nobody could ever be like his master.

As he stood next to the bed, his gaze traveled slowly over the sleeping form before he carefully slid onto the bed. Trying not to awaken Ashley yet, he sat beside his master, running his hand lightly over the sheet covering Ashley's stomach.

Not quite awake, Ashley rolled onto his side, essentially wrapping himself around Shaun's bent leg. A few seconds later, he nuzzled Shaun's knee, mumbling, "Mmm, hi, babe."

"Didn't want to wake you," Shaun murmured as his hand drifted over Ashley's back. Shaun had noticed Ashley had been more quiet than usual lately. "You feeling okay?"

Ashley nodded, snuggling closer. "Yeah. Yeah, I am, Kitten." He shifted and opened his eyes, smiling up at Shaun. "Sorry about breakfast."

"No reason to apologize. I understood everything." Smiling, Shaun leaned down, brushing a kiss to Ashley's hair. "You did impress Cain, though. And I think Élan, as well."

Chuckling, Ashley rolled onto his back, though he stayed pressed up against Shaun's leg. "He saw my scars. I told him about Illian, and he took me to the House of Illumina. He let me use his private prayer room."

Shaun pressed a quick kiss to Ashley's lips, whispering, "You're growing on him, too. Just like you did me. What's the House of Ilumina?"

Ashley returned the soft kiss before answering. "It's a chapel where spirits of weres go when they die." Ashley held Shaun's gaze. "I let myself remember…and I feel I've

183

KITTEN

reached closure."

"You've never said all that much about him to me, but I knew it troubled you." Shaun studied his master's face. His fingers gently combed through Ashley's hair, meaning the touch to be comforting.

"I think that was more my way of shoving it to the back of my mind. I was forced to watch them torture him, and they whipped me. Then they slit his throat right in front of me." Ashley closed his eyes and turned his head toward Shaun's hand. "But I'm finally able to move on."

Ashley had never given him the full details, though Shaun knew Ashley had been whipped. "That will never happen here. And I want to do my best to change things in Noramerna."

"So do I, Kitten. Did you find the books you needed?" Ashley asked as he opened his eyes once more.

"Yeah, I did. Cain also told me that Élan wants him for his consort." Shaun fell silent, simply staring at Ashley.

"I know that look," Ashley said, smiling slowly. Wrapping his hand around the back of Shaun's neck, Ashley tugged him down. "Out with it, Kitten," he chuckled, licking Shaun's lips.

Finding his heart had started beating more rapidly, Shaun licked at the taste of Ashley left on his lips. "I...I want to ask you to be my consort, Ashley."

"In a heartbeat." Ashley cupped Shaun's face with his other hand, thumb running across Shaun's lips. "Love you, Shaun."

"You will?" Shaun's voice rose slightly in his excitement. After kissing the tip of Ashley's thumb, Shaun buried his face against his master's chest. "I love you so much."

Ashley chuckled and, sliding his arms around Shaun, rolled over until Shaun landed on his back with Ashley hovering over him. "Of course I will. I'm proud of you, Shaun, and honored to stand beside you."

* * * *

Élan took his time getting back to his room, his

184

thoughts darting between Ashley's past and Cain. Ashley Winters had proven himself, to say the least, without having to verbally make his case anymore than he had. While his temper was a bit touchy, which was something Élan couldn't quite begrudge the man since his own was rather short, Ashley's past and his present were enough to convince Élan that the man was true.

Then there was the issue of Cain. Élan smiled as he opened the door to his chambers. He'd been waiting for Cain—watching the man for nearly Cain's entire life—and now he was trying to convince Cain of his love. Lost in his thoughts, Élan stopped suddenly in the bathroom doorway, riveted by the sight of Cain bathing.

Cain stood and stepped out of the pool, water running down his body and dripping to the floor. He seemed unaware of Élan's presence as he reached for one of the smaller bottles at the edge of the pool and poured some of the liquid into his hand. Then he began rubbing the oil over his skin. Staying where he was took every ounce of Élan's willpower. He watched the motion of Cain's hands, his own itching to run over the muscular body before him.

Reaching for the towel, Cain began drying off the excess water and oil from his body. Turning slightly, he looked up and saw Élan standing not too far from him. His face turned red as he hastily wrapped the towel around his hips. "My lord."

Élan opened his mouth, but nothing came out. All he could do was grin sheepishly. When he could finally speak, he said, "Sorry. I didn't mean to surprise you, but…" His gaze swept over Cain slowly. "Well…"

To have Élan's attention so completely on him left Cain warm and tingling, and a bit embarrassed. "I'll just get dressed, my lord. I wanted to talk to you. I'll do that after I get dressed."

Just as Cain started past him through the bathroom doorway, Élan stopped him, one hand on Cain's hip. "Wait. Just…one kiss, love. Please."

Turning slightly, Cain found he couldn't resist the faintly pleading hint in Élan's eyes. Nodding slightly, he raised his face to the werelion. "One kiss."

"Just one," Élan whispered, "I promise." Cupping Cain's face with his other hand, Élan leaned down and licked Cain's lips before parting them slowly with his tongue.

A soft whimper sounded in Cain's throat and he instinctively moved closer to Élan. Drawing Élan's tongue into his mouth, Cain suckled lightly at it as his arms slid around Élan's neck. Élan leaned back against the door frame, pulling Cain to stand between his legs. When Cain became aware that the effect Élan had on him was apparent, he pulled away. Turning on his heel, he went to the bedroom to get his clothes. In his hurry, it took him less than a minute to put on the pants and vest.

"Thank you."

"My lord?" Cain heard the muttered words, but wasn't sure why Élan said them.

Élan smiled and shook his head. "For the kiss, for not running in the other direction when I said I wanted you as my consort."

"Something I wanted to talk to you about, Élan." Clasping his hands behind his back, Cain shifted from foot to foot, suddenly unaccountably nervous. Finding his tongue tied in knots, he couldn't continue and tried to clear his throat.

Élan walked over to the bed and sat down. "Have you changed your mind?"

Cain slowly approached the bed as he asked, "You still wish me to be your consort, my lord?"

"I want nothing more," Élan said quietly. Then he sighed. "Cain, I've waited for you since you were born. Call it fate, call it what you will. I loved you then, and I love you now. I want you by my side, if you will have me."

Kneeling in front of Élan, Cain pushed between the were's legs to get closer. "I don't understand any of that,

186

but I know how I feel about you." Lifting his hand, he cupped Élan's cheek in his palm. "I would be honored to be your consort."

Élan smiled and leaned into the touch. "Thank you."

Smiling back, Cain's fingers caressed Élan's cheek before his arms draped over Élan's shoulders. "I believe you should also expect an announcement from Shaun soon."

"It wouldn't surprise me. Ashley Winters is a better man than I gave him credit for, I think." Élan leaned down and kissed Cain's forehead. "Is that what you wanted to talk to me about? If so, then I have something I'd like to discuss with you."

"I'm coming to believe Ashley will be the perfect partner for Shaun, in many ways." Closing his eyes, Cain fell silent with the kiss, then lifted his face, taking one of his own. "What did you want to talk about?"

Élan hummed before pulling back a little. "Would you have me in a unification ceremony?"

"You don't even have to ask. For the first time in my life, I've found the happiness I've always wanted."

Élan smiled and tilted Cain's face up for another kiss, whispering on Cain's lips, "Thank you."

* * * *

"Weres run the assemblies, and in part, it's because the mortals allow them to. There's an equal balance. In a lot of human matters, weres are asked to weigh in with opinions, just as in quite a few were matters, humans are asked to do the same. Each side allows the other considerable freedom in their own lives and choices." Cain sat across from Shaun and Ashley, explaining their method of governing.

Shaun held Ashley's hand as they listened to Cain. "How do the assemblies work?"

"During the month, each lord holds their assemblies for everybody within their household and jurisdiction. Each house handles a particular part of governing. Criminal matters are sent to the House of Justice, legal matters are taken care by the House of Trials. Your house once dealt with matters concerning any issues between weres and mortals, Shaun. Currently, the House of Mirra holds that power, but when problems arose five years ago, it was split between Mirra and Earth. The first day of every month, the werelords of every house hold a session to discuss different matters."

"I want to know more about the House of Mirra, Cain." Shaun had read information about the houses, but nothing in depth.

"Yeah, I'd like to know about those guys, too. Like how much power do they really have?" Ashley leaned forward in his seat.

"Most of their power comes from the fact they were able to bring down the House of Light. Decades ago, it split the houses and nearly toppled our way of life. Those who remember still fear Mirra could do the same again."

"Can they?" Shaun asked quietly.

"Anything is possible, Shaun. But I believe, with the House of Light restored, the other houses will fear Mirra less. Élan has found enough information to convince others that Noramerna funding the House of Mirra before and during the wars is closer to truth than rumor."

"Why would Mirra have worked with them?" Ashley asked.

"Trafficking in weres is a very lucrative career path. I'd say the money was irresistible to Mirra. No doubt they believed it would gain them the same prestige and power of the House of Fetters."

"That didn't happen, though. Why?" Shaun wanted to learn all he could before he faced the counsel assembly in two weeks.

"Élan has always kept a very close eye on Mirra. In part, because he never believed your father would betray us in such a way. He didn't believe Lord Tyr-Set would sell his own people into slavery. Mirra only laid the crimes they were guilty of at Lord Tyr-Set's feet. However, several houses were guilty. Shock divided the houses and civil war followed."

"And in the chaos, my father and mother had to flee for their lives," Shaun added.

Cain nodded sadly. "I was taken from my home to safety, but my parents refused to desert them. In the aftermath, the houses in Euroas began to crumble. Noramerna took advantage and declared war on them. The weres and mortals were in such chaos, that Euroas fell, and the were lines were forced into hiding."

Ashley nodded. "I was young at the time, but I remember my parents talking about the war. They didn't approve of it."

"During the war in Euroas, Élan realized Ausafca would be next. He literally forced the houses to reunite. At the time, he basically became a dictator and ruthlessly suppressed any dissension. Not a period he is proud of or talks about much. By the time the war in Euroas ended, Ausafca was too strong for Noramerna to risk war—especially with their coffers depleted by the first war. Our military was larger than theirs, and still is." Cain paused, waiting for any comments.

"Now Noramerna has a steady supply of pets from Euroas." Shaun sighed. It seemed like there was so much to do; he didn't know where to start.

"Some of the houses are steadily growing stronger. Italy has thrown off the oppression of Noramerna and is holding its own. Southern Spain is becoming stronger, and possibly within five years, the rest of Spain will follow," Cain explained.

"Does Ausafca help any of them?"

"No, not really. Other than giving safe refuge to were and mortals who come here, Ashley."

"Ashley told me he sold everything he had to come here. Why aren't there routes for safe passage? Most weres don't have access to the kind of money it would cost to get here."

"Those are things you would need to address in assembly, Shaun. Perhaps the House of Light will someday stand for those issues." Clearly, Cain didn't have all the answers.

"Oh, I will see that it does."

Cain smiled. "Noramerna can't hold both continents forever. The rising opposition will increasingly make Euroas a more and more expensive proposition to maintain."

"Are there figures available concerning possible funding, and what can be achieved?" Shaun had absorbed a great deal of information and now worked with the ideas in his head.

"No," Cain murmured, "but I can tell you the assets of Ausafca are vast. Prying some of it from the houses wouldn't be a bad thing."

"It's about time Ausafca shared the wealth," Ashley chuckled, eyeing Shaun.

"Élan told me to work out a proposal to present at a council assembly. Any recommendations on who can help me, Cain?"

Cain seemed to think on that. "David Tyr-Set. He is the one who took you to Noramerna, and he is still very loyal to your house. David could find the information you need and recommend others who will help."

MYCHAEL BLACK / SHAYNE CARMICHAEL

# Chapter Eleven

"My lords, I welcome you." Élan bowed toward the others before sitting. "I have called this Assembly for a purpose…" He looked at each member in turn. "To introduce a new lord."

As Lord Rian sat, he nodded to Élan. "Thank you, Lord Élan. We are all quite curious, considering your announcement was vague, at best."

Élan smiled and gestured to the doors. "Please, Cain. Would you bring our newest member in?"

Smiling faintly at Élan, Cain bowed his head, turned, and walked across the room to an inner chamber door. Pulling the door open, he stood slightly to the side. As Shaun stepped into the room, a gasp of surprise rippled through the assembled crowd. Most of the elder members recognized the young man simply from his markings. A buzz of whispered conversation preceded Shaun as he slowly approached them.

Pausing in the middle of the chambers, Shaun smiled at them. "I am Lord Shaun Tyr-Set, House of Light."

Immediately Lord Nostra jumped from his seat, yelling, "Why have you brought the traitor's son into the assembly?"

"Enough!" Élan roared from where he sat. "Lord Tyr-Set has every right to speak here, as do all of you." Nostra dropped into his seat, glaring at Élan.

As the others fell silent, Shaun spoke again. "I am here to rebuild the House of Light. As the son of Aldar Tyr-Set, I have that right. If any of the council wishes to dispute my claim, address Houses Fetters, Earth, Trial, and Nine with your complaint." While Shaun recited the

191

names, each lord of the four houses stood.

"Nothing good will come of this," Nostra growled under his breath.

"Then take your concerns to the aforementioned lords," Élan reminded the lord of House Mirra none too gently.

Talon stepped forward. "If you have a complaint, you will take it up with us and fill out the appropriate letters for the House of Trials."

As Jareth, Simon, and Élan stepped from their places, they all focused on Nostra, waiting silently. With no further word, Nostra nodded abruptly to them. A moment later, several voices rose in chorus and echoed in the chamber: "We have no complaint."

Clearly Mirra would be seriously outnumbered on the matter, and it only increased the scowl on Nostra's features. Turning his baleful eye on Shaun, a growl rumbled deep. Shaun calmly eyed his father's killer, refusing to break eye contract. He stood in silence, folding his arms across his chest. The tension within the room rose several degrees as the others waited silently. Several long moments later, Nostra finally backed down and looked away from him.

Élan watched them both, and only when he looked at Shaun did he smile and nod slightly. "If all the lords are in agreement..." He looked at the lords, then glared at Nostra. "Then so be it. Let it be hereby known that there is a new lord of House of Light."

The thuds from the wooden staffs of the lords drowned out any other sound in the room. Shaun bowed to the others before he moved to take his place in the tier of circular seats beside Ashley. Glancing at Élan, he smiled back. They'd won, and there was little Mirra could do openly about it.

* * * *

A week after the announcement of Shaun's ascension to the House of the Light, all four of them walked up the steps to the House of the Gods. Shaun and Cain seemed the most notably nervous, but Élan and Ashley appeared quite calm. They stepped into the outer chamber and the doors shut behind them, and they were greeted by complete silence.

Élan led the way through a pair of large mahogany doors. Inside, the huge room was completely bare except for a rounded set of stairs that led up to a doorway at the far end of the room. The outer walls of the room were made of stained glass. Each god was portrayed in all of their glory within the sanctity of the room.

When they stopped in front of the stairs, they waited in silence. Élan took Cain's hand, and Shaun took Ashley's. A few seconds later the Lady of the House came through the doorway. Dressed simply in a white gown wrapped around her form, small dazzling lights danced in the fabric and in her dark hair as she moved. When she stopped at the edge of the top of the stairs, she looked at Élan and Cain.

"Why are you here?"

"To become as one," they answered in unison.

Then she turned to Ashley and Shaun. "Why are you here?"

"To become as one," they answered together.

"And do you all come of your own free will?" When they all answered "We do", the Lady smiled. "Then present yourselves to the gods, with open hearts and open minds."

As she turned and moved back to the doorway, they followed her and entered the small hallway lined with doors. Stopping in front of one of the doors, she waited for Élan and Cain to go into the room before she walked further down the hall and gestured for Shaun and Ashley to enter another room.

* * * *

Élan closed the door to their room and took Cain's hand. Smiling, he led Cain to the center of the circular marble room and looked up. Stars shone above them through the open roof.

"You ready?" Élan asked, stroking the top of Cain's

193

hand lightly with his thumb.

The clasp of his hand tightened as Cain stepped closer to Élan so that they were side by side. "Yes, I am more than ready to be joined with you, Élan."

A glow within the depths of the white marble suffused the room in a golden color and bathed them in the warmth of the light. No more words were necessary for the ceremony. They themselves were the ceremony.

Élan got down on his knees, easing Cain down with him. Kneeling and facing, they held each other's gaze, their fingers entwined. The light enveloped them and began swirling slowly, creating a sphere of gold. Drawing on them, the energy folded within them, and they became the energy. Within, nothing could be hidden, their lives and all they were laid bare and blended, to be shared with one another. Cain lost all sense of himself as existing as a separate entity. In their merging, their hearts opened to each other. The love Élan held for him mirrored his, deepening it.

As they stared at one another, the power drew the lines of their lives and intertwined them, separate in the past but together for the future. They shared memories, dreams, and hopes, and gave them understanding of one another. The light began pulsing in time to the tandem beats of their hearts, echoing the steady rhythm. Though he didn't speak, Élan smiled. Then he tipped his head back, the power gathering strength. A few seconds later, Cain felt the power rushing through him, and he gasped with the surge of energy. It built inside until it seemed as if he would burst. Then Élan kissed him.

As the power bound them, it also left them free. The burning rush flooded them both as they kissed, and the golden light became blinding, leaving them alone together in the majestic force that now resided in both of them.

The light faded slowly, leaving them once again beneath the night sky. Opening his eyes, Élan simply stared at Cain before resuming the kiss. It would be a good while before either of them was ready to leave.

\* \* \* \*

Shaun stared at Ashley as they knelt together, the depth of his own feelings clear in his eyes. The ceremony wasn't a union of words, but an expression of themselves that would become an extension of each other.

"I love you," Ashley mouthed, squeezing Shaun's hands in his.

Shaun whispered the words back to him. Ashley closed his eyes and threw his head back, shuddering as the energy filled him. The golden light swirled and pulsed, spinning around them both. He felt Shaun jerk suddenly and seconds later his Kitten was kissing him. Ashley's eyes opened with the rush of Shaun's power, his own flowing into Shaun through their kiss. It was dizzying and intense, taking Ashley's breath away as it fused his soul to Shaun's. The pain of their existence alone had been taken and replaced with the life they had together.

Shaun lifted his hand to cup Ashley's cheek, capturing Ashley to keep him still. The power flowed through them, enriching as it bonded them to be truly equal. They belonged to one other in accordance with their own wishes. A union that could never be taken from them. As the golden flare faded, the open emotion on Ashley's face was the first thing Shaun saw.

Ashley opened his mouth to speak, but when nothing came out, he just shook his head helplessly. The look on his face didn't fade and all he could do was stare at Shaun.

This far exceeded the mark Ashley had put on him. Shaun discovered Élan had been right about that. His arms encircled Ashley and Shaun pressed a gentle kiss to Ashley's lips, the soft stir of his breath warming Ashley's skin.

\* \* \* \*

Closing the door behind them, Élan turned to Cain. "If I asked for a kiss now…?"

"I believe you're allowed to, Élan." Stepping closer to Élan, Cain ran his hands over the front of Élan's shirt. "You're allowed to ask for whatever you want." Face lifting for a kiss, Cain pressed his lips lightly, teasingly, against Élan's.

"As are you," Élan whispered.

Without giving Cain a chance to answer, Élan pulled him into a kiss, tongue parting Cain's lips as the werelord slipped the vest off Cain's shoulders. A shiver ran through Cain and he opened to Élan, his tongue circling the werelord's. He'd dreamed of them being together, but the reality was so much more satisfying. Letting the vest drop to the floor, Élan ran his hands back up Cain's arms, then over his shoulders to cup his neck. Élan ended the kiss slowly, mouth moving in light kisses over Cain's throat, breath heating Cain's skin.

Tilting his head, Cain encouraged the further exploration of Élan's mouth. His fingers kneaded Élan's muscles as he pressed against the werelion's body. Just their closeness was enough to arouse a deeper need. Élan slowly went down on his knees, the kisses sliding downward as well. He exhaled over Cain's left nipple, then sucked the small bit of flesh into his mouth, sucking and nipping. His hands left Cain's hips and pushed into the loose pants, easing the thin material down Cain's legs and to the floor. A low moan rose in Cain's throat. Naked before his lord, he stood proudly, watching Élan. One hand moved to Élan's shoulder, continually kneading his flesh.

Standing, Élan started backing Cain toward the bed, hands on Cain's hips. "I want to taste you."

"Anything and everything you want, my lord." With an impish grin, Cain let Élan guide him back toward the bed. When the backs of his knees hit the edge, he slid onto the covers and stretched out. There was no shyness in him now. He wanted everything as much as Élan did.

"How do you want me?" Élan asked, parting Cain's legs as he crawled onto the bed. "Do you want the man? Or do you want both?" Élan leaned down and drew a line up Cain's inner right thigh with his tongue, stopping just short of his balls.

Highly reactive to what Élan did to him, Cain couldn't answer at first. Squirming slightly, he stared down at Élan, a heated flare rushing through him. "Both. I love both, I want both, Élan."

Smiling slowly, Élan began to shift. His face, while remaining primarily human, took on a somewhat feline appearance. Golden hair covered his body and his nails lengthened. Pushing Cain's legs up and further apart, Élan lowered his head, drawing his rough tongue up along the hard, heated flesh of Cain's cock.

"Oh, gods." Cain's hips jerked, seeking the heat of Élan's mouth. Reaching down, he ran his hands over the silky fur of Élan's shoulders before grabbed his legs to hold them up for the werelion. The wriggling of his body opened him further to Élan, leaving him completely exposed. "I love every way you are."

A deep purr answered Cain and Élan shifted downward. Hands beneath Cain, Élan tilted him up a little and began lapping at his hole. The teasing only heightened the rush of need as it swamped Cain. Eventually he would demand the same taste of Élan, but right now he couldn't concentrate worth a damn. A small push of his hips tried to edge nearer to the enticing sensation of Élan's tongue, and a small, pleading sound escaped him.

Chuckling softly, Élan gave Cain exactly what he wanted. Tongue pointed, Élan fucked Cain with it, licking and sucking on the puckered skin before plunging back inside. His hands spread Cain open wider, letting that tongue push deeper. Soft moans poured from Cain's lips as Élan's tongue repeatedly pushed into him. Already hard and leaking, he dug his fingers tightly into his own skin, and the rock of his body continually encouraged the werelion. Élan slowly moved up, sucking one of Cain's balls into his mouth. He rolled it gently over his tongue, then released it to continue upward. As he took Cain's cock into his mouth, one clawless finger eased inside Cain, curling forward. Élan purred around the hard flesh, sending small vibrations up the shaft. When Élan hit a particular sweet spot, Cain cried out, a cascade of sensations rippling through him.

Pulling his finger out, Élan released Cain and slid up, taking his mouth in a deep, heated kiss. A hand pushed between them and long fingers curled around Cain's cock, giving it a long, torturous stroke. The press of Cain's lips and body became more demanding with the arousing pressure of Élan's hand. Ending the kiss, Cain stared hungrily up at Élan before he pushed at the werelion less then gently. He rolled Élan onto his back, then straddled him. He tugged at the edge of Élan's shirt, pulling it up over Élan's head and tossing it to the side. The pants were the next to go. Once the clothing was taken care of, Cain settled back on Élan, his body pinning the were's to the bed. He dragged his nails slowly over Élan's nipples, taking his own enjoyment from the feel of their cocks rubbing together with the grind of his hips.

Élan hissed, fingers digging into Cain's hips as he rocked his hips up. "Cain. Gods…"

Pinching lightly at Élan's nipples, Cain leaned down, flicking his tongue over Élan's lips. "Want to ride you, my lord. Ride until I scream for you."

"Yes," Élan growled. "Gods, yes."

Cain grabbed for one of the jars that had been placed on the side shelf near the bed. As he stared down into Élan's eyes, he opened it and dipped his fingers in the gel. Shifting slightly, he ran his hand slowly over Élan's cock, slicking it. Watching the intense expression of the werelion's features and the glowing gold of Élan's eyes, Cain smiled slowly. Closing the jar, he set it aside as he raised his hips slightly. His finger remained curled around Élan's cock as he guided it slowly into himself. It had been some time since he'd been with his male lover. Taking his time, he carefully eased himself fully onto the werelion's hard flesh.

Élan's eyes rolled back slightly and his grip on Cain's hips tightened. "Cain. So tight…gods…"

As he settled against Élan, body stretching out over the werelion's, Cain stopped all movement except for the light pinching and twisting of Élan's nipples. Feeling the full pressure inside him, several small shudders ran through him, and Cain closed his eyes, focused on the feeling. "Perfect. So fucking perfect."

Élan's rumble of agreement was muffled as his lips sealed around a spot on Cain's neck and sucked up a mark. His fingers traced Cain's spine, finally coming to rest on his ass, holding him open as Élan rocked his hips up the slightest bit. Just the slightest movement sent a chain reaction through Cain, and with a deep groan, he ground back against Élan, then began slowly riding his lord's cock. Each exquisite inch filled him over and over, his breathing quickening.

"Yes," Élan whispered. "Mine. Always have been, love."

The possessive tenor of Élan's words went beyond the sound of them. A vibration of power weaved through them, sinking deeply into Cain. In answer, he shuddered and gasped out, "Yes." Cain rested his forehead on Élan's shoulder, and the rock of his body sharpened the needful feelings overtaking him.

With a deep growl, Élan rolled them. He braced himself and caught Cain's lips in a kiss as he drove deeper inside Cain, staking his claim. "Love you. Now let me hear you."

"Élan." His lord's name became a soft chant, falling from Cain's lips. The deep thrusts drew the hard arc of his body, and the tension became near unbearable with the friction trapping his cock. Suddenly Cain shuddered hard and his orgasm rolled him under. A sharp cry threaded through Élan's name as Cain shook with the rush of pleasure.

Élan roared and thrust harder, hips jerking as he filled Cain. When he was spent, he collapsed onto Cain's chest, breathless and shuddering with the last of the tremors.

## KITTEN

As Cain held tightly to Élan, soft brushes of his lips feathered against his lord's throat. Emotionally and physically, Cain was complete. After lightly nipping at Élan's ear, he whispered, "You are my other half, Élan. As it was meant to be."

# Chapter Twelve

"Kitten." It was the first word Ashley had spoken since the bonding had taken place and they'd returned home. Back against the door, he reached out for Shaun. "I can feel you, Shaun. Everywhere. Inside me."

Leaning against him, Shaun pinned him to the bedroom door, pressing several kisses to his lips before answering. "The way we wanted to be. For always now."

Ashley nodded and smiled against Shaun's lips. "Yes." He slid his hands up Shaun's sides, humming softly in appreciation. "Want you, love."

Shaun's fingers slowly unbuttoned Ashley's shirt, then slid it from his shoulders, caressing his bare skin. "However and whenever you want."

Meeting Shaun's gaze, Ashley traced his fingertips up Shaun's arms, over his shoulders, to cup the back of Shaun's neck. "However I can get you, and for the rest of our lives."

A soft, playful growl sounded in Shaun's throat as he took hold of one of Ashley's hands. Drawing it to his lips, Shaun nipped lightly at the tips of Ashley's fingers before pulling two slowly into his mouth. His tongue teased around them before letting them go. Turning, Shaun looked back over his shoulder at Ashley as he moved toward the bed. Pushing away from the door, Ashley chuckled and took off his pants, letting them fall to the floor before he followed. Coming up behind Shaun, he snaked his arms around Shaun's waist and nipped at the nape of Shaun's neck.

"I want to taste you everywhere, Kitten. Inside and out."

Their moods matched each other perfectly, and Shaun could feel that. Leaning back against Ashley, his backside nudged tighter to his lover. Turning his head slightly, he quickly licked at Ashley's lips. "As long as I can taste you all over, too."

Ashley returned the lick, then sucked Shaun's tongue into his mouth as one hand moved lower to cup Shaun, giving him a gentle squeeze through the thin loin cloth. "Shift for me? I want the man, Shaun," he said, finally releasing Shaun from the kiss.

Smiling as he pulled away, Shaun did what Ashley wanted. His body slowly changed into his completely human form. After taking off the loincloth, Shaun slid back onto the bed, gazing at Ashley the whole time.

"Gods, you're gorgeous." Ashley crawled onto the bed. Pushing Shaun's legs up, he settled down, flicking his tongue over Shaun's ass.

Squirming downward, Shaun slipped his hands around his legs, holding them for Ashley. A whimper escaped him as he wiggled his ass, begging for more. Ashley's tongue pushed into him, Ashley's hands gripping Shaun's hips to lift him up. Pulling away long enough to wet two fingers, Ashley slid them inside, licking around the stretched hole.

"Ashley," Shaun gasped out his lover's name. A tremor raced through his body and he closed his eyes, sinking into the arousal sharpening with each deep push inside him.

"Yes, Kitten." Ashley surged up Shaun's body, taking his mouth in a heated kiss. Those fingers pushed deeper, spreading Shaun open.

Shaun lifted his hips, rocking on Ashley's hand as he hungrily returned the kiss. A moment later, he rolled them, Ashley landing on his back. Nipping sharply at Ashley's lower lip, Shaun tugged gently on it before letting go. Shimmying down slightly, he pressed kiss after kiss to the warm skim, his tongue tasting the salty-sweet flavor. Ashley moved restlessly beneath him, and Shaun's heated breath stirred over Ashley's skin before his mouth surrounded his lover's left nipple.

"Shaun!" Ashley's fingers buried in Shaun's hair as Ashley pushed his chest up for more. He spread his legs, cradling Shaun between them, hips rocking to slide their cocks together.

"Want to love you," Shaun whispered as he released the nipple. His fingers twisted and pinched at both nubs. As his lips traveled lower, he rubbed against Ashley, loving the sensation of their cocks rubbing together. Taking his own sweet time, a path of licks and nips scattered over Ashley's stomach, then slowly further down. He just couldn't get enough of the taste of his master.

Ashley simply groaned, fingers stroking Shaun's hair. He didn't push, just held on, hips not quite still. "Please…"

Soft sounds interspersed with each lap of Shaun's tongue as it twirled around the head of Ashley's cock. Gently, he suckled just the head into his mouth, teasing. His hands slid downward over Ashley's thighs, thumbs massaging over Ashley's inner thighs.

"Shaun…don't stop…" Ashley shuddered, hips lifting a little more. "Gods, please, Shaun."

Drawing Ashley deeper into his mouth, Shaun glided over his lover's cock in a deliberately slow movement. With each buck of Ashley's hips, his mouth closed tightly, swallowing the hard flesh.

"Oh, God…" Ashley gasped, hands tightening in Shaun's hair. "Fuck. Shaun."

Finally releasing him, Shaun lifted his head and pinned a heated look on Ashley. He moved slowly upward, rubbing their bodies together, then rolled them once again. Stretching beneath Ashley, Shaun captured his master's mouth, tongue pushing hungrily between Ashley's lips. Ashley deepened the kiss, sucking on Shaun's tongue. A moment later, he broke the kiss and sat up to kneel between Shaun's legs. Holding Shaun's gaze, Ashley slicked two fingers, easing them deep inside Shaun. Knowing his master was intent on drawing things out, Shaun's hands clenched tightly in the covers beneath him. A slow rock of his hips drove the fingers deeper, and a particularly loud whimper escaped him with the graze across the most sensitive spot.

Ashley leaned down, nipping at Shaun's belly just beside his navel. He exhaled, heating Shaun's skin as he added a third finger. "What do you want, Kitten?"

"Whatever you want to do to me, Ash..." Shaun didn't care as long Ashley kept doing it. Breaking off with a groan, Shaun grabbed his legs and opened himself further to Ashley.

Shifting lower, Ashley swallowed Shaun down, throat working around Shaun's cock as a fourth finger was added, all four scissoring apart, stretching Shaun open.

Each push inside him and the mouth around him drew several low moans from Shaun. The nearly painful stretch of his ass focused his attention on the feelings. With every slide of Ashley's mouth, the sensations tightened more sharply in Shaun, driving him toward desperation. "Please, Ashley. Oh, please, Master."

Pulling up slowly, Ashley gripped the base of Shaun's cock with his other hand, steadying it as he licked the tip. "What do you want, love? Tell me." He flexed his fingers in Shaun's ass, moving them in and out.

The jerk of Shaun's hips became more frantic and he cried out. "You! Please. I want you. Now."

"You've got me." Ashley eased his fingers out, slicked up his cock, and sank deep inside. "All of me." Then he took Shaun's lips in a kiss, hands linking with Shaun's to draw them above Shaun's head to the pillow.

Shaun's legs wrapped tightly around Ashley's waist, pushing into the slow penetration of his body. The feeling short-circuited his brain and left him writhing hungrily for more. His fingers curled tightly around Ashley's as Shaun drew his lover's tongue into his mouth, teeth scraping over it. Ashley shivered, groaning into the kiss. He pulled out slightly, then thrust back in, fingers digging into Shaun's hands. The slow rhythm of their bodies joined them over and over again as they made love. The emotions between them spilled over, entwining between them. Dropping his head to the pillow, Shaun stared up at Ashley.

"I love you, Ashley. With everything, I love you."

"Kitten…love…" It was all Ashley said before he cried out, hips jerking against Shaun as he came.

Taking in the sound of Ashley's pleasure and the sight of his rapt expression, lost in his own world, Shaun's body strained tightly against Ashley. A quicker, persistent rock of his hips sent him over the edge into his own release, and Shaun cried out sharply with it. Every pulse rippled through him, heat slicking between them as his body shuddered.

Breathless, Ashley rested his head to Shaun's shoulder, shaking with the last of the tremors. "Love you so much, Kitten," he whispered, kissing Shaun's shoulder.

"You're everything to me," Shaun whispered back, turning his head slightly toward Ashley. Freeing his hands, he wrapped his arms tightly around Ashley, refusing to let go of him just yet. He could still feel the minute throbs of Ashley's cock and was reluctant to separate from his master.

Ashley nodded, arms sliding under Shaun's shoulders to hold him. "Everything."

* * * *

It had taken them a week to finally settle in the House of Light. Shaun missed the closer proximity to Élan and Cain, but they weren't that far away. There was a lot he needed to learn and know, and he still relied on the other two for wisdom. Once it became well known that a Tyr-Set had returned to the House of Light, the hidden family members slowly came out of hiding. Most of them wanted to return to service under Shaun. The enormous palace they moved into was far more than Shaun had ever been used to. It hadn't taken him long to decide to put the larger portion of it to another use. As he entered the library, Ashley and David were already waiting for him.

"I've already gone over the ledger of finances, Shaun," Ashley said as Shaun sat down next to him. "The council has allotted the necessary funds for reconstruction of our House. Let me tell you, the amount set aside for just maintenance of the building is unbelievable."

"Figure out how much we actually need for physical maintenance and servers' pay. The rest I want diverted to necessary supplies for the refugees we'll be taking in. We need at least a figure of what it will take for retraining, food, and finding work for whomever we take in."

"Next month's session, you're scheduled to address the assembly to obtain additional funding, my lord. I've already gotten a hold of several of my contacts in France, Spain, and England. They're working on the quickest, safest routes from those points." David opened his folder and pulled out several sheets of paper, placing them in front of Shaun.

"Has Chester answered you yet?" Shaun asked as he skimmed over the list David had made.

"Yes, he did, my lord. He sends his love and says he'd be very interested in what you can come up with."

"He'll be our main contact in Noramerna. I trust him to make the judgment calls on the disbursement of what we send his way."

David nodded. "He did mention he already knew of two weres who needed help. One, he said, was a pet of someone you knew. Woman by the name of Illa Jacobs."

Without hesitation, Shaun growled out, "Tell Chester to take the were. Immediately."

Gazing steadily back at him, David replied calmly, "I gather it's already been done. Chester has Adam in a safe house. He's just waiting for the money he needs from you to get Adam here. I have Chester's bank information here. Thankfully he has an account in England. They're more concerned with the privacy of their customers than where the money is from."

Shaun relaxed in his seat, and Ashley looked relieved as he said, "Tell Chester to notify Enforcer Narson about the problem with Illa Jacobs. And ask him to check into the most immediate needs cases."

Unfortunately, they all knew they couldn't save every were at this point. Shaun had made the decision to focus on the worst cases as they became aware of them. "Since the route won't be in place for another month, find out if Chester can hold Adam for that long. If not, transfer the funds to his account and have one of our agents in New Roth make the arrangements for getting Adam here."

David made several notes on his pad, then set his pen down. "That reminds me, my lord. I've already had three servers approach me, asking to help with your project. Two of them said they were willing to go to Noramerna and act as your agents."

Shaun frowned slightly. That wasn't something he'd considered. Exposing an Ausafca to the way things were in Noramerna would be extremely rough.

Seeing Shaun's expression, David continued quietly, "It is something to consider. You could have trusted family in key positions."

Shaun hesitated, but after a moment, he finally said, "I'll think about it."

David nodded. "Yes, my lord."

Ashley waited until David had left again, then he stood and went to lock the door. "As much as I hate the thought of anyone going there, David's right. To have trusted people in place in Normerna would help us tremendously if this is to work."

"You know what it's like here, and what it's like there. It would be a very hard adjustment to make. A lot harder than the one we had coming here." Sighing, Shaun reached for Ashley's hand and stood.

"I know."

Ashley smiled and sat on the edge of the desk, tugging Shaun to stand between his legs. It amazed him how much Shaun had grown in the short time his Kitten had been here. Shaun's level of self-confidence before had been virtually nonexistent. Now, Shaun was someone completely different, in a sense. Ashley couldn't be more proud. He smiled and cupped Shaun's cheek, stroking his Kitten's lower lip with his thumb.

"I'm proud of you, Shaun."

Draping his arms over Ashley's shoulders, Shaun's voice dropped to a whisper as he leaned down, nuzzling against Ashley's ear. "Thank you, master."

Ashley suppressed the shiver. "Kneel."

Shaun went to his knees and his head tilted up to look at Ashley.

Crossing his arms over his chest, Ashley's expression became stern. "Take your cock out and stroke yourself. Do not come."

Quickly unzipping his pants, Shaun pulled out his cock and slowly began running his hand up and down its length. His gaze remained on Ashley.

"Unbutton your shirt, but do not stop stroking."

With his other hand, Shaun unfastened the buttons, revealing the rest of his body in slow glimpses. He greatly enjoyed the intent fixation his master had on every movement of both of his hands. As he continued pumping his hand around his cock, the speed quickened and a soft moan of need escaped him. He looked pleadingly up at Ashley.

"Twist your left nipple. Let me hear you."

Obedient to Ashley's every command, Shaun's fingers slid across his skin to his nipple and began twisting the nub. He shivered with the pulses of pleasure and pain strengthening in him. A soft sound rose in his throat, the pitch changing to a needier tone as he whispered, "Please, master..."

Standing, Ashley popped the button on his own pants. "Suck me, but do not stop what you are doing." He pulled out his cock and stroked it slowly. "Use only your lips and your tongue; no hands on me."

Staring at the hard, leaking flesh in front of him, Shaun wet his lips but waited until Ashley rubbed the head against them. He opened his mouth, tongue circling slowly as he leaned forward to draw his master's cock in deeper. He obediently kept his own hands occupied with teasing himself as he'd been told.

Ashley groaned, one hand cupping the back of Shaun's head, holding him there. "Fuck, yes." Ashley began thrusting in and out, fucking Shaun's mouth with quick, shallow strokes. "Suck it," he commanded.

Suckling more tightly, he met the rhythm of Ashley's thrusts, and the pace of his own hand matched. Shaun felt his increasing need for release, but he couldn't vocalize it. To still it, he focused on the hard flesh in his mouth, tongue and lips gliding more rapidly over Ashley, eager for the full taste of his master.

"Shaun." The name was growled and Ashley pulled away. "Bend over the desk and spread yourself for me."

Standing, Shaun stepped out of his pants as he moved to the desk. Bending over the desk, palms on his ass, Shaun spread his legs as he opened himself to his master. A small shudder ran through him at the thought of Ashley inside him, and a soft moan accompanied the restless shift of his body. Ashley walked around to the other side and pulled open the bottom left drawer. Glancing up at Shaun, he took out a small wooden box and opened it. He seemed to take his own sweet time, leaving Shaun in the somewhat vulnerable, exposed position.

"I have something for you." From the box, Ashley lifted a plug, larger than the one they normally used, and a tube of lubrication. Then he set the box to the side and went back around to stand behind Shaun. Without warning, he landed a sharp smack to Shaun's left ass cheek.

Shaun jumped slightly because he had been expecting something entirely different, and the sting of Ashley's hand surprised him. In reaction, he tried to find some point of friction against the desk for his painfully hard cock. His ass cheeks were spread and two slick fingers pushed inside him, Ashley stretching him open. Then a third was added, all three scissored, opening Shaun's ass wider.

"So tight. Hot and slick," Ashley said, working his fingers in and out, twisting them to loosen Shaun up.

With a slight jerk of his hips, Shaun pushed back against the pressure. Unable to bite back a deep groan, his hips rocked, wanting his master to be inside him. "Please, Master. Fuck me, please."

"In time." Ashley withdrew his fingers and something larger and harder replaced them. "Bear down," he said as he began pushing the large, slick plug into Shaun's ass.

Swallowing down his impatience was difficult, but the painful stretch of his ass accommodating the new toy accomplished that. Biting at his lower lip, Shaun tried his best to relax his body as he felt the plug sliding inside him. It was far larger than the others Ashley had used on him. Though it did hurt at first, a rush of pleasure enveloped Shaun when the plug was fully inserted. He knew his master was pleased as well and probably relishing the sight. The trembling of his body betrayed Shaun's closeness to the edge, yet he controlled it.

Once the plug was firmly situated, Ashley skimmed along the sensitive skin stretched around it. "Very good," he purred. He went back around to stand before Shaun and reached into the box. With one hand, he tilted Shaun's head up. Then he held the leather collar so Shaun could see it. It was nearly an inch and a half in width, with a silver buckle. Ashley opened it and revealed the silver-painted inscription tooled into the leather inside:

*To Kitten, with Love. Master Ashley.*

Across the front of the collar, Shaun's pet name of 'Kitten' was spelled out in silver studs.

Shaun stared at it for a few seconds as he read the

inscription. Tears welled in his eyes as he looked back up at Ashley. "Please put it on me, Master."

Ashley smiled and slid the collar beneath Shaun's hair, buckling it in back. Drawing his hands back, Ashley traced the studded name with his fingertip. "Show me how proud you are to wear my collar. Come."

It took no more than the one word to trigger the chain reaction in Shaun. He released his own control, and with a sharp cry, the already tightly-wound tension inside him broke. His hips rocked against the desk as he came, crying Ashley's name.

"Beautiful." Ashley rose and walked behind Shaun. He eased the plug out slowly, slicked his cock, and thrust inside. Fingers curling to Shaun's hips, Ashley fucked Shaun hard and quick, hips slamming against Shaun's ass. "Kitten!" With a final thrust, Ashley buried himself deep inside Shaun, his cock throbbing.

As his master used him for his own fulfillment, Shaun lost himself in the deeper mindset of giving himself completely to Ashley. The knowledge itself became a powerful pull on Shaun's senses, and his body responded completely. When Ashley shouted his name, Shaun's body shook with a more intense orgasm and he incoherently cried out to his master.

Shuddering, Ashley remained plastered to Shaun, practically draped over Shaun's back. Breathless, he rested his head on Shaun's shoulder. "So good," he murmured. "My beautiful Kitten."

Exhausted, Shaun laid limply on the desk, feeling the weight of Ashley's body against him. "Master, I love you." He could barely form the words, but he had to say them. Ashley had taken him to a place deep within himself, and forever Shaun's soul would be branded as his master's Kitten.

"Love you, too, Kitten. More than life itself."

# About the Authors

**Mychael Black** never set out to write erotic romance (or romance or erotica, for that matter). When Mychael first started writing (way back when), it was to be a fantasy author—someone along the lines of Tolkien or Mercedes Lackey. Mychael even thought about breaking into horror. Then, somewhere down the line, Mychael got hooked on gay porn.

The rest is history.

Born in Alabama in 1976, Mychael is known by many names. At this point, most people in the e-publishing world (readers and authors) know Mychael as Kay Derwydd.

The name Mychael Black came about when Mychael started working with Shayne Carmichael. (See Shayne's bio for the progression of that whole thing.) To date, Mychael has written countless works with Shayne, plus several single-authored works as Mychael Black.

When not writing, Mychael can usually be found researching anything medieval—arms, armor, history, religion; anything Welsh—culture, language, history; languages—namely Welsh, Hebrew, German; and only God knows what else.

Aside from research, writing, and editing, Mychael spends most of the time chasing down two young children and fighting off the plot bunnies left and right.

More information can be found at the following places:

http://www.geocities.com/mychaelblack
http://mychael-black2.livejournal.com

Who is **Shayne Carmichael**? His real name is Shayne Lee Smith. He was born in Itazuke, Japan to American parents. (ie - Dad was in the Air Force). From the age of three to eight, he lived in Taiwan. He's traveled a lot, and only discovered even more he wants to learn about the world.

When not writing, Shayne is a self taught PHP and MySql dynamo. Or at least one would think from the number of scripts he's been begged to write for free. With any spare time left to him, Shayne runs ERWI (Erotic Romance Writers International), aggravates his co-author, Mychael, to no end, often drowns under Mychael's plot bunnies, and holds a forty hour a week job.

Currently Shayne is working on a six book series, The Legends of the Romanorum. Blood Ties, Blood Magic and Blood Sins are being written by Shayne. The Prince's Angel, And the Two Shall Become One, and Forever May Not Be Long Enough are being written by Shayne and Mychael. Included in the writing list are a few other books, Magic and the Pagan, Night Song, and numerous novellas and shorts.

Shayne writes under the pen names of Sable St Germain and Shayne Carmichael. Sable was an RP character he used to play. Shayne Carmichael is a combination of his first name and Cian's (Angel/sorcerer in The Prince's Angel) last name. The character Shayne writes for in The Prince's Angel is Mael Black. That would explain why Mychael's last name is Black, and the character Mychael writes for is Cian.

# KITTEN

Shayne's first official publishing contact is with Phaze for the Power of Two. A vampire D/s, BDSM story written with Mychael Black. The status of Phaze author has been one of their goals. Having achieved that, their next goal is to take over the world.

Over the last nine years, Shayne has rped (roleplayed) and written both male and female characters. Gay, lesbian and het (vanilla and non vanilla). You could say he runs the gamut.

He's never believed whatever gender he happens to possess dictates what he can and can't write. And he pretty much ignores anybody who thinks that way. Especially since he's never been a vampire, were tiger, ghost or guide, but he writes about them anyway.

Hell, he could be a woman pretending to be a man, or a man pretending to be a woman. He might be a 21 year old sex crazed female or a 60 year old dirty old man. It's the world wide anonymous web, remember? In the anonymous vacuum of web space, nobody can hear you scream. They can't tell your age or sex either.

In the publication of most of his books and for advertising, his persona is male. In the comic strip The Beleaguered Lives of Mychael and Shayne, his persona is female. Why? He likes confusing the readers. Then again, maybe he's a bit of both.

Whether he's a man writing gay, lesbian and kinky het or a woman writing gay, lesbian and kinky het, doesn't matter. If he can draw you into a story with his words, he's done his job.

Who is Shayne Carmichael? Does it really matter?

Shayne shares a website with Mychael Black, his partner

in crime at http://www.theprinceangel.com.

Excerpts for other works and several freebie stories are available on the site. To contact Shayne, email shayne@ theprincesangel.com.

Printed in the United Kingdom
by Lightning Source UK Ltd.
135906UK00001B/42/P